A Deadly Chain of Events . . .

It all started with a letter. A letter that had been sitting undisturbed in Holding for a quarter of a century. A day before Ford died in a so-called accident, he wrote to tell his wife not to believe in accidents. That was the starting point. No, that's not really true either. The starting point was a blue-eyed blond stunner named Justine Ford. That was the real reason it had gone any further. If Joe Blow or Irene Nobody had walked into the Command Post, the mystery would have kept on gathering dust for another twenty-five years. After all, he thought, we were postal inspectors, not military police, not homicide detectives, not Schwarzenegger and Stallone. . . . Let's face it, we knew more about going after the perpetrator of a chain letter than we did about going after a killer.

And that wasn't the worst part. The worst part was that Eamon wasn't at the top of his game. He finally got one of the all-time great cases—it had everything, explosions, suicides, murders, threats on the president's life, you name it—and he was in love with the dead lieutenant's daughter. . . .

Books by Sean McGrady

Dead Letters
Gloom of Night

Published by POCKET BOOKS

GLOOM OF NIGHT

Sean McGrady

POCKET BOOKS

New York   London   Toronto   Sydney   Tokyo   Singapore

An *Original* Publication of POCKET BOOKS

POCKET BOOKS, a division of Simon & Schuster Inc.
1230 Avenue of the Americas, New York, NY 10020

ISBN: 0-671-74268-X

First Pocket Books printing November 1993

10 9 8 7 6 5 4 3 2 1

Cover art by Simon Galkin

Printed in the U.S.A.

Ingebjørg

They lay alone or in clumps in the high grass of the field and along the road, their pockets out, and over them were flies and around each body or group of bodies were the scattered papers.... There were mass prayer books, group postcards showing the machine-gun unit standing in ranked and ruddy cheerfulness as in a football picture for a college annual; now they were humped and swollen in the grass.... Now they were scattered with the smutty postcards, photographic; the small photographs of village girls by village photographers, the occasional pictures of children, and the letters, letters, letters. There was always much paper about the dead and the debris of this attack was no exception.

—Hemingway, "A Way You'll Never Be"

He steered the little golf cart past the long winding tracks of conveyor belt, through the angry rumblings and grim, soot-stained landscape, past the heapings of mailbags and parcels, letters and crates and boxes in the hundreds of thousands, all of them awaiting Removal and Transport, toward the heart of DL country, ten football fields away. With dazed familiarity he maneuvered the Byzantine maze that surely would have had any newcomer crying out for a map, driving determinedly down those narrow, congested, poorly lit aisles for the dark, open fairways of Dead Letters.

At times, in shadowy sections, where too many burned-out bulbs—naked, dangling things of low wattage—had been neglected, he used caution, opting for headlights. It was quite a little cart, no doubt about it. Five speeds—up to forty miles per— leather seats, walnut dash, a sparkly gold paint job. But it was the odd domed roof, made to look like a golf ball, white with nifty scalloping, with *Titleist* written in red script across its front, that Eamon Wearie liked best of all.

The Bob Hope Special, as it was referred to by the boys in blue—regular army, the guys who did the loading and lifting, the only real work at Depot

349—had just appeared a few months ago in the Holding Station. Word was that it was confiscated from some billionaire Colombian powder king who had managed to call a tad of attention to himself by erecting his own private Augusta in the back of his Jersey home. That kind of thing was happening more and more. Treasury and FBI and IRS, on the frontlines of the new seize-and-procure orders, had been hitting the drug dealers where it hurt most. Taking their cash and their cars and their homes, sometimes auctioning the loot off, but just as often dumping the stuff at Dead Letters. There weren't too many warehouses that had the size and breadth to hold helicopters and Learjets and classic car collections and those ubiquitous high-speed cigarette boats. Actually, lately, come to think of it, they'd been landing a lot of great stuff. Even one of Elvis's old gift Cadillacs, tail fins ablaze, had managed to find a home in Holding.

Eamon knew he must be a comic sight in his duckbilled cap with Golfers Have More Fun lettered over the beak, at the controls of the garish cart, weaving his way through the strange netherworld of Dead Letters. He'd never even played the game himself. The closest he'd come was to putt his way through a date at one of those miniature jobs. Federal postal inspectors just weren't known for their country club ways, all those pink and lime La Coste shirts and their falsely reverent caddies. Not that he didn't like watching it on television, the soft surreal colors of Florida and California providing perfect somnolent backdrops. Why, drink in hand, he had passed many an afternoon in that sweet pastel glow, falling asleep to the pseudo-British intonations of supercilious play-by-play men. He tried to think of such perfect things now, of Pebble Beach and Doral and other places that he had never been and would likely never go, of those things not occupying the steel-gray drawer of his workaday mind. You couldn't really blame him. After all, it was his lunch hour.

In recent weeks Eamon had looked forward so keenly to lunch and coffee breaks that it embarrassed him. To think that these idle moments, along with trips to the restroom, were the high points. Every day now he was leaving work minutes earlier, wondering if the others were catching on, as if in some body-snatcher movie, as if he was not one of them anymore. It had to be the drinking. Since he had given it up—three weeks ago Monday—he had not been the same.

His nerves were jangled from the coffee; he was drinking it by the quart now, as if somehow to compensate. And he was smoking twice as much. And there was the matter of his newly developed sweet tooth, always craving ice cream or fudge in the evenings now. But that was just the physical side, the unimportant. He wondered more about his mental condition. At first he thought giving up the booze would make him sharper, more perceptive, acute. But the only difference he could see was that he was getting good at avoiding people. Like some wounded soul, he'd taken to hunkering down, to retreating.

In fact, he'd reverted to some old habits. When he'd first arrived at Dead Letters a decade ago, when he was just a new cadet and didn't know anyone, in an effort to avoid the awkwardness of a lunch with strangers, he'd ride one of the official mopeds back, deep into the letter wasteland, away from all ordinary concerns. Today, as he passed the North Pole—that twinkling way station for Santa's mail, the year-round blue spruce lit up for business, Yellow Team giving him the thumbs-up—he wondered about that young man and where he had disappeared to. He had turned thirty-three in

3

September, and it seemed to him that the years had passed without anyone so much as consulting him, just gone thataway, you know.

There were things he remembered about first coming here. The awestruck cadet who couldn't quite believe the magnitude of the place, of a building that stretched out like a highway, that some said was the largest single structure on the entire planet, that looked from the outside like a desolate mile-long bunker. Without so much as a window. Without so much as a spattering of sunlight in the entire hellish place. Just gray cement and a linoleum floor of mysterious color—no one could quite fathom it under the layers of grit and shoe scuff—and that marvelous asbestos ceiling that never seemed to hold its own on a rainy day.

But there was magic nonetheless. There were things in the United States Postal Service's Eastern Seaboard Mid-Regional Bulk Management Depot, Postal Depot 349 in Permanent Sector 4D (known as Dead Letters to the rest of the country's mailmen, final resting place for the nation's undeliverable mail) that practically defied imagination. In these cavernous catacombs were misaddressed letters by the millions, shelf upon shelf, acre upon acre dating back to the Pony Express, with jewels and wallets and rare artworks and television sets and credit cards and processed film and stuffed animals and whatever else one could possibly dream up. All of it lost in the mail, lost forever and dispatched finally to Dead Letters to be interred in the dust and cobwebs of the ages.

He scooted past the Financial District, which included Sector 1040, the repository of all matters relating to the IRS. Mostly the redwood picnic tables, which were cordoned off by state, were littered with the returns of pissed-off taxpayers who, in a most foolish form of protest, refused to put postage on them. There were also stacks of un-claimed refunds, mainly the result of dead tax-payers. On the outskirts of the Financial District, under armed guard, were those things that glittered and beguiled, a plenitude of wallets and purses, having been shoved in letter boxes by the more con-scientious pickpockets, then the glass cases of diamond rings and golden timepieces—somehow disposed of in the mail, engagements gone sour, gifts returned in rancorous fits, without return address, without so much as a second thought, RETURN TO SENDER, RETURN TO SENDER—ever so darkly glowing, the closest thing to radiance in the dull, heartless void.

Besides providing colorful diversion, mere riches really didn't interest Eamon. He liked the things in Dead Letters that were weirdly personal, that struck the deeper chords, the letters most of all. And when he first arrived, fresh out of the Bureau's training program at Quantico, starting his first real job with that peculiar eagerness and naïveté that is recognized only in memory, he thought, like Gehrig in the hollows of Yankee Stadium, that he must be the luckiest man alive. God, he got paid to read the mail.

Like every new cadet, he went through a period of apprenticeship, spent in the bowels of the Depot, more clerk than postal inspector, paid to locate those misplaced missives of importance, usually something with a check in it, nothing that couldn't be handled with a minimum of effort. Mostly, though, no one watched over him, and he was left to his own devices. He liked to wander aimlessly, hiking back into that vast paper forest, going where the feeling took him, lost in a wilderness of old letters and dated emotion. He often felt like that Jack Lemmon character in *Mister Roberts*. In fact, the first time he met Bunko, Bunk said, "Why, if it isn't Ensign Pulver." Which turned out to be a pretty hard nickname to shake.

Thinking back to those strangely lackadaisical days had him vaguely regretting the present and longing for a past that seemed so largely carefree. Whereas Lieutenant Wearie had just finished an arduous eight-month-long investigation into mail fraud, Corporal Wearie had been a man of entirely unsupervised, unspoiled leisure. Spending his hours in the dark nooks and sweet crannies in worthless pursuit, opening the ancient, yellowing letters, deliriously snooping about, eavesdropping on the lives of his fellow citizens. In the cool damp dark with other people's secrets—what could be better?

But Eamon was respectful of these motley treasures, even if most of what he came across was Big Two–related, almost always Love or Money, one or the other. Either Cupid's poisoned arrows or the slings of outrageous fortune. People seemed so little interested in anything else. He recalled too many tormented letters from jilted lovers, stinking of dime store cologne, signed in red lipstick and green blood. Ex-lovers, it seemed, never forgot a cherished moment, no matter how short-lived. Their sad, tender remembrances always called back the lost magic, moonlit nights and summer sand and winter longings. They could never let go, Eamon thought, and so they could never go forward. But that wasn't the worst of it. The sort of letter he'd encountered most frequently was entirely obsequious in tone, full of uneasy fawning, all oily lubrication. The request for a loan—"just until I'm back on my feet again," as they never failed to add—was such an old and unhappy sport. The gambit for money, so often unsuccessful, recounted unpaid hospital bills and past-due mortgage payments, warned of imminent car repossession and deranged-looking kids growing up without the service of orthodontists, described old familiar wolves at the door. Still, to Eamon Wearie, guardian of the sacred trust, it was only human to reach out for help in such a hard-boiled world. And for those deemed worthy, a precious few who stood out, those lovers with love in their heart, those borrowers with genuine need, he performed his special service, sending the long-detained letters on their rightful way with God's speed.

To Corporal Wearie there had been an almost unimaginable beauty in this vast subterraneanlike universe. There were things only he knew. Like the very smell. You opened a letter and the very heat of life rushed up to greet you. And he wasn't just thinking about those flowery pieces of pink stationery sent from girlish lovers, with their obscenely fragrant promises. Always smelling of that fiendish split personality, Innocence and Corruption; of ripe strawberries and Chanel No. 5. Whole stories, whole lives unfolded when he inhaled. Too many times it was someone else's poverty. An odor you couldn't help but recognize, like sickness and cough syrup, like litter boxes and last night's cigarettes. It wasn't hard to imagine fetid rooming houses and scrawny cats, terrible loneliness and atrophy, the pain of being forgotten. That other smell, so much harder to attain, he encountered far less often. Money had a special freshness, like newly laundered linen and Harris tweed and the good sea air. At times it was fine cognac and cigars in the private library. Other times it was spearmint mornings and yellow roses. Still, you didn't open too many of those babies. Perhaps because the rich had less to worry about, they wrote less often. Or more likely, they just sent off "Having a wonderful time, wish you were here" postcards.

Although the years had slipped by, the next too much like the last, leaving him grizzled and marked on the inside, Lieutenant Wearie looked no different really from that young corporal who'd arrived at Dead Letters with such perverse enthusiasm. In that way he was like some kind of Dorian Gray, none the worse for the wear, still darkly handsome, his hair just as thick and unruly, his deep, hypnotic eyes still pulling in the stares. It always seemed that women wanted to believe in him, wanted him to be the person he looked like. He knew that; he knew a lot of things that didn't help him worth a damn.

So now Lieutenant Wearie was spending his lunch hours in that saddest of pursuits, trying to recapture a past already behind him. He went back through the years, past Sectors 32 and 33, looking for the late seventies, a time period he much preferred. He liked the letters from that seemingly worry-free time, when that peanut farmer was in the White House, when disco was all the rage, when the Bee Gees were actually popular, when hair was long and sloppy, before the advent of that yuppie thing, when no one owned any fashion sense, wide collars and the miracle of Dacron, the good old days, when his Yankees were winning pennants on Reggie's bat and Guidry's arm, hell, when he was just a kid, still in school, still fixated on Jenny, the girl of his dreams.

He was just about there, a block away from Sector 36, his own personal time machine, when Sanchez appeared a few yards away, flagging him down.

"Hey, stud," she said. "Where've you been keeping that nice ass of yours?"

Shit, he thought. All he needed now. He'd been trying to avoid her ever since that bad night, the last time he'd had a drink. Three weeks and counting. Sure, she'd left messages on his machine and tried corralling him in the parking lot a couple of times, but so far he'd gotten away with telling her that he was swamped with work, that lame old excuse. Though he had to admit she was one very sexy-looking woman, that black waist-length hair, the shapely body that couldn't be concealed by the shapeless, regulation Confederate–gray uniform. Still, it'd probably been a mistake.

"Eamon, how come you don't call me anymore? Wasn't I good enough in bed for you, stud?"

That's what he meant. She was just so straightforward, so unapologetic in the face of life's awkward moments. He liked her, though, he had to admit. But his heart didn't seem to beat any faster, who knows reasons why.

"Good to see you, too, Sanchez," he said, low-key as possible. "I've been meaning to call—"

"Yeah, I'll just bet," she said, suddenly pugnacious. "Hey, you're the one missing out. We could have some good times together—if that night was any serious indication. I like you, Eamon. God knows why. It's not like you're big on sending flowers and all the little things a girl likes. You know, there's lots of boys who call me up, you know."

"I'll bet," he said, a small smile forming, the first one in weeks. "Listen, Sanchez—"

"And that's another thing I don't like. It's Lita from now on. Especially after the way we've been together."

She was looking at him with the strange and knowing look of an old lover, conspiratorial and scolding at the same time. He knew what she meant. He missed her, too. Why did he always want so much more? Tell him that. They'd gone bowling with the Depot team, the Ball Breakers, like any other Sunday night, and then, with Bunko in tow, they'd gone down to the Marlin, just like always, but somehow different this time, somehow different in that primeval moonlight, in the demented glow of a big round moon. Funny things started to happen, starting with her dancing eyes, all that funny green light, playing such tricks with him, and it wasn't long before he felt the fur sprouting up his body. She matched him drink for drink—it must have been witches' brew—and soon they were oblivious to everyone else, just two groping, pawing werewolves in the middle of a neighborhood bar. How they got back to his place he'd never know.

"So Eamon," she said softly, "I remember every little thing you said to me. You said a lot of nice sweet things that night."

He found himself staring at her, asking for trouble. She was a bodacious-looking woman, he'd give her that. He didn't know what it was, but he'd get close to someone, and then that someone would start wanting to know all about him, all his secrets and hidden places, and he'd get sort of almost frightened, like they were discovering too much too fast, and then he'd have this overwhelming need to bolt. But he forgot all about that for the moment. She was something else, this girl.

"Hey," she said, "you didn't even congratulate me on my good work down here. You must have heard about it. They even did a little story in the newspaper. You see it?"

He'd seen it, all right. In fact, it was one of those things he wished she hadn't brought up. Her little find had caused nothing but headaches for them. Bunko wanted to shoot the girl on sight. Usually you never even heard from the new cadets, but he had to admit Sanchez had made quite a discovery in the Holding Station. In the back of an army jeep—the damn thing had been there at least as long as he had, covered with all sorts of shit, God knew how it had gotten there in the first place—she'd found a large canvas mailbag. The thing was, this was no ordinary sack of mail. The letters were all from August 1967, by way of Saigon. All from the 27th Infantry. In some cases they were the last letters of young men who'd never made it back from Vietnam. Words from beyond the grave. It was some spooky shit, the way these old letters affected people, wounding them all over again. Jesus, it was unbelievable. And even though they'd expected some kind of reaction, they hadn't counted on what had followed.

"You wouldn't believe the kind of crap we've been dealing with," he complained. "Christ, you've never seen anything like it. We got all sorts of people calling up about their dead sons and shit and why did we have to remind them of all the pain all over again, and God knows what I'm supposed to tell these people. Yeah, so good work, Sanchez. Just beautiful, kid."

"Oh, don't give me that shit, Eamon. You're just mad because you had nothing to do with it. And I'll tell you something: If I lost my son or my man or whatever and somebody found something he wrote from a long time ago, you bet your ass I'd want to have it. Even if it was just some nothing little thing they whipped off twenty years ago. Because it would mean even more now."

"Well," he said, more stiffly than he would have liked, "maybe people don't want to be reminded of—"

"I don't care what people want," she said forcefully. "That's not the point. Maybe what's important is that people never forget, you know. You can bury the past, but that doesn't mean it's going to go away."

He almost laughed, how serious she looked. He liked that, the fighter in her, never taking any guff, always at the ready to deflect your next jab. She was a beautiful piece of work, he thought as his eyes wandered over her blue-gray uniform, recalling those racy curves and the demented glow of that full moon.

"I didn't mean to get all touchy about it," he said, working the apology angle and some others besides. "It's just—hell, it's caused a little extra mop-up duty. I even got some kid coming in later on about those damn letters. Lost her dad and shit in the war. I don't even know what the heck she wants. Hell, if she's like the others, she probably just wants somebody to talk to. I guess there's nothing wrong with that."

He paused, searching her out with his big bad eyes, working all the angles. "Lita," he said, "I'm really sorry for not calling you." Once more he looked at her that way, with everything. Time to close the deal. "You know, I think my schedule is beginning to clear up. How's Friday night for you?"

As the pretty twenty-four-year-old looked over the man she most wanted to be with, she was overcome by two separate and distinct feelings. On the one hand, Lita Sanchez would have done almost anything to be with Eamon Wearie. He had the way, the look, the feel, the thing that just sometimes happens. On the other hand, something told her this was just the guy to hurt her bad.

Please don't, said the little voice inside of her as they negotiated the time and the place.

Back in the office after lunch, Eamon and his partner went back and forth over their next case. A bunch of things had been collecting on their desks while they'd gone after Ridgeway, that long, tedious ordeal, but now Bunko only wanted to do one thing, which meant going out to California.

"C'mon, get with the program, Wearie," Bunko bellowed. "Thing's a piece of cake. Some goon's gone overboard on this babe—he's probably harmless, for all we know—sending this TV star, Miss

Whatever Her Name Is—course, I don't watch the boob tube, so I wouldn't know who the fuck she is, but she's quite a looker I gather . . . So anyway, what was I saying? Oh, yeah. So some hard-up creep is sending bizarro letters every day. How fucking difficult can this be? A little sun, a little sand, a little pussy. Do us some good, whatayasay?"

"I just don't know, Bunk," he said, tired of the whole thing. "I really don't want to go all the way out to L.A. Who knows how long we'd have to be out there and all."

"What's with you, Wearie? Ever since you stopped drinking you've been a real drag, buddy boy. I remember, not too long ago, either, when I used to enjoy your company. Christ. Whatayasay? Let's get on a jet and do that Hollywood thing— you know, hit the beaches, ride around in a convertible listening to the Beach Boys, the whole surfin' salami."

Eamon got a comical picture in his head of the Bunko on a surfboard, all six-foot-five, two-hundred-and-fifty pounds of him.

"What the hell you snickering at?" Bunko demanded.

"Nothing, big guy. Just thinking of you hanging ten. Riding through that tunnel of white. Sort of an updated version of the Melville classic: *Moby Dick Goes Surfing.*"

"Hardy har har, Wearie. I'll have you know I've lost a little poundage lately, in case you haven't noticed. I'm on that Tommy LaSorda thing. You know, you drink these chocolate shakes for breakfast and lunch, and then you get to have normal stuff for dinner. And I'll tell you something: I feel and look a whole lot better. So fuck you."

Eamon always forgot how sensitive the big galoot could be about his weight. And he had to admit that the Bunk was looking good lately. The guy had been touching up his gray bristles, just leaving it distinguished at the temples, had even bought some new clothes, a most shocking development, exchanging the checked sports coat and tacky bowling shirts for a classy Brooks Brothers look, today donning a navy blue blazer with charcoal slacks and one of those precious button-downs in a most muted pigmentation. Had to be someone new in his life, had to be.

"We could help Green Team with that letter bomb thing in West Virginia," Eamon suggested.

"Christ, they don't need our help with that. Forget coal mining country. Let's go west to the promised land. Whatayasay?"

"No, I'm just not into it," Eamon replied coolly. "We got plenty to do here. How about all those social security checks that were found missing in that Ohio ZIP?"

"Fuck that shit. That's just some dumb-ass mailman trying to be too smart. They'll catch him without our help. Let's go to the beach, soak up some rays, check out all that blond action."

"No way, Bunk. We got lots of things right here. There's Mister Postage Due. We never solved that one. In fact, never even came close. I'm sure the Bureau would appreciate it if we got cracking on that."

"Ahhh, Christ," Bunko let out, clearly exasperated. "Not that psycho job. Not another fucked-up Vietnam vet bullshit thing. Take it from me, guy's just some fruitcake that ain't gonna do dork to nobody. Threatening to kill the president, what a bunch of bullshit. You saw those letters. Guy's wacko, but not that wacko. Mister Postage Due, give me a break."

"How do you know it's not for real?"

"I've been in this business long enough to know. Guys who spend too much time talking about it don't got the nerve to do jack shit. And fuck it, I'm sick of goddamn Vietnam. Ain't bad enough that I had to spend fourteen fucking months over in that shithole when I was just some stupid kid, now I gotta hear about it for the rest of my fucking life."

"Hey Bunk, what is this? One of those delayed stress syndrome things? Like are you back in Nam? You know, in the jungle again, tracers going off, the whole *Apocalypse Now* deal?"

Eamon was laughing, but Bunko didn't say a thing for a long, uncomfortable moment. "Fuck you, you smart aleck know-nothing," he finally said without humor. "You're a lucky son of a bitch to be born so late. Just another punk who doesn't know nothing about nothing."

Undeterred, Eamon said, "Hey, speaking of Nam, since it's obviously a favorite subject of yours, we got that Ford girl coming in an hour or so. You know, the daughter of that guy who got killed over there. Something about those old letters, you know, the ones Sanchez found in the jeep."

"No way, pal. That one's for you. I ain't going to have nothing to do with it. Now as I was saying about California before I was so rudely and unhappily interrupted ..."

Bunko went on like a travel agent from hell, continuing to try and sell him on all that golden pussy wandering around the beach. Eamon could hardly blame him. He understood that Bunk was just sick of being cooped up in the office. That whole unfunny mail fraud business had kept them holed up for the better part of a year. The fucking Ridgeway Concern. It was a sad case in which a lot of middle-income and retired people had wound up losing their life savings. The Ridgeway Concern was a mortgage banking corporation owned by one Stanislav Ziegewski, and to those foolish enough to buy in, which mostly included Stanislav's fellow Polish

Americans, Ridgeway promised a too-good-to-be-true annual interest—twenty-three percent—on mortgage-secured investments. Bunko and Eamon had followed Stanislav's staggering paper trail, perusing bank statements and computer transactions, which finally led to the incriminating evidence, the forged documents and forged signatures they'd been searching for all along. It had been another pyramid deal, the type of thing inspectors saw all the time, where Stanislav paid off old investors with the money from new investors and pocketed the difference.

It had been a complicated, frustrating, intolerable case that tried every ounce of their patience. Fortunately, it was time to move on to the next one.

"C'mon, whatayasay?" Bunko pleaded for what seemed like the hundredth time. "We get to meet this famous television actress, Miss Whatever Her Name Is, which I'm sure you'd enjoy, knowing how you love all that celebrity bullshit. And then it's an all-expenses-paid week of beautiful sunny smog and string bikinis. I mean, what's not to like? C'mon, all I'm asking is that you think about it, partner."

"All right," Eamon said, knowing he'd regret it, "I'll think about it."

"That's the boy," Bunko said, sure that he was halfway home. "Now you're talking."

Justine Ford arrived at the Command Post at a quarter to five. She stepped off the elevator to find herself in the Depot's newly renovated operations center, a spacious central area that looked very much like the city room of a large metropolitan daily. Middle-aged men, scattered about, separated only by flimsy colored partitions, sat at their IBM computers, tapping in reports or analyzing data, their faces dark with concentration and late-afternoon shadow. It was a new world for the inspectors; less and less did their work take them out into the field; more and more they belonged to the new corporate race, plugged into phones and fax machines and the strange radiumlike glow of the display terminal.

Justine Ford seemed lost. She noticed the executive offices, glass cubicles encircling the perimeter, but their curtains were drawn for the most part, and there didn't seem to be a main reception area. She didn't move or say anything until Percy Sedgewick, Depot 349's temporary supervisor-in-command, spotted her and approached.

"How may I help you?" the slick bureaucrat asked. He did not usually take an interest in the goings on of the Command Post, but like most men he was simply struck by Justine's looks. She was devastating, an icy blue-eyed blond beauty like Grace Kelly or something. She was, Percy decided, like a chilled double Finlandia with a twist. Or perhaps he was just thinking of his favorite drink; it *was* almost that time of day, wasn't it.

"Well," she said, practically ignoring him, used to wolflike leering, "I'm here to talk to either Lieutenant Wearie or Lieutenant Ryan. Can you direct me to them?"

Percy was more than a little disappointed. Oh, those clowns, he thought with his trademark condescension. At the mention of the two field agents he visibly stiffened, preferring to look down at his burgundy Bass loafers with the trademark tassels. God, how he hated to deal with the inspectors. They were just so uncouth. Why hadn't his appointment at the State Department come through yet? What was taking so long, he wondered. After all, his father had put the word in.

"Excuse me," Justine said again to the arrogant young man in the expensive Italian suit, "can you help me or not?"

Percy looked up with unconcealed annoyance. "Of course," he said. Then he turned to face that silly mess of partitions and announced: "Oh, Mr. Wearie! Mr. Ryan! Wherever you are! If it wouldn't be too much trouble, there is a very attractive young lady here to see you!" Then he turned back to Justine to say with great and trademark smarmyness, "It's been a pleasure, of course. If those two dodos turn out to be of no use—which wouldn't surprise me in the slightest—then you might try calling on me. Just ask for Percy. I'm sort of top dog around here, if you catch my drift."

Eamon and Bunko were in the back at their adjoining desks, those newfangled bright red slabs from Scandinavia that had replaced their cherished lead-gray metal units. They were smoking Marlboros and watching with undue interest the big hand of the Command Post's central clock as it inched toward the magic moment, the end of their daily purgatory, when Percy interrupted their reverie.

"What a complete Harvard fuckhead," Bunko commented just before noticing the beautiful and gorgeous Justine Ford at Sedgewick's side. "Jesus," he said, in evident awe.

"Yeah, I hate it when the bastard calls me Mister Wearie," Eamon said. "It took me a long time to make lieutenant, and I wouldn't mind—" He stopped midsentence, seeing her.

"Listen," Bunko said, "I was probably being too hasty there before. Passing off all the work to you. God, why should you have to deal with this Ford girl and whatever the hell she wants. Listen, you go home, cut out early, leave this one to me. It's only fair—"

"Not on your fucking life, Bunk," Eamon said, eyeing this stunner from across the room. "A deal's a deal, pal."

18

"Shit," he said as Eamon went to retrieve her.

Eamon couldn't believe his luck. He felt like he was on the razor's edge of sensation, the way this sublime creature smelled, like a field of spring violets, the way she looked, like Venus di Milo with the arms, the way she walked, like nothing else he'd ever seen before.

"I'm sorry I'm so late," she said apologetically. "I couldn't get away from work any sooner."

She was dressed elegantly and discreetly, in some kind of Chanel-looking suit, a string of pearls, most probably real, a sedate Rolex, silver without the flash, but the girl had gams, majestic gams that wouldn't quit and couldn't be hidden.

"What kind of work do you do, Miss Ford?" he managed to inquire.

"Stockbroker. Over at Legg Mason. Do you know it?"

Sure he knew it. That big emerald palace on Baltimore's Inner Harbor was hard to miss. Thirty stories of green, the only green building in town as far as he could tell.

"Lieutenant," she said, "is there someplace quiet we can go? What I have to tell you, I'd like to do in private."

"Sure, sure," he said, leading her into one of the darkened glass cubicles. Most everyone had left by now, and what was the harm? The placard on the executive desk said Huntington Marsh. One of Percy's Harvard classmates, no doubt. He snapped on the desk lamp. She sat directly across from him, so close.

"So Miss Ford—"

"Call me Justine, please."

"So Justine, what brings you here anyway?"

Quite suddenly that composed and sublime face started cracking. "Something's wrong, something's very wrong," she said in quick gulps. "You see, my daddy—who I don't even remember, I was too young and all—but my daddy, Lieutenant William Ford, well . . ."

She paused, reaching for some tissues in her handbag. Then she dabbed at her blue eyes, although he couldn't see any sign of tears.

"Well," she said, newly composed, "we got those letters. Those letters from the summer of 1967. I was just a baby then, back when we lived on the Eastern Shore, that's where I grew up and all. Well, Lieutenant, I'm sure you don't want to hear about any of that. But that's when my mommy was alive. Mommy died just a year ago. Cancer, from the smoking I'm sure. I told Mommy, I told her, but she wouldn't listen . . ."

Eamon was struck by the way she referred to her parents, just like a little girl. But her voice was lilting and very feminine—with more than a trace of Southern hospitality—all woman.

"But my point is that the letters were to Mommy, but since she died these matters have fallen to me. I should tell you first that I was most glad to receive them, to have something of my daddy's, and I read them like they were precious gifts, savoring every word, trying to imagine who Daddy was, the man behind them. Ever since I can remember I've spent hours trying to imagine him, trying to make him real as it were. I had pictures, of course, and Mommy told me what she could, just as Grandpa and Grandma Ford did. But you know how it is with family, Lieutenant. They are the last to tell you their faults. And so I knew my daddy was handsome and smart—West Point, in fact—and kind to animals and all the rest of it, but I was always curious about his other side. We all have another side, don't you think, Lieutenant?"

In the dim light she looked at him hard, almost

beseechingly. The silence felt awfully strange to him, so much more was going on here.

"Do you mind if I smoke?" she asked, not waiting for an answer, already dipping into her bag. Her cigarette lit, she turned to face him again. "I know, I know, after how Mommy died. Well, what are you going to do?"

Her voice was lighter and different, could have been taken for frivolous, as if they were no longer talking about her father, as if they had already moved on. "You know, Lieutenant, you're most handsome," she said, holding her aim on him. She was smiling wickedly. Yes, wickedly. "Well, never mind about that. I'm sure you get it all the time, from shop girls and waitresses and whatnot. Girls will be girls will be girls."

She was like some mood ring on the blink, flashing yellow caution one moment, red-hot the next. It threw him. On the surface she was wintry and contained, bordering on a kind of human perfection. The type of woman he had always desired, almost unattainable. He saw her strolling down one of the more fashionable avenues, reflected in the storefront windows, every hair and expensive fiber in place, catching the light like the hood ornament on a Rolls-Royce.

"You were saying about your dad's letters that—"

"Yes, well, that," she said, snuffing out the unsmoked cigarette. "Perhaps I'm rushing to conclusions, Lieutenant. It seems quite mad to me the more I think about it. I probably shouldn't have even come down here, wasting all your valuable time, Lieutenant."

Usually he would have told her to call him Eamon. But he liked the way she ended her sentences deferring to him. It was as if she was putting herself in his hands, his competent hands. "I'm sure you're not wasting my time, Justine," he said sooth-ingly. "Now why don't you just tell me what was in those letters that's got you so upset."

"Thank you, Lieutenant. I'm sure you're just being nice. But you are easy to talk to. Very." She continued to look into his eyes, deeply, sexually. "You know, even though I'm probably overreact-ing, something is quite wrong. There were three letters, two of them just the usual thing, missing me and my brother and Mommy and all that, but the other one, the last one, is something else entirely. It was full of, full of, all sorts of, uh, strangeness."

"What do you mean?" he asked. He was begin-ning to feel sort of like her shrink. He could easily picture her on the sterile black couch. Probably went twice a week.

"Well, for one thing, Daddy seemed quite sure he was about to die, quite sure."

"I'll bet that was a common feeling over there," Eamon said. He was beginning to think that this wasn't leading to anything, that he'd been right in the first place, that she just needed somebody to talk to. "I mean, it was war, wasn't it. In wars people—"

"No, no, Lieutenant. Daddy thought that one of his own men was going to do it. Can you imagine? He was the platoon leader—but I don't know why anyone would've wanted to hurt him. From all I know about him, he was a good and truly decent man. There's something else, too. He said some-thing about giving testimony, that he hoped he lived long enough to give testimony. But he didn't say what it was about, he didn't give a clue. But he did say one thing: Daddy said in the letter that if any-thing should happen to him, that we should have it investigated, that we shouldn't just take it at face value."

"So what did happen to your father, Justine?"

he thought to ask. Even though he was listening to every word, it was hard to ignore that imploring face. She never took her eyes off of him, never gave him the chance to ignore her, as if that was even possible.

"That's the other thing I was going to tell you. He was killed. And here's the really peculiar part. He was killed the next day, the day after that letter was written. In an accident. At least that's what the government told us. They said one of his men was cleaning his gun, and that it went off accidentally. That's all they told us. And then you know the rest. They wrapped his body in a flag, and they shot off guns, and it rained, and our family was left to go about its business without him."

She seemed to fluctuate from child to adult, missing the entire range in between, one or the other. It did seem strange, though, what she'd been telling him, her father dying that way, especially after what he'd said.

"Am I crazy?" she asked plaintively. "I just feel like I owe Daddy this. He'd want me to look into this. And I tried the Defense Department. They told me that everything relating to Daddy was classified, that they were sorry but that they couldn't help me. I didn't know where to go. I came here. Will you do something, Lieutenant?"

"This," he said, careful to phrase it well, not wanting to upset her further, "is a little bit out of our territory. I really don't know what I can tell you about—"

"Oh, Lieutenant, please," she cried. "There's nowhere else I can turn. I must find out what happened to him. Don't you see?"

This just wasn't Postal's jurisdiction. This was the army's ball game. That's how he saw it. "I'm sorry," he began, "but—"

She chose that moment to take one of his hands

in hers, to hold it. "I just know you can help me," she said softly. Her eyes were blue ice melting. "Sometimes you just know."

He found himself obeying. "Okay, I'm not promising anything. I'll do what little I can. Do you have the letters with you? They might provide further clues for us."

She took the rubber band-wrapped bundle out of her bag and stopped just short of passing it to him. "You could never know what these mean to me. You really couldn't. To hear from him all these years later. Please handle them with care. As you know, they've come a long way, across miles and years. And I would be beside myself if anything happened to them. Thank you, Lieutenant. For all your kindness."

She got up from her chair and reached across Huntington Marsh's desk to give him a kiss. And he did nothing to stop her. Justine Ford kissed him lightly on the lips and then just as quickly took her leave, leaving Eamon Wearie dizzy and disoriented.

Things like this did not happen every day. Things like this maybe happened to Phillip Marlowe or Sam Spade, but never to a federal postal inspector.

What was left of the day was cruel and vivid. The sky was a merciless blue, and the sun still had the power to blind. The harbor water, usually a murky, unpleasant brown, gleamed and refracted, hard with the white light. It was golden late afternoon in October, sharp and clear and dazzling with a smoky little bite to the air, and it was painful to think that he'd spent most of this God-given day in the world's biggest and darkest warehouse.

It was the time of year Eamon liked best, as far back as he could remember. Cobalt days, so piercing you've got to squint. Big cumulus moving swiftly across that bluest of horizons. Nights with the chill of premonition, whole galaxies of stars studding a black universe. The clarity, the unbelievable clarity. Jesus, what wasn't to like?

Such a cool, burnished day. With all the talk of global warming, it was simply nice to have such a seasonal throwback. Part of it, of course, was living in Baltimore, just the difference a degree or two in latitude makes, but it was hard not to be nostalgic for the Long Island of his youth. It just seemed there had been more days like this one there. Great piles of leaves crackled and burned in the driveways of memory. Weekend warriors, potbellied dads and their Pabst Blue Ribbons, leaning on their rakes and wiping sweat from their brows. Kids playing pickup ball in the middle of the yellow-striped road. So many of those fine nippy afternoons, the sun darting in and out from behind churlish clouds. All those grand, dumb-looking colonials cramped on their quarter-acre lots, all those suburban dreams of the bigger and thus better life. And hell, hadn't his dad moved them out of Queens for that very reason, looking for his little piece of the action, wanting nothing better in this world than a back-yard barbecue pit and a good school district? Yeah, his dad used to get into his old beat-up Maverick and head into his cop job in the city, slogging through the morning rush, lost in that famous sea of lost souls. And every evening he came back through the door a little grayer, a little more worn, a little less there.

Cities sucked, Eamon thought. Crack addicts and big gray rats in the alleyways and that hard, un-friendly look in everyone's eyes. Someday, with any luck, he'd get to leave, too. Still, it was a beautiful Monday, the way the water glinted, the way it felt in the good choppy air. He didn't know what to do with himself, though. At first he went home, to his tiny brick row house on Sycamore, a pleasant enough place on one of the many quiet side streets of Fells Point. But it was much too nice outside for that, for settling back with a newspaper and one of those chirpy, early-edition TV news fests. So he went down to the docks, only a few blocks away, content to shuffle about with his hands jammed into the pockets of his windbreaker, checking out the grimy red tugs and remaining fish canneries, staring off into the brilliant distance, a man without a game plan.

The problem, of course, was that he wasn't drink-ing. Just three weeks ago he would have known what to do. Head up to the Marlin and start in with the tap beer and the darts and the juke and the slow fade. He thought of his buddies, Timmy Longley and McCleary and Donnie D., everyone slumped in place on the usual stools, telling the usual lies. Then that primitive male bonding thing where everybody had to do a shot with everybody else so that they could prove they're bestest buddies in the whole world. Bar life was like that, sloppy and sodden, spilt drinks and spilt feelings, none of it too easy to wipe up. When you were sober, as he was now, you felt left out, and it was hard not to be judgmental. You saw it for what it was. You saw the loneliness most of all. You saw the way heads turned whenever the door opened a crack, hoping against hope for something pretty, something vaguely real; yeah, right, like *she* was going to glide in at two in the morning and save your soul, whoever the hell she was.

He felt like he was coming out of something, like he'd been away for a while. Still, he missed his friends, missed the old ways. It wasn't even six yet, but the sun, a big red job, was sinking into the harbor, bleeding over the darkened water. It got cold in a hurry. Suddenly there wasn't any more of that autumnal splendor, and the place reeked again of the old industrial, smelling of brine and gasoline and the hot dogs from the vendor over there.

A trolley pulled up. It was one of those fakes done up to look old-time, another bright idea from the Chamber of Commerce. He hopped on, not thinking much about it. It wasn't like he had anything much to do. Going home meant another paperback mystery or flicking through the channels, another one of those nights. Besides, Pinkus, his tenant, was probably hanging about with his girlfriend. He felt weird about that, like he was intruding or something, even if it was his house. Pinkus's girlfriend, Muffie or whatever the hell her name was, was always trying to bring him into their little twosome, like she felt sorry for him or something. She'd suggest renting movies or a popcorn party or some such shit, and even though she meant well, it just wound up making him feel that much more pathetic, like he didn't have friends or a life of his own.

As the trolley—just another city bus without shock absorbers—creaked and groaned its way out of Fells Point, stopping every other block or so, leaving behind the low-slung, brick-brown landscape, its myriad restaurants and taverns winking benignly in the deepening twilight, Eamon Wearie found himself once again contemplating life without the drink. In fact, he seriously wondered how much longer he could stand it. All that blinking neon tubing, promising the High Life and the simple, frosty, anxiety-leveling joy of a cold one. It sent shudders through him, that it came down to just this, to choosing one way over the other, as if there were to be no satisfactory compromises this time.

Trying to think of anything but the one thing, he spied the young woman across the aisle, a mousy-looking nurse locked into the pages of Stephen King's latest. There was something all too breakable about her, he felt. Like she was a victim waiting to happen or something. Maybe it was the sensible hospital shoes, or perhaps it was the thick prescription lenses in drab designerless frames. You could tell a lot just by looking at her, all kinds of psychic vibes. For one thing, she was still living at home with her folks, ostensibly to save money. But this was a girl with a long history of timidity, too often running scared in the face of life's many challenges. Nor did she have much of a social life, hardly ever going out on a Saturday night. But she had a damning, shaming secret all the same. A married doctor. Twice a week at one of those motels that advertised special day rates. That old deal, telling her to wait and hang on, just a matter of time before he told the cold and unfeeling wife. But that would never happen, of course. Their affair would drag on for years, and the mousy nurse would let other opportunities pass, paying little heed to other more promising suitors, letting her youth slip away into that larger pool of bitters. Finally she'd write her letter to Ann Landers, the one warning other mousy nurses about the dangers of lying, conniving, married doctors.

Eamon smiled at the thought. Just some girl engrossed in a book, for Christ's sake. It wasn't like he could look into her soul or anything, he'd never claim that. But shit, you could just see it in her. Hell, might just as well have been stamped FRAGILE: HANDLE WITH CARE. A victim waiting to happen. It was like with that Ford girl today. As beautiful and contained as they came. Put together like a Cartier diamond, hard and brilliant and seemingly flawless. And yet there were things swirling around in there, crazy things all hidden in the dark center, nothing you could fathom with the naked eye. He was sure of it somehow.

And that was the one thing he *really* didn't want to think about. Forget the drinking, forget everything else. Here's this goddess, one of the forever unobtainable, and she's got to do something really stupid and insane—like kissing him. What the hell was that all about? Here's this world-class beauty, the kind Greek shipping magnates kept on the sun decks of their yachts, and she's all fucked up somehow. That was all he could figure. And the really awful part was the way he felt. When Justine Ford kissed him, it happened, that whole pitter-pat, thump-thump deal. Goddammit. Wouldn't you know.

But it had been such a very long time. Had to go way back, high school and all that. With Jenny. After cheerleading practice. Under the bleachers. In his football uniform, second string forever. A grubby fall day, threatening black rain. Taking her in his arms, as if he knew what the heck he was doing. Then all that staring into each other's eyes. Then the rest of it. One of those moments. One of those things. Never could have imagined how much it would mean later on, how many times he'd rewind it and hit the play button again.

Even when he was married to Trish, that brief disaster, he never once felt that feeling.

He took her father's letters out. He'd been saving them, or maybe he'd been avoiding them. He wasn't sure what he'd find, or if there was really anything there at all. Maybe he'd find out something about what she came from at least. Even that seemed like a lot to hope for. Justine's mom and dad were dead, that was what he knew. That was what was real.

Her mother's name was Kinnan, which was nice and unusual. They were all addressed to Kinnan Ford in Crisfield, Maryland. In the right-hand corner of each envelope, in lieu of stamps, Lieutenant Ford had simply scrawled FREE, postage being one of the very few advantages of war. The letters had a worn quality, like they had been read over and over, like the very life had been squeezed out of them.

The other thing that struck him was the handwriting, the strong, straightforward stroke of Lieutenant Ford. It was true that he crossed his *t*'s and dotted his *i*'s with military precision, but it was also true that great sincerity registered in his smooth, even-tempered hand. With a certain amount of trepidation, Eamon began to read:

Gloom of Night

Darling Heart,

I think I'd go crazy if I didn't have you and the kids to think about. Just knowing that you're all okay, I can't find the words even. That there is such a place. I fantasize about it all the time, coming home, home sweet home, taking you all on a picnic or to a ball game or just to church on a beautiful Sunday morning. Imagine me fantasizing about one of old Halabash's sermons, the way he goes on forever in that barely audible monotone of his. Hard to believe, isn't it? I remember when my fantasies used to be slightly naughtier, usually involving you and that skimpy teddy of yours. God, I miss you. You must know that, darling. In your wise and kind heart, I'm sure you know much more than you let on, even if most of the time I try to steer clear of this war and all its jungle rot.

I'm not sure what good it does to tell you that you and the kids are the only things that matter to me and that all the rest of it is hardly worth the time of day. I cannot even begin to tell you how much your wonderful, courageous letters mean to me. You put on such a brave face and you fill them with the greatest and most wonderful trivialities, and I live to hear every blessed little thing, all the funny nonsense Justy and Bobby say and how the vegetable garden is coming and all the people who have bothered to remember me in passing. It does my heart good to know that you are all under one roof, even if it is the roof of my parents' house in good ol' Crisfield. Someday, someday darling, I'll be there with you again, and we will buy a little house of our own. And

I can tell you something else: I will never complain about any of it, whatever it is, if it is the car breaking down or if one of the kids needs braces or if the roof leaks or whatever it is that we're always worrying about. Because, and I tell you this truthfully, it does not matter, not at all. What matters is to love your family and to have good friends and to live a good life. Don't listen to anyone who tells you different. What I wouldn't do. Just to take you all to the beach, just lying there on our towels listening to the ball game on the radio, everybody smelling of cocoa butter. Then later we all go over to Buddy's for their all-you-can-eat crabs, with that good sweet summer corn, and don't forget their special spicy shrimp, and now that I think about it, we'll need to wash it down with some cold beer, too.

Oh, darling, these are the things I fantasize about when we are hacking our way through the muck with our machetes, not seeing three feet in front of us, not knowing if the NVA are right there on top of us or if we're about to step on some goddamn mine. The vines and trees are so thick that even when it rains, which is all the time, if you ask me, that it mostly never reaches us in the ordinary way. It is like some kind of invisible rain where the air is always slimy wet. We are like swamp creatures, and our days are spent "humping the boonies," as everybody calls it here, looking for Charlie because Charlie's way too smart to come to us. It is all kind of beyond me now, to tell you the truth. I just have to believe in God and believe that God will see me through. I used to believe certain things, but I must say, and believe me I don't like saying it, that my faith has been shaken. I have seen some shit now, and I will not get into it, not now and not ever, but I have seen some things that would never happen in a world created by God. But I still pray and hope and try to believe in whatever better places there might be. Because if it all came down to this, to dying here, so far from everything that I have loved and cared about, then I would have to say it was all a waste, a fucking waste.

Darling, you must excuse my language. And please don't pay much mind to what I've just written. It is just that I am more confused than ever about some things, about some serious things. I must believe that the president, my commander-in-chief, knows better than I do about such complicated matters. I certainly hope so. Actually, today is one of the better days, although you'd never know it from this letter. We're at base camp, the first time in weeks, which means showers and a decent night's sleep on something other than the moist ground. My men are happy to just strut around in dry underwear, to write their sweethearts. They are just kids, I find myself thinking a lot, even if I am just a few years their senior. But a month over here will mark you in ways you cannot—thank God—imagine. I will let it go at that. You will just have to read between the lines, like you always do. But for the most part, with perhaps the exception of one or two bad apples, they are truly some of the finest and most decent young men that I have ever had the pleasure of knowing.

*America has a lot to be proud of, whether
she knows it or not.*

*Darling, I'm afraid I'm getting tired. I will
try to write some more later after my nap.
Just know that I love you. With all my heart.
With everything that I have.*

Your loving husband

As Eamon finished the first letter the trolley
came to a stop in front of the National Aquarium.
He felt just a little startled to realize where he was,
sort of like that feeling you get when you exit a
dark movie house into bright sunshine, seeing that
the world has gone about its business without you.
He watched as that mousy nurse got off. He wasn't
surprised. This was part of her story, too. The
lonely part, the killing time part. He got a mental
picture of her, standing in front of one of the giant
glass tanks, her face pressing into that strange watery world of zebra-striped fish and painted coral,
silent except for a few bubbles percolating to the
surface. Besides the big old Enoch Pratt library,
that vast mausoleum off Cathedral, this was the
place she could most often be found.

Eamon got off at the next stop, and as he did it
struck him, in belated enough fashion, that he was
really no better off than the mousy nurse. He was
out there, too, just as alone and probably just as
lonely, all the more ironic in a big city full of people, but somehow separated from that greater community, somehow outside of it all, left to peer in
without a clue.

He'd landed in the middle of Baltimore's glassy
downtown, a corporate skyline that hadn't been
there ten years ago. In the bright fluorescent window panels, in sharp contrast to the deep, dark
blueness of early evening, he could see them in
their rolled-up white shirts and loosened ties,

ghostly figures who, from a distance, seemed beyond hope or beyond even the fringes of time. These shining new towers, mostly banks and hotels, were bunched close to the Inner Harbor, taking full advantage of the safe and well-lit tourist haven. The city fathers had spent a bunch to pretty up the waterfront, cleaning out the riffraff and bringing in the klieg lights. Now there were giant malls filled with spanking new restaurants and boutiques. Now there were suburban families wandering about with ice cream cones. They pointed at the sights, at the U.S.F. *Constellation,* an ancient warship permanently docked on the gray water, at the mimes who performed in the same tired spots every day for the same tired people. They snapped away with their Canon Sure Shots, and they whittled off more time going up and down escalators in the Gallery and the pavilions across Pratt.

And it wasn't like Eamon had any problem with that. It was just that he'd lived here a while, knew a little about what lay behind the rich glass facade. It was no great big secret, the plight of the inner cities. The grim litany—the drugs the homeless the unemployment the Saturday Night Specials the AIDS the daily despair—was delivered every evening by the TV people, solemn-sounding hairdos who could just as deftly switch over to sports. *Just a terrible tragedy about little six-year-old Chris Hitchens. Another senseless victim of the ongoing drug wars. To recap: His young life snuffed out by a stray bullet while playing tic-tac-toe. We'll have more on that at eleven. But how 'bout those high-flying Birds? Now here's Chuck with the sports to tell you all about it.*

He walked up Charles, through a deserted downtown. No one lived in this part of the city. The stores and even many of the restaurants were already closed, their metal barriers drawn tight, firm acknowledgment of the fact that no one bothered to hang around after work. The suits and suitettes grabbed their imitation-alligator briefcases and rushed directly from the office to the parking garage, then sped away in their locked Toyota Camrys for the outlying suburbs. The cowards retreated to the likes of Putty Hill and Donnybrook and Silver Creek, to their two-car garages and dewy lawns, trying hard to hang onto that tarnished American dream.

He imagined that Justine Ford was among them on that freeway going out of town. She probably drove something like a BMW or a Saab and she was probably plugged into her Blaupunkt at that very moment, off in her own cool and shimmering world, removed from it all. And if she didn't live out in those green suburban pastures, she surely lived in Federal Hill, in some pricey brownstone. There was just something about her that implied money, even if he couldn't quite figure where it came from. Okay, he knew she was a broker, but even that didn't quite explain it. And there wasn't anything snobbish or off-putting about her father's letter, nothing in it that pointed to that kind of family wealth. Her dad sounded like a real decent guy, you could tell how much he loved his wife and kids, somebody with a heart.

The whole Vietnam thing, to be truthful, was just a bit beyond him. It was hard to picture it, not the part about Lieutenant Ford chopping his way through a muggy jungle, not that, but the whole being there, the whole head trip of winding up there, a zillion miles away from everything you knew and gave a shit about, in the middle of some crazy war, *just being there*. Everything Eamon knew about Vietnam seemed to come from movies and television and crap like that. Like everybody else he'd seen *Platoon* and *The Deer Hunter* and *Born on the Fourth of July*—but what did that really tell you about anything? Just a bunch of movies, no matter how good they were.

He knew a couple of vets, come to think of it. There was Toby, a carpenter who did his drinking at the Marlin. But Toby was like Bunko in that he never brought up the war, not a word, and Eamon would never have known about him if it wasn't for all those tattoos. Then there was Big Norris, a real hard-on when he was doing the Wild Turkey, all over anybody who made the mistake of initiating conversation:

"Yeah, well I was in fuckin' Nam. But what the fuck would you know about it? You weren't there. You don't know nothin' about what I've seen or haven't seen, and you sure as hell don't know shit about shit. I was there, I know what the fuck went down. And listen, brother, I wasn't up in no fuckin' pussy Canada with my tail between my legs. You know what I'm sayin'?"

Talking to Norris was a mistake a person only made once.

Hungry, Eamon opted for an anonymous greasy spoon, red vinyl stools and a Formica counter. He ordered breakfast for dinner, eggs over easy, sausage links, hash browns, toast, coffee. The waitress, a large pasty-faced woman with dead pinkish eyes, took it down without once looking up at him. "Make that whole wheat toast," he said as she turned away. Sometimes he didn't feel like he was in the same world as everyone else, like he was living in some parallel universe where nobody could quite hear him.

At least he had something to read while waiting for his eggs. Eamon noticed that Ford's other two letters, like the first, were dated the same day, August fifth, 1967.

Darling Heart,
I tried to sleep but just couldn't. I guess I've gotten used to the not sleeping, to grabbing an hour here and there. Besides, every little thing, whatever it is, seems to startle me awake, as if all my sleep was on the very edge of consciousness anyway. To tell you the truth, somebody opened a beer and I jumped awake, as surely as if that beer can was a live grenade.

It's just as well. My dreams haven't been so good lately, if you really want to know. This last one, though, started out promisingly. I was in my Charger on a great big bridge, something like the Golden Gate I think—which reminds me, darling, please take the car out anytime you like; there's no sense in keeping it in the garage; who knows when I'll be back, and I feel funny about you always having to deal with that clunky wagon of yours—and anyway, back to my story, I was in my Charger with the radio on to something loud and bad, and I had that Magnum V8 roaring, and it was sunny and beautiful out, and that big old bridge just seemed to go on forever. Man, it was beautiful. I was up over a hundred, no problem, not even working up a sweat, cruising with the blue angels, and all my problems, whatever they were, they were back there, behind me, in the wind and exhaust. And it went on for the longest time, this fine wonderful feeling, all this sunshine and highway and bridge, and the only thing really weird about it was that there was nobody else out there on the road, just me.

But you know what happened, don't you? Sure you do. The sun went away, and it started to rain something terrible, and I was having trouble keeping the car under control, skidding all over the place. And I couldn't slow down for some reason, couldn't get my foot off the gas. And then suddenly there was no more bridge, just this abyss. I slammed the brakes, but by then it was too late, and I fell for what seemed like forever, right into eternity.

Darling, I don't think I'm going to make it, I really don't. I love you, I love you. There are some things I feel I must put to paper, just in case. I know it probably won't make much of a difference, being that words are just words. Still.

Darling, if I had never met you, then it all would've been for nothing. No one ever had a better friend, or lover, for that matter. In fact, I never knew a better person.

I have been so fortunate. I have the greatest parents in the world. No complaints there, no, sir. It's the one debt that I cannot ever repay. I don't think they ever denied me a thing, at least that I can remember. And if they did deny me anything, they did it only because they truly knew better.

I thank God for everything.

But most of all I thank God for my two little babies. Justy and Bobby, you're much too young to understand any of it, but whatever happens, whatever it is, good or bad, your daddy loves you and will always love you. I will always be there, even if you cannot see me. You must trust me on this one; as with so many things in life, you must have faith. There is so much I would like to tell you. You're both so young, and already I have such high, wonderful hopes for you.

I want you to live long, healthy, prosperous lives, and I want you to marry with the kind of amazing luck that I've had. I want so much for you. But let me tell you something right now: There'll be bad moments, times when things don't go right, times when you fail yourself and others—it's unavoidable, I'm afraid—and the thing I want you to know is that I'll love you just the same, just as much as ever. Life can deal such bad cards sometimes—there are cruelties that I pray you will never be exposed to—but I ask, no matter what, that you try to carry yourselves with honor and dignity. You are Fords, after all. One last thing: Good manners still mean something, regardless of how the rest of the world acts. Remember to say thank you and please because, believe me, the small kindnesses are always appreciated.

I keep thinking I should be telling you something else, that I'm forgetting something. But I don't know what it is, what I can tell you that will make any difference later on. Just trust in yourself and in your family and in God. Take care of your mama always.

Your loving daddy

Eamon looked up, a little teary-eyed, to see that his food was already there in front of him, that in fact it had already grown cold.

He arrived home shortly after eight. He could tell right off by the way all that weird blue light played in the windows that Muffie and Pinkus were in the living room watching television on his big Zenith. Just great. Another night in fucking rehab. It was bad enough that he wasn't drinking. But then you had Pinkus with all his crazy neuroses. That guy was a fruitcake, absolutely scared of everything. Made the Cowardly Lion look like a man-eater. Eamon couldn't believe it when they finally released him from that hospital. The only thing he could figure was that Pinkus's insurance must have run out. And then you had his loopy girlfriend, Muffie whatever the hell her name was. It was a helluva love story, the bulimic meets the obsessive-compulsive. They would have to tell their future children that they met in group therapy.

"Oh, you're just in time," Muffie cried enthusiastically. "I've got the popcorn popper popping, and Daniel and I have just been to the video store, where we lucked out again. Considering how late it was, I just couldn't believe we were able to get our greedy little hands on *The Way We Were* and *Yentl*. Oh, as you know, Barbra is just my absolute absolute favorite favorite! This is turning out to be quite the night, if I do say so myself. So won't you please join us, Eamon? Oh, pretty please."

He could hardly stand to look at her. Muffie was one of the eternally cute, a grown woman who went through life believing that she was just gosh darn adorable. Her cherry hair was done up in extravagant Shirley Temple curls, and the rest of it was just as girlish and off-putting, the sweet-sixteen angora sweater over the peaches-and-cream turtleneck, then that Minnie Mouse–patterned skirt along with the Annette Funicello saddle shoes. The original Mouseketeer. God, she was a picture. And when Eamon told her he was just too darn busy to attend a popcorn party, she gave him one of her world-class, lemon-sucking pouts.

"Oh, that just *really really* bites," she whined.

Eamon quickly collected his mail and retreated to the relative sanctuary of his upstairs bedroom. Those two ... he'd about had it with them. And he probably would have given Pinkus notice except that his rent was always early, and then there was the matter of his relationship with those damn cats. God, why did Trish have to leave him with two strange and obese cats named after Italian-American movie stars? The thing was, Pinkus didn't mind feeding them or even emptying out their daunting litter box. Pacino and Brando were big as raccoons and followed Pinkus everywhere he went. It was this whole Little Bo-Peep thing—and, if you asked Eamon, it was a little scary, the way the guy was always talking to them, going on and on as if they understood every word. Why, just the other day he'd come home and found Pinkus telling them about his latest grant proposal—this was how the guy made his money, applying for every government loan and little-known grant that came under the heading Career Deadbeat Graduate Student—like those two overstuffed rodents were *colleagues* or something, like they might even have something *essential* to add.

It was a bit much, but then again, everything about Daniel P. Pinkus seemed to be overdone. After all, this character had just gotten out of the loony bin for something called obsessive-compulsive behavior. Eamon wasn't really sure what the hell it was all about, but from what he could gather, Pinkus was in a constant state of anxiety, spending almost every waking moment worrying about all sorts of weird shit. To top it off, he was always washing his hands even when they were clean and redoing things he'd just done, like checking and re-checking to see if he turned off the oven or the iron, doing it hundreds of times, as insane as could be.

God only knew. Just leave him alone, for Christ's sake. Nights like this he just wanted to take a six-pack up and nod off with some nostalgic old favorite on the stereo. He closed the door on them, hoping they'd all just go away. Nonetheless, he couldn't block out the drifting, cloying chords of Barbra Streisand's "Memories." There would be no justice tonight.

Then to check out the mail. Of course, wouldn't you know it, the first item was a catalog from Victoria's Secret, as if he was to be continually tormented. All these beautiful and serene maidens in their panties, stretched out in their lovely sunlit boudoirs or wading through yet another sun-dappled meadow, scenes of such exquisite lighting and texture that it was as if some mad combination of Hugh Hefner and Claude Monet had produced them. Flipping through it, he not only thought of the paucity of such women in his life, but he also longed for them in that strange, not quite real way, longed for the unrealness of garter-belted beauties with sanguine, knowing smiles. For a quick, indelicate moment he wondered what Justine Ford looked like beneath the Chanel duds, in her white frilly stuff. Then he laughed at himself, at the very idea, like it was even a possibility.

The rest of the mail was the usual crap, the phone bill, the Visa statement, a plea for money from something called Citizens For A Better America—yeah, he thought, why don't I just write you out a check for about two trillion billion dollars, because that's what you're going to need just to get started—and then there was another freakin' postcard from the folks. They'd moved down to North Carolina a couple of months back, some condo village on the coast near Kitty Hawk, and since they weren't really letter-writing types they just sent postcards instead. Great bunches of them. They were usually like this one, sea-inspired shots with a hard-to-explain dated quality, a washed-out look that made him think early sixties. Here a grim, cadaverous fellow displayed his prized catch on the charter *Golly Miss Molly*. Eamon decided that he'd seen this one, that they must have sent the exact card a short while ago. Scrawled on the back in his dad's rough hand: *Fishing's Great! When you coming down, boy? Your mother—a fine woman, in case you've forgotten—misses you for some damn unfathomable reason. So get your ass in gear. Love, Your Old Man.*

Eamon guessed that they were lonely, for all the usual reasons, missing friends and family, in over their heads on this one. They hadn't really thought it through. His dad hadn't wanted to wind down his life in Miami Beach, like so many others. But just the same, it was weird to think of them out there on the Carolina dunes, so far away from their previous life. He felt bad for them. They'd been there for him all those times, and now in some odd twist they needed him. He'd get down there for Thanksgiving, without a doubt.

What a night. It wasn't even nine o'clock yet. Same old choices. McBain's new one from the 87th Precinct just sat there on the nightstand, all shiny new and unopened; hell, reading took effort. And there was never anything on television, the whole fucking world knew that. He felt such a giant blankness inside him and all about him. Even his room looked unlived-in. There were some personal mementos above the fireplace, that was about it, pictures of his brothers and old girlfriends and the one wife. He didn't think about Trish too much anymore, at least he didn't think he did. Okay, sometimes he'd wonder, just for the briefest second or two, where she was, what she was doing, and who she was with at that very same exact moment. He knew she lived out in Los Angeles now, and when he'd think of her he'd imagine her at some really dazzling party somewhere, somewhere he didn't know where, but outdoors with Japanese lanterns and champagne and fireflies, and then he'd see her dancing under the stars with some crummy stranger.

Despite what a lot of people thought, you couldn't just erase the years and pretend that certain things hadn't happened. And he'd certainly put his time in with Trish, doing all those lover things, cooing all the sweet words, talking about the kids they'd have and all the things they'd do and so much more.

He wouldn't have minded getting married again. Even if the first time was such a bonehead play. It didn't matter. Still didn't stop you from dreaming the little dream, the little house, the little family, little moments. He wondered if Justine Ford had ever walked down that big aisle. He kept coming back to her. He didn't know what it was. It was more than just the fact that she was a great-looking gal. Had to be. There were plenty of lookers out there, if that was the only thing you were after. He didn't know, he just didn't know.

Besides, what was he going to tell her? There didn't seem to be much of a case in the letters he read. It was damn moving and all, and it wasn't like he didn't feel for her for losing her father, who was obviously a first-rate guy, but it just didn't seem to merit official involvement from a postal inspector. How did he get into these kinds of things anyway? A pretty girl smiles at him, and he promises the moon, and when she kisses him his whole world goes upside down. What a jackass.

Except, he remembered, he hadn't gotten to Lieutenant Ford's last letter. But he just couldn't see it changing things, since it wasn't much, just a few short paragraphs. But there was something different about this one. As Eamon held it up to the reading lamp he couldn't help but realize that these were the last words of a dead man:

> *Darling Heart,*
> *I'm sorry to bother you again. I know I've probably bewildered you already with all my ramblings. But this is the P.S., and it's an important one at that.*
> *I can't get into it, I've probably already said more than I should've, but if anything should happen to me in the next few days, I want you to muster all your available courage and strength to find out the truth, whatever the hell it is. Things may not be as they seem. In fact, count on it.*
> *I just hope to give testimony, that's something I've got to do. Darling, I just wish I'd never even heard of what happened there with that little Vietnamese girl. Just some kid, you know. They called her Angel Girl. In some damn place called Phuoc Linh, which sounds about right when you come down to it.*
> *I wish I could tell you more. I wish for a lot of things. Love is eternal. That's what I know.*
>
> *Your loving husband, Billy*

Holy shit, Eamon thought.

Phuoc Linh just wasn't the name of a place that you'd soon forget. Not when Bunko was always calling it Fuck City.

And Angel Girl wasn't something he was likely to forget either. The motherfucker always ended his letters with that. Every single psychotic one of them. *For Angel Girl.* Mister Postage Due's own twisted way of saying Very Truly Yours.

Holy shit.

Bunko simply wasn't buying any of it.

"I don't care what the fuckin' thing says, it's a bunch of horsebleep. And I don't think we should be wasting everybody's time chasing after something that's all in the forgotten past. Dead and buried, as far as I'm concerned. Besides, I don't see what good it does anybody. I really fuckin' don't, and I mean that sincerely. I say we go out to Hollywood and do some real good with somebody who's living, for cryin' out loud. And not only is she still with us, this famous TV actress whose name I can't quite think of at the moment, but she's a total stupendous knockout."

"Bunk," Eamon said, more than a little unhappy with his partner's attention span, "I really can't believe you. Just forget California for a fuckin' minute. Have you listened to a word I've said about anything?"

Now Bunko didn't like the kid's tone. He wasn't used to Wearie giving him a hard time. But then it occurred to him that something else was at work here. Yeah, had to be. Nothing else made sense.

"Listen, buddy," he said to the kid, trying to soften the edges. "I think I know what's got your clock all wound up here. Yeah, I do. This all has to do with Trish, right? Hey, am I right? Look, *mano-a-mano* here. Your ex is out there in L.A.—don't think I don't know that; I know a lot more than I let on, *compadre*—and so this whole thing has got you, like, uh, profoundly troubled. Fucked up, as it were. That's it, isn't it?"

Eamon could hardly believe his ears. "What did you do, Bunk?" he said loudly, jabbing a finger into the big galoot. "Leave your brain at home this morning? This has nothing to do with *fucking Trish.* She's a *fucking memory* as far as I'm concerned. But this has a lot to do with Mister Postage Due and a woman named Justine Ford, you big moron. Haven't you been listening to anything I've said this *fucking morning?*"

Well, that was that. Bunko looked over the kid, his partner and good friend for the past seven years, and decided he'd lost his mind. Sometimes it just happened like that, with no particular warning. Besides Wearie losing his mind, it did not thrill him to discover that they'd taken center stage in the Command Post. Santos and O'Brian and Williams and several others had gathered on the periphery, ostensibly to enjoy the show. But Bunko, as he himself well knew, did not have to say a word. When the two-hundred-and-fifty-pound giant glared, grown men scampered.

"So here's the thing, Bunk," Eamon said, as if he hadn't noticed any of it. "It could be a coincidence—granted, an awfully big coincidence—or otherwise, if it's what I think—and I don't see how it could be otherwise, really—these two cases are totally connected somehow, as unbelievable as that might seem."

Bunko took his chair, the new specially designed one that had just come in from Italy. It was supposed to be good for your back. But he knew the real reason why that Harvard fuck Sedgewick had ordered them: It was an insidious attempt to get more production out of everybody. Ignoring Wearie, he turned to face the IBM and its luminous blue screen. Clicking through the menu, he finally found something appropriate.

"So my point is this, Bunk: Mister Postage Due and Lieutenant Ford were both in Fuck City. They both knew something about this Angel Girl or had heard of her or something. On the one hand, we've got this psycho job Vietnam vet who's still very much alive and threatening to kill the president. Then we've got Ford, who's obviously dead, but who went down in a pretty damn suspicious way. Now you've at least got to admit that. Bunk? C'mon, Bunk? I could use a little input on this sucker."

Bunko continued to play computer tennis, oblivious, delighting in the soft plinks and pings.

"C'mon, give me a break, Bunk. Hey, look, I'm sorry. I didn't mean to hurt your tender feelings back there. Listen, maybe I got a little carried away. It's just, you know, this case is important to me. I read those letters last night, and I can tell you that William Ford was one of the good guys. It came through loud and clear. And then there's the thing about his daughter. Okay, you got me there. I like her. Is that so terrible? And I want to help her. What's the big deal?"

"The big deal," Bunko said finally, swiveling around to face him, "is that this ain't our business. This really has nothing to do with Postal or anything else. Nam is old news, brother."

"What are you talking about, Bunk? What about Mister Postage Due? The Bureau wants that one solved, man. Montrez's been on our cases for weeks about it, and—"

"Give me a break, buddy boy. Get with the program. It's a nothing case. Threatening to kill the president, him and twenty million other unimaginative guys. If you ask me, just another disturbo who's shooting his mouth off. Just another guy without a day job. And let me tell you something else, since we're on your favorite bullshit subject and all: There ain't no connection between this Ford guy and Postage Due. Not a fucking strand connects the two—"

"How can you say that? What about Fuck City and Angel Girl? What about that, huh?"

"Wearie, obviously some battle took place there, okay. Phuoc Linh, right? Up in the middle of the country somewhere. Yeah, sure, that's it. Probably involved tons of GIs. Tons of 'em. And that Angel Girl probably isn't even a real person. Probably their name for something else. Hell, Angel Girl could be a fucking building or a bomb dropping out of the sky for all you know."

"Bunk, I know she's a fucking person. It says so right there in Ford's last letter. He says something about how he wished he never heard of what happened to Angel Girl, a real live honest-to-goodness person. Here. Take a look at it. I've got it right here."

"I don't give a shit. I have no interest. Just leave me alone. I've got important things to take care of right here. In fact, I'm losing to myself in tennis, which is a new kind of embarrassment."

"C'mon, Bunk. Let's take this case on."

"I'm not listening to you anymore."

As a form of illustration, he shoved fingers into those big cauliflowers of his. The big guy was a sight. In his new houndstooth tweed jacket. Along with those fine English twill pants. That perfectly conservative tie. He was trying hard. And yet nothing would ever save him from that face, from that wonderful, wonderful face. The nose was an honest-to-God tragedy, all fleshy and broken to hell, a nose to make even W. C. Fields wince. Then those ears, those magnificent boxer's ears. Featured even more prominently with those thick forefingers jammed into them.

"Oh, that's just great, Bunk. Real fuckin' mature. C'mon, let's discuss this like grownups. Or I might have to send you down to the principal's office, big guy."

"There's nothing to discuss. I want to go to California and ride around in a convertible. And you, on the other hand, are a prick."

"At least you were succinct."

"Fuck you. How's that for succinct?"

"Bunk, I'm surprised at you. This thing's got to be explored a little, and if you won't do it for me, then how about for Justine?"

Suddenly Bunko turned on him: "See! That just shows how little you know, Wearie. How very little you know. That girl's another one, another one if you ask me."

"You better spell this one out, big guy. Because I, for one, have no fucking idea what you're talking about."

"I'm talking about your new wacko girlfriend. Don't get wrapped up in that one, that's my advice, buddy boy. I didn't want to have to get into this with you. But I bumped into that Justine girl in the parking lot last night. I had some things to take care of in Holding, so I was a little late getting out of here, and—"

"So what's your point?" Eamon said, tensing.

"Easy, there. I'm almost sorry I brought it up. But maybe you should hear it anyway. Maybe it'll do you some good. That girl ain't right, if you ask me. Now I ain't going to say this to hurt you or any other shit, because you know we've been through lots of garbage, and that ain't my way. But listen, old buddy, she was coming on to me something awful, and—"

At this, Eamon broke into great spasms of laughter. Catching his breath, he managed, "Oh, right," and "Yeah, that's a good one," and "Where do you come up with this stuff?" Even for Bunk, this was reaching. Yeah, right, the wondrous Justine making a big play for Bunko in the parking lot. Only in his dreams.

"Kid," he continued, "I wish I was kidding. I mean, don't get me wrong. She's one prize specimen. So believe me, I was just as flabbergasted as you apparently are. I know I ain't Kevin Costner or fuckin' Tom Cruise or—"

"Bunk, you ain't even John Candy."

The moment he said it, he regretted it.

"You just go to hell," Bunko sputtered out before returning to his tennis game.

He just wasn't getting anywhere with it. He'd spent most of the day on the phone to the Pentagon talking to low-level public information officers. He'd been asked to "hold, please" dozens of times and had wound up telling his story just as often, only to be transferred time and again to someone just a stripe higher on the military ladder. "I'm sorry, sir, you'll have to talk to my superior about that, sir. Please hold, please."

Late in the afternoon, having spoken to perfunctory corporals and unhelpful sergeants and officious lieutenants, Eamon Wearie landed a full-fledged captain. Unfortunately, Captain Williard was standard issue.

"I'm not sure what you're after, sir. Is it your intent, sir, to disparage or in any way use this information to discredit the United States Armed Services? And sir, if it is true, as you say, that you are somehow working in conjunction with the Federal

Bureau of Investigation, then how is it, may I ask, that the FBI, an organization known for its ability to procure information, cannot supply you with the data you have requested? Now I must admit, sir, to a healthy amount of skepticism on my part and on the part of the United States Army.

"So let us begin at the beginning, shall we. You say, sir, that you are an official with some sort of branch of the Post Office that I, for one, have never heard of . . ."

It was hopeless. All he wanted to know were some old and dusty facts. He wanted to hear the official version of Lieutenant Ford's death for himself. He wanted to know what Ford had meant about giving testimony. Before what commission or review board? To do with what? And did he or didn't he testify on the day of his death?

That was to begin with. If he even ever got that far.

He also wanted to know the names of the men who'd served under him. Maybe somebody knew something or remembered the little detail that would pay off later. Maybe a lot of things.

But Eamon was starting to think that he wasn't going to get very far without Bunko's help. The man just knew how to cut through all the baloney and red tape. Bunk would've just grabbed the phone and pretended to be some eleven-star general. Just bully and B.S. his way through the ranks until the nitwits were saluting and yessirring up the old gazoo. If only he'd kept his mouth shut this morning; if only he'd given the big guy his due.

He'd just about run out of ideas. In his mind he kept going back and forth over the same tired possibilities. He was in headache country now, the dull, persistent throb of pressing too hard. All he had were the damn letters anyway. And he must have reread Ford's a dozen times. That was no problem. A mite sad, but no problem otherwise. There just didn't seem to be enough there. On the other hand, Mister Postage Due wasn't exactly easy reading. He cranked the hatred out on his old portable Smith-Corona, sending the sick missives directly from his tortured soul. Eamon had examined a lot of anonymous letters in the course of his job— everything from the harmless crank to the sexual deviant—but he hadn't seen anything to match this. Mister Postage Due was an American original, in the way that Hinckley and Oswald were originals.

They had five in all, five threats mailed out at monthly intervals with the same secret White House code. This was the main reason the Bureau had taken the matter so seriously. Anytime somebody says they're going to dispense with the president, the Bureau gets on it, pronto. But this was different. This was very different. The five-digit code was not common knowledge, not something Joe Public was likely to possess. It was used to disassociate the president's personal correspondence from the tonnage of mail that came in every day simply addressed 1600 Pennsylvania Avenue. Ordinarily the deranged stuff would just be weeded out by staff and handed over to the appropriate authorities. But in this particular case, the president was actually receiving and even reading these twisted pieces of mail.

That was the infuriating part. Or, depending on your point of view, the beauty of it. To the Bureau, it was something that simply had to be nipped in the bud. Even Montrez, who was like gray slate, just as hard and impenetrable, seemed on edge. It was Eamon's guess that the director himself—who regularly hit the links with the prez—had come down hard on this baby. It was the only explanation for the lengths to which the Bureau had already gone. Three full-time agents assigned to a special task force. White House staff and their immediate family members subjected to lie detector tests. Every kind of analysis known to man and computer on the letters themselves.

The lie detector tests had seemed like so much overkill. Considering that there were plenty of others, besides just staff, who were aware of the code. Friends of the president knew, of course. His lawyers, his accountants. The code even appeared on his monthly bills and credit card receipts. So there were plenty of ways it might get into an ambitious person's hands. Eamon figured that Montrez wanted to at least give off the appearance of leaving no stone unturned. Cover Your Ass, after all, was the motto of any self-respecting government agency.

They were more successful with the lab tests. It was almost unbelievable what they could do these days in the Bureau's infrared rooms. They had no problem discovering that he'd used a Smith-Corona typewriter, in this case a fairly common model from 1979. The paper, subjected to a battery of ultraviolet and chemical tests, was found to be a high-grade, easily smudged brand produced by the Papier Company of Buffalo, New York. Their products were primarily sold in the Northeast, and that fit in with the rest of their geographical-limiting finds. In fact, the paper—which had highly retentive qualities—was free of prints, suggesting that their man wore gloves in the process of handling it. Almost certainly, agents theorized, this was because his prints were on file with Selective Service.

The paper was also the basis for other leads. The lab found several hair samples from the same source, which DNA typing established as a balding, brown-haired male in his late forties. Coffee rings on one of the sheets revealed that he was a drinker: The lab guys were able to determine that he'd been putting away Irishes during that particular letter-writing session.

The postmarks on the plain white letter-size envelopes were all stamped New York City, which led them to wonder if he lived there or worked there or was just shrewd. He did not bother to affix stamps, somehow knowing that the special presidential code ensured delivery. It was another odd bit of insider's information, and of course it had led to his nickname. "Mister Postage Due" wasn't even up to their notoriously low standards, but it had stuck, and there wasn't much they could do about it now.

By far the most important clue was the trace of a telephone number. The number, which had been written on something else, was etched into one of the letters like it was a carbon. The absence of an area code had made things more difficult, but not impossible with the aid of AT&T computers. There were over seven hundred possibilities nationwide. But within New York's 212 area code there was only one. Unfortunately, it didn't turn out to be a residential number, as the Bureau team had hoped, but belonged to Con Edison, the city's electric company. It was their complaint bureau or, as corporate euphemisms went, their office of consumer affairs.

The investigators immediately requisitioned all of the consumer complaints Con Ed had on file for the previous year. If this guy was making a nuisance of himself in one place, their reasoning went, why wouldn't he be doing the same crap somewhere else? But so far they had been unable to make a match.

Eamon shuffled through the pile of copies—the Bureau had held on to the originals—arranging them in chronological order. He wasn't looking forward to going through them again, and he found himself fighting boredom and fatigue, all-too-familiar feelings in his line of work. Any job could wear you down after a while. Even going after would-be assassins.

May 5

Dear Mr. President,

I'm not quite right anymore. Something has gone out of me. I was once somebody too. It's a long time ago now. But I miss who I used to be. I know you don't give a shit. But I think I might have to do something about it for my little Angel Girl.

These things are not under my control anymore.

June 13

Dear Mr. Bigshot,

You better start thinking about us LITTLE PEOPLE, if you know what's good for you.

WE COUNT for something. You can't tell me we don't.

I grew up just like you, playing ball and doing things and dreaming of stuff.

The girls used to really go for me. But Phuoc Linh changed all of that.

Oh, what do you know about anything?

Me and Angel Girl NEVER HAD A CHANCE.

July 9

Dear Draft Dodger,

I'm coming for you. You might've avoided serving your country. But you're not going to avoid DIVINE JUSTICE. You don't even know what I'm talking about, do you? You, you lucky fuck. You didn't have to serve. You didn't have to be there that day. It was hot, MURDEROUSLY

HOT. The smell of SMOKE AND CHARRED FLESH.

God help me.

God help my Angel Girl.

And God help you. Because you're going to need it, YOU FUCK.

August 3

Dear FAGGOT,

You're not going to get away with it, you hear me? You don't have a FUCKING PRAYER. I'm coming for you.

I have killed before. But this time I'm going to do it for Angel Girl. And for what's left of me.

I have the means at my disposal.

And, when I get you, I'm going to COME RIGHT in your fucking mouth.

Choke on that.

Sept. 17

DEAR HOMO BOY,

You're not safe. You're going to DIE very soon. Nobody, not even your PRECIOUS palace guard, can save you.

You should have been there with me in the JUNGLE that day. You should have done your PATRIOTIC DUTY, just like the rest of us. Instead, you wind up in the White House, sucking off YOUR SECRET service agents.

Which only proves there's no God.

I'm going to fuck you up the ass.

And then I'm going to do your wife, too.

I'm going to do it for Angel Girl.

Somebody's got to pay the price for what happened.

Eamon was concerned with the technical aspects. He wondered if there was some sort of code at work, the way he capitalized certain words and phrases. He knew the Bureau's cryptographers had worked it all over, playing their own versions of Anagrams and Scrabble, and had discerned nothing as yet. Still he wondered.

He was interested in the letter's neatness. The guy knew how to type, that was for sure. There were no mistakes that he could find, no white-outs or type-overs, nothing like that, which in itself was unusual. It wasn't like he was using a damn word processor. So even though it sounded like blind rage, perhaps it was a bit more premeditated than that. Maybe he wrote it out in longhand first or something. Or maybe he was just the world's greatest typist. Who knew? Eamon made a note, adding it to that ever-growing list of things to come back to later.

He wanted somehow to keep his distance. Preferring to focus on those rigid, perfectly contained rows of print, black on white, only the bare essentials. It sure got complicated the further away you went from that and the closer you got to what he was saying and who the hell he was. Moving in on all that human strangeness.

You tried to make it like a little game. Like all those sick, pissed-off words were just building blocks. Like the whole thing was just one big Erector Set. You took it apart piece by piece. There was no other way.

You're going to DIE very soon. Sure as hell didn't sound like an idle threat. Bunko be damned.

I have the means at my disposal. What did he mean? That he had a gun? A plan?

I have killed before. No trouble there. No trouble believing that part. But did he mean in some battle? Or something far worse?

The girls used to really go for me. But Phuoc Linh changed all that. Had he been wounded in Vietnam? Is that what he meant? Or was he talking about his soul or something? Too damn cryptic to figure.

Phuoc Linh was key. *The smell of SMOKE AND CHARRED FLESH.* If only he could get something out of Defense about what went down in that damn place. Was it some big battle? Or something more isolated?

He noted the changes in tone and urgency, how each subsequent letter had become increasingly more hostile and ugly. It certainly didn't go by Mister Postage Due that his commander-in-chief had missed serving in Vietnam. Not to mention the blatant homophobia. Eamon didn't know what to make of it, other than the usual, which was that it almost always pointed to an unhealthy amount of self-loathing.

He was just going to have to keep trying. He picked up that goddamn phone again. He girded himself for all that military bullshit. The Pentagon just wasn't in the information business, that was for sure. No sir, sir. But this time he wasn't getting off until he got some answers. This time was going to be different. No more puffed-up corporals and reticent sergeants. This time he was going to land a major, and a talkative one at that.

Bunko was already five chapters into it. There was really no trick to the writing game, so far as he could see. He just tapped it in the way he remembered it. And God knows, he'd lived a colorful enough life, a real page turner. Hell, people wouldn't be able to put it down. God, he'd probably have to write like about nine sequels to it. They'd turn it into a movie, and he'd have to go on TV talk shows and all sorts of other celebrity bullshit. He hadn't even gotten to the good parts yet. Shit, he'd lived a life, all right. All the babes he'd had, not to mention the three wives from hell. He'd been a damn honest-to-God war hero. Saved lives, took chances in that jungle, you name it. Even had his own detective agency back when. Sure, broke some big cases. Got involved in some real gunplay. Killed a man, damn straight. Not that the clown didn't deserve it. Cheating at cards, Jesus H. Christ. Yeah, his life was a whole Mickey Spillane number. Now *there* was a writer. There was a son of a bitch who could write. Short and to the fucking point. No bullshit.

He'd have to come up with a real Spillane-sounding title. Call it like *Bullet Hell*. Naah, too easy. Not subtle enough. Maybe something like *.38 Special*. That was good, if he didn't say so himself. Or had they already used it? That was the thing with the good ones. He'd have to work on it. With any luck he'd have this sucker finished in a couple of weeks, the way he was going.

Besides, it wasn't like he had much else to do. What with Wearie losing his mind and everything. What was with that guy? First he gives up drinking, then he goes nuts. There was some correlation, had to be. There he was on the phone all day with the same narrow-minded, anal-retentive, idiot bureaucrats. He wasn't going to get anywhere with those bozos. Anyone could have told him that.

Still, he stuck with it. Bunko had to give him credit. He almost felt bad for the kid. Except. Except they could've been out in Southern California, the promised land. Listening to gentle waves lap ashore. Drinking funny-colored drinks. Making passes at women who looked just like Vanna White. Jesus. It was too much. Here, they just finished up with that Ridgeway crap, and now Wearie wanted to go on another cockamamy wild goose chase. Jesus, they'd just spent practically a whole year reading bank statements. What more did the kid want from him?

What they needed around here was a little leadership. Bunko couldn't get over the lack of interest from the top. In the old days assignments were just dished out. None of this back and forth crap, him and Wearie at loggerheads. But that Percy and his Harvard cronies, like they could care less. He couldn't figure them. Like they had nothing to do all day. Always slipping away for these marvelous three-hour lunches. Come back in such a good, bubbly mood, smelling of martinis and the good life. Then it was sit around and read the papers until it was time to go home. Which came at exactly four-fuckin'-thirty. Just beautiful. Watching these bonny princes hop into their fancy British roadsters and zoom away, as if they were all on one long permanent vacation together. Hell, he just couldn't figure it.

And then you had someone like Wearie over there. Actually gave a shit about his job. Christ, he suddenly felt lousy seeing the kid on the phone, going after it all by himself. Eamon was many things, but mostly he was true blue. And they'd been through some things, plenty. The worst part was the shit about that wacko, that Justine girl. The worst part was it was all true, just like he tried to tell the kid. She was making the big goo-goo eyes and all the rest of it that didn't go down too well.

Eamon was on hold again, cradling the receiver and listening to "Stars and Stripes Forever," when Bunko called over.

"Hey, kid," he said, "how about we make a little deal?"

That was how easy it was. A whole day with their

backs to each other, and it was over in nothing flat.
And it wasn't like Eamon had any trouble agreeing
to terms. Bunko was willing to help on one condition. One condition only. If they didn't come up
with something quick, real quick, they'd head out
west, to Bunko's version of the holy land.

Eamon watched in awe as his partner made ex-
actly one telephone call. To George G. Wilkenson.
Flapper to his friends. A bona fide two-star general.
"Owes me one," Bunko said matter-of-factly.
"Saved his big fat ass in the war."

He thought he handled it pretty well, considering. Of course, he could have gone with something pricey, say one of those hotels with a glassed-in French restaurant at the top, candlelight and a single long-stemmed rose, the whole damn city twinkling below. But then he'd have had to pretend to know something about wine and how to tip that haughty maître d' and all sorts of other nonsense.

The other choice was to go downscale, one of those crab places with newspaper on the tables and beer by the pitcher, which was more his way of doing things, if you really wanted to know.

But this was okay, just fine. He wouldn't have had it any other way. Busy little restaurant up on Charles Street, filled with suits and suitettes, everyone oblivious to the recession. He knew he'd made the right choice; it was her kind of place. It wasn't his usual terrain, but what the hell, it was just perfect for the getting acquainted stage. They talked like old friends and called out for more sushi and more Kirin beer and just rolled merrily along.

Okay, maybe he shouldn't have started in with the drink again. That was one thing. But when she asked him to join her in some sake, he didn't debate it, like he'd known all along it was going to

64

happen, one way or the other, sooner rather than later. It had seemed almost predetermined, set off in the genes like some silent alarm clock.

But that was another matter. Not something he was going to deal with tonight. Tonight was for being with an outrageously beautiful woman at a sushi bar. Tonight was for all things possible.

Oh, he had to admit, the whole thing was totally unlike him. Chasing after her the way he had. Even if he made it sound like official business. Nothing but the facts, ma'am. A masterful piece of phone work. And she kept saying, Thank you, Lieutenant. I knew I could count on you, Lieutenant. Almost as if she was playing along with him. Then he sprang it on her, trying to sound casual as hell, his heart racing like some damn adolescent's. What do you say we get together over dinner to discuss it further? Like it was nothing, no big deal. Like postal inspectors were always taking gorgeous members of the general public out on the town. Just part of the job, ma'am. The Postal Escort Service. More wine, ma'am? Or would you prefer a back rub?

Christ. But there she was, and she was really something, all right. The way she shimmered and glimmered, the way the light caught her emerald earrings and that golden necklace, the way it danced off those pearly whites and baby blues, the way it flashed on everything else. He'd be checking out those long, long legs, trying not to linger on their seeming endlessness, and then, embarrassed by his own admiring gaze, he'd suddenly look back up again, only to settle on that perfect, startling face. From those elegant cheekbones he'd work his way back to that sublime neck, and of course that led him to her breasts, which pressed forth into indigo silk, which gave him more reason for pause. He just didn't seem able to hold her fully, to capture her whole. All Eamon Wearie knew were dazzling fragments.

He tried to keep his mind on what she was saying, but the words just seemed to go right through him. He was all gone in the lights, and he stared, perhaps foolishly.

"Are you sure you don't want to try some of the fried eel?" Justine asked again. It wasn't the first time she'd had to repeat a question to him. "It's just divine. Absolutely scrumptious."

She dipped it in soy sauce and ate it with a bunch of her own personal lip-smacking sounds. He watched her every move, enthralled. He liked the fact that she wasn't dainty with her appetite. He couldn't stand it when he took someone out and she ate like a mouse, a nibble here, a sip there. Justine loved to eat, and she loved her sushi, mostly going for the real odd and messy-looking ones, sea urchin and quail eggs and salmon roe, anything that would have made him think twice. Eamon, on the other hand, played it safe, opting for the California and cucumber rolls. He just couldn't face those thick, bright slabs of raw fish that Justine was so keen on. When she forced him to try a bite, he'd smother it first in that hot mustard and ginger and soy. Actually, if Eamon had his way, he'd go for the shrimp tempura, or maybe the negimaki.

"What are you looking at?" she asked impishly, knowing damn well he was just interested.

"You," he said, for lack of anything better. "I like watching you, that's all."

"I'm not all that fascinating," she said, still smiling mischievously.

"Oh, but you are. You are."

He wasn't used to saying things like that, dumb foolish boy-likes-girl things. It had been all downhill since that first sake. Before that it had been more than a little awkward. He'd gotten there late, only to find her waiting outside under the restaurant's awning, a dark, unhappy look eclipsing her face. They played it pretty straight at first, doing a little dance of Q and A, everything aboveboard and duly official. Of course, she wanted to know what progress had been made, and she was mighty persistent at that. But he was doling out only the absolute minimum. That was how it had to be for now.

Flapper Two Stars, Bunk's old war buddy, had come through for them big time, delivering the goods by messenger. But instead of providing answers, the coveted files had only opened up an economy-size can of worms. There were worms crawling all over this one. He told Justine what he could. Like for one thing, that of the fifteen men who'd served with her father, only two were still alive. That wasn't the best ratio they'd ever heard. But they figured it was a war, and in wars people die. The way of the world, right?

Or so they thought. Then they dug just a fraction deeper into those gray, wordless files. The paperwork was numbing, pages and pages of computerized codes, cold and practically indecipherable. The men of Company A, 3d Battalion, 18th Infantry, 1st Infantry Division had been reduced to social security cards and birth dates and payment schedules. The numbers told the bare-bones story, beginning with each man's entry into the army—draft board classifications and aptitude scores and medical exams—detailing the stops along the way, from basic training camps to the strange, unfamiliar-sounding encampments in-country, everything up to their discharges or last fateful steps.

But those same matrix dots yielded up quite a story if you somehow managed to hang in there. In fact, pressing on through the official and quite dreary documentation, they discovered that a total of six men from Ford's old platoon—not just the two remaining members—had made it back to the States. All of them very much alive. But the numbers had three dying in the summer of 1969. On American soil. This seemed almost unbelievable on the surface of it. Three soldiers from the same platoon dying within months of one another and within months of arriving home—not the kind of thing you could easily dismiss with that all-inclusive word coincidence.

Though that's just what Bunko tried to do. Eamon was more than a little surprised that he was so willing to classify it as one of those things, just another series of unconnected, unrelated events as far as he was concerned, the type of thing life was always dealing out. But then again, Eamon knew Bunk had been doing his fair share of California dreaming lately, and the last thing the big guy wanted was some time-consuming investigation into something that had taken place more than twenty years ago.

And so far, Eamon had to admit, the facts seemed to bear Bunko out. Going after it by phone, they'd managed to put together much of what had happened to the three men. Donnie Bunce, a charter boat captain from New Jersey, had lost his life at sea. They didn't know all the details yet, but the authorities had ruled it an accidental death. Earl Shad, living on disability outside of Pittsburgh, had suffered a brain aneurysm. This they got from a very reliable source—his mother. They also discovered that Jackie Jay Robinson, the third luckless soldier, had lost his life in a house fire in Detroit. They were still looking into the fourth and final casualty, a guy named Chick Hurly, who had been living out in San Francisco. The thing was, Chick had left this world three whole years after the others.

Certainly, on the face of it, none of it seemed to

spell conspiracy or anything. Not counting Chick, three guys die in three different states in three completely different ways. But all the same, Eamon had real problems with the time frame. He wasn't calling it a day until he found out a few more things, like a few particulars.

He just couldn't bring himself to tell Justine any of this shit. He didn't know what it was, if it was just not wanting her to get worked up over a probable zero or if it somehow went a whole lot deeper. She was too beautiful for words, and sometimes she'd look at him in a certain way, like she believed in him and thought maybe he could help her, and somehow that just made him want to clam up. It was hard to explain. But he didn't want to blow it, steer her wrong. So he kept it inside and didn't say anything. When people believed in you, the worst thing you could do was give them false hope.

He did what little he could. He gave her some dope on the two remaining members of Ford's old platoon. He'd spoken to Coleman Briggs himself, a wonderful, affable sort with whom he had no trouble hitting it off. In fact, Cole—as he was called—owned a little hardware store out in Montauk, a picturesque little town on the eastern tip of Long Island, a spot the Wearie family knew well. Eamon and his dad had gone to Gosman's Dock plenty of times when he was growing up; they'd taken charters out and gone after the big ones, tuna and mako and anything else that thrilled. So he and Cole got along famously, talking about fishing and all sorts of shit, so much so that he almost forgot the reason he'd called in the first place.

But even though Cole tried his best, he still wasn't that much help. Said he didn't really remember no Phuoc Linh, that it sounded like any other Vietnamese town to him. And he didn't know anything about Lieutenant Ford testifying to anybody.

Though he did add that there'd been a lot of tension in the air just before Ford got killed, he did remember that. Cole hadn't been around when the gun went off, but he felt pretty sure that it was an accident, that nobody would be so dumb or crazy as to try and kill the commanding officer. Besides, it was Earl Shad's gun that misfired. Earl seemed to be a pretty sensitive kid and took it hard, as could be expected.

It was tough to talk about after all these years. That's what Cole kept saying. He even said he attended a weekly meeting with other veterans to discuss that very kind of thing. Because Nam was something you carried inside of yourself always. It was battery acid in your soul. Always eating right through you. That was how he put it, just like that.

Eamon tried to tell Justine that that was the part of the job he liked least. Prying where he didn't belong, getting into Cole's old festering memories, bringing back all the bad shit for him. Justine didn't seem all that interested in how Eamon felt on the job. She wanted to know what else he'd learned. Wanted to know about that other guy from the platoon. When he told her that they hadn't been able to locate him yet, that all they knew was that his last known address was New York City, she seemed disappointed and maybe a little annoyed to boot, like they hadn't done nearly enough.

That was how their evening started, under the restaurant's dark red awning, suits and suitettes brushing past them, so many little dissatisfactions on the cold night air. It wasn't until they were inside and the kimono-clad girl had brought the sake that the world warmed over and she remembered how to smile again.

"I loved my mommy, God I loved her, you know. She was just never the same, you know what I mean? She just wasn't. And for the longest time she never went out with anyone, just never. It was the whole martyr thing, wearing drab colors and not ever wanting to have a good time, like she wasn't entitled to it. She spent her days polishing the silver picture frames on the piano, the pictures of him. And every Saturday she went to Heavenly Gardens, the place where he's buried. It's not a bad place, really, a green hill that looks out over the town, and you can almost even see the water from there. His grandparents are buried there, and several generations before that. Not a bad place, really. I guess real far away from whatever he knew as his last minutes . . ."

Justine's voice trailed off, but it wasn't like she was about to cry or anything. She just seemed to be picturing the place, seeing that green hill again. She took Eamon's hand in hers.

"You're so easy to talk to. I feel like you know me somehow, like I've known you before. That I can tell you anything . . ."

He was in her blue eyes, their deep, surreal blueness, trying hard to fathom her mysteries, so great and so small. The Irish coffees didn't hurt matters, everything a warm, wet glaze now. In that artsy-fartsy bookstore-café across from the Japanese restaurant. At the art deco bar. Served by a bartender in a paint-spattered smock with a Vandyke. While all around them the young and the chic and the restless were drinking cappuccino from an elaborate golden machine and feigning unimaginable interest in the works of Dylan Thomas and Sylvia Plath. But dead poets were no match for those wondrous eyes of hers, so blue and alive and so blue again.

"You're so sweet, Eamon. You are. The way you listen to me, even if I just go on and on. Oh. So. With my mom. Mommy never ever went on a date after my daddy. Except. Except this one time. And

I really remember it, because Bobby and me were real happy that she was finally going to go out on a Saturday night. We were teenagers by this time, and we just wanted what was best for our mom. Because we really didn't know him. Because we knew her, and she didn't have much. She read the Bible a lot, and she kept the house cleaner than ... cleaner than I don't know. Just smoked her Salems and read and cleaned and cooked and walked around a little vacant-looking, really. Anyway, anyway. It doesn't really matter, it's all gone now. You're just sweet to listen to me. You are.

"It was a Saturday. Did I tell you that? And it was a lovely, warm night in May, one of those first really wonderful spring nights when all the wisteria and honeysuckle are perfuming the air, the kind of night when you feel like the world is just starting to open up to let you in. And I remember it like it was yesterday, like it was just yesterday, really. And Mr. DeShays came in his car, and it was a nice car, although I couldn't tell you what brand it exactly was, but me and Bobby were in the window watching her get into that car, and she was all dressed up that evening. She bought a new dress. This sweet polka-dot thing from Ursula's Dress Shop. And I helped her do her hair, pinning it back, which was the best way for her, and I tell you, we were all in it together that night. And there we were, waving from the window, and Mr. DeShays even gave us a nice, good-natured toot on the horn, and that's why it was so awful later on when they came back.

"They must've only been gone an hour or so, no more, I don't think, when poor Mr. DeShays pulled back into the driveway in that nice big car of his. At first I thought something truly terrible had happened because Mommy could barely look at us, and she just ran up the stairs to her bedroom without explaining a thing. Why, at first I thought maybe the man had tried something funny. But of course that wasn't it. Mr. DeShays owned the stationery store and was a widower himself and wasn't the type to hurt a flea. It was just because of Daddy, that's what it was.

"You know, she never went out with another man as long as she lived. Mommy just never got over him, and that's all there was to it. Isn't that something?"

It still threw him a little. The way this elegant grown woman got when she talked about her mother and father. Almost like a little girl. And it did something strange to him. Made him just want to draw her close and hold her tight and protect her from all of life's miseries. It was as deep and primitive as it got, a feeling that was probably just as familiar to Cro-Magnon man.

"Your dad must've been a great guy," he said. "It was there in the letters, it really was. The way he loved your mom and you guys. You and your brother Bobby. Which reminds me, what's your brother up to these days?"

It was the pause, the way she paused that gave her away. It probably didn't last a second, but Eamon knew the mind could travel over whole oceans and continents in that beat of time.

"Oh, he's doing good. Real good. Out in Minnesota now. Likes it out there a lot. Oh, you know what? I'd love another coffee. Can I talk you into it?"

She could have talked him into anything. That was the problem. The bartender with the goatee— who was quick to inform his customers that he wasn't really a bartender at all but an important new painter of abstract expressionism—set about the task of preparing their Irishes. Eamon watched in mock-horror as the goatee added Chivas to cappuccinos and then went crazy with a can of Reddi Whip. In a final stroke of tormented genius he trickled crème de menthe over the whole mess. On another night Eamon might have demanded that the mad painter do them right, strong black coffee with more than a splash of Old Bushmill's, topped off by a dollop of freshly whipped cream. But tonight he just felt too good for that, for starting up with someone.

"These are abstract expressionist Irish coffees," he said, touching his glass to hers.

"Well, I guess we can be glad we didn't get a cubist," she said, right there with him.

"Have you ever noticed that you can never find a realist when you need one?"

"Boy, isn't that the truth," she said, the smile forming.

"Next we'll do some shots in pop art colors."

"Seriously, though, do you like any particular school?"

"Harvard's a good one," he said, smirking. Then he saw that serious, well-intentioned face and took another tack. "Well, personally, I've always gone for impressionism. The Monets and Manets and a bunch of those Dutch guys besides. Something about that rich golden light and those lush meadows and when they do lily pads and shit like that. To tell you the truth, I've always been a sucker for anything pretty."

"I own a Renoir," she said.

"Auguste?" he said, taken aback.

"That's the fellow," she said, clearly enjoying his reaction. "Very lovely. A nude. It was a gift from my husband."

"Husband?"

"Don't worry, it's not like that. Been over for some time now. Very amicable and all that. And you? Are you married?"

"Not recently," he said, suddenly realizing they didn't know a hell of a lot about each other. "Geez, your ex-husband must've been in the chips to buy you a Renoir. Probably wasn't a postal inspector, right? Just a guess there. Incidently, Justine, I don't know if it'll come up, but I usually just send red roses. Okay, maybe, if I really went nuts, I might splurge for Godiva chocolates, that's about it. I can't really remember the last time I sent somebody a Picasso or something. Oh, wait a minute. Yeah, right. I almost forgot. I did send this one girl a Van Gogh. Yeah, couple years ago. Good day at the track. Some damn picture of sunflowers. Nice, though. Maybe not worth fifty million, but hell, it made her day. You know how women are. Nothing like a museum piece to brighten their day."

She had a funny look on her face. "I like you, Eamon Wearie. You're just demented, and I really go for that in a man. And besides everything else, you're so damn good-looking. I can't imagine how your wife ever let go of a package like you. I'll bet she regrets it now."

He felt uncomfortable when she mentioned his looks, even though he had been staring at her all evening for the very same reason. It just seemed like a dumb thing to rely on somehow.

"Yeah, Trish," he said, as if reminded of some other lifetime. "Old story. Mistaking sex for love. Young and foolish and hot for each other and just letting the world happen to us. Well, at least we didn't have kids and screw up their lives, too. At least that. You don't have any children, do you, Justine? Now'd be a good time to get that out of the way."

"No. Just the Renoir. That's my baby."

The moment came. Just looking into each other's eyes. Both thinking along the very same lines. Moments come and moments go, but Eamon Wearie made the most of his opportunity. He kissed her now, while he had the chance, while she was still there.

They went for subtlety, brushing each other's lips with eyes closed, believing perhaps that magic happens only in the dark.

When they drew apart she said softly, "When we finish these, why don't we go somewhere more private?"

He knew just what she meant, of course. But his first horrible thought was of Pinkus and Muffie and those humongous cats. She was way too classy for his place and all that it entailed.

Then she saved the day by saying, "We could go to my place and have a nightcap there, if you'd like. I'm not far."

It was much too good to be true. And with it came the unsettling quiet. Eamon was just afraid of blowing it at this point. As they finished their coffees he wondered if everything was indeed leading up to where he thought it was leading. He also knew things were happening way too fast, and that if personal experience was any indication, they should just call it a night.

Justine seemed to realize his uneasiness and tried drawing his attention elsewhere, asking him what he thought about the big canvases strewn about the café. "I believe they're the work of students over at the Maryland Institute of Art. Rather good, don't you think?"

He just couldn't see it. Most of them were so angst-ridden, full of wild black tornado swirls and skull bones and bloody slashes, representing Armageddon and terrible plagues and all other frustrations of the very young. There was one he liked. Some autumn squash on a windowsill, lovingly rendered, reminding him somewhat of Cézanne. It was something he could see putting up in his living room, see spending some time with.

"You like the still life, don't you?" she said, watching him. "I should've guessed. A man set in his ways. Not wanting to be encroached on by a rapidly changing world. Finding safety in the warm late-afternoon light. Right?"

He just nodded, never one to like being analyzed.

"You know, Eamon," she said, deftly changing the subject, "there was one thing I've been meaning to ask you about. It's about my daddy's letters. I was actually kind of wondering where you found them. Like, where were they exactly?"

"Well, I'll tell you, I wasn't actually the guy who found them. Somebody I work with, Lita Sanchez ..."

Hit him like a thunderbolt. Couldn't believe it. Forgotten all about it. They had a date tonight. Supposed to go over to her house and have some supper. Friday night. Christ. Just stood her up. How could he have been so stupid?

"Justine, I'm sorry. I've got to make a call. Be right back. Only take a minute."

There he was with the young, chic, and restless, calling in his apologies. In line for the pay phone, trying to think up something quick, something damn good. A girl in a crimson beret and a huge afghan sweater and these skin-tight black leotards got on right behind him. And she just started staring at him, he could feel it. Oh, great. Just what he needed now. The student artist from hell. Her eyes didn't let go of him, and he did his best to ignore her.

The Friday night crowd swirled about them, noisy and unrelenting, not allowing him an alibi. It would be pretty difficult to tell Sanchez he was home sick in bed. A minor car accident might work. Unconscious for a couple of hours, something like that, maybe. He didn't know. Have to see how she sounded, how pissed off, proceed from there. That was the best way.

He dialed. Christ, he was feeling guilty as hell. Kept seeing her there with her ruined dinner, the candles melted down, tears screwing up her mascara.

"This better be good, Eamon," she said with fire. "You better be in the fucking hospital. That's all I have to say, you fucking shithead."

Worse than he thought. No two ways about it, he'd have to go with a major five-car collision, maybe even throw in a little tractor-trailer action.

"Boy," he said groggily, trying to get it down, "how'd you know? Did Bunk call you? Oh, man, I'm sorry. But you know, they wanted to keep me for observation—"

"Eamon, are you okay?" she asked, concern suddenly edging in. "What happened?"

"Oh, yeah, I guess so," he said, taking full advantage. "You never know with these head injury things. Funny part is it doesn't even look that bad. But once you're out for a couple of hours—"

"You were unconscious?"

"Listen, I'll be all right. At least that's what Dr. Jacobs says. I just wanted to make sure I somehow got to you to explain—"

"Never mind about me, Eamon. What happened? Are you okay?"

Success. She believed him. Perfect.

The only trouble was that student artist from hell. She was listening to his every word and scowling at him something fierce. Her eyes were ablaze, like in a comic strip or something.

"Yeah, Lita, that trouble spot on Route 40. Right. This Alpo truck just comes flying out of nowhere. God, maybe the driver was drunk, I can't figure anything else. First he smacks into this family in this van, and then all hell breaks loose. Oh, it was horrible. Crushed metal, glass everywhere. Christ, it was an absolute miracle nobody was killed. But everybody's going to be okay, that's the main thing."

"Eamon, what's all that noise in the background? What's going on over there?"

Shit. Doubt was creeping back into it again.

"Christ, it's that kid in the next bed. He's got the remote control, and he's got it on some goddamn MTV dance-party thing—"

The student artist from hell picked this opportune moment to rip the phone from his hands and scream into it:

"DON'T BELIEVE THE MOTHERFUCKER! HE'S IN A FUCKING BAR! JUST ANOTHER PIG LYING THROUGH HIS DICK!"

Eamon didn't even bother to retrieve the dangling receiver. He could hear Sanchez's disembodied voice calling out his name. But it was too late, much too late for that. The damage had already been done. The student artist from hell just glared at him, almost challenging him to do something. But he already knew he was no match for this babe. She'd cut him to shreds in that knife fight.

She pulled the costly sedan—a burgundy Jaguar with a leather interior that had to be seen to be believed—into the garage of her Bolton Hill townhouse.

"You're so quiet all of a sudden," she said. "Is everything all right?"

He didn't know. He felt it was all somehow out of his control, almost like he was wandering about in someone else's dream. That weird. He was just going to go with it, whatever. There was no turning back now. No turning back in someone else's dream.

They entered the foyer. He stood on the marble

floor and gazed up in wonder at the huge crystal chandelier overhead. She led him through French doors into a dark, oak-paneled library. An elaborate Oriental rug rested in the center of the fine parquet floor. Leather furniture from another era, two large armchairs and a psychiatrist's couch, were in deep forest green. Shelves were loaded down with ancient-looking books, probably chosen for no better reason than their sturdy, regal spines. A fireplace with a fancy set of bellows and prods completed the picture.

She poured him a drink from a crystal decanter. "I hope you like cognac," she said. "I'm going to change into something more comfortable."

She left him standing there, mid-dream. He drank the cognac and waited for its searing warmth. He examined a Ming vase in the corner. He wondered all over again what he was doing there.

It wasn't long before he heard her calling out for him, a hoarse whisper across rooms.

Justine was on the staircase. That was where he found her. But it was how he found her that he'd never forget.

She could have stepped out of one of those lingerie catalogs they were always sending him. She was one of those serene, garter-belted maidens. One of the unreal and untouchable. At last Eamon would find out for himself about that sanguine, knowing smile.

5

"It wasn't the worst idea you ever came up with, I'll tell you that, buddy boy. Not that I think it's going to add up to meat loaf, if you know what I mean."

Bunko was at the wheel of his new Ford Bronco, looking right behind all that horse. It was a gloomy gray afternoon, the sky low and oppressive, but he was in an expansive mood nonetheless.

"Actually, Wearie, you're starting to use the ol' fuckin' noggin again. I'd almost given up hope on you there. But let's make it quick with this Bunce guy. Let's not waste too much fuckin' valuable time with somethin' that I happen to feel is totally unnecessary. Because I feel lucky, I swear to Christ I do. Like I could break the fuckin' bank. I'm not going to go easy on those bastards today. I'm not walking out of those casinos with anything less than three million. That would put me just about even for my lifetime."

Frank Sinatra belted one out about how he'd been a pirate and a poet and a pauper and a bunch of other things. Bunko sang along, in his usual loud and unperturbed way. Frank was always in the tape deck when they went to AC. Nothing else would do. All part of Bunko's preparations and gambling

81

superstitions. He had at least a thousand of them. For example, they always had to stop at that little coffee shop in Absecon, no matter what time or inconvenience. Because that one time he won big he'd had breakfast there. And it was good luck if you found any coins on the ground heads-up. Tails-up, you just left well enough alone. Then there was the thing about the dead birds. He actually believed that if he saw a dead bird on the drive up, he was doomed at the tables. God, his face would go absolutely white if he noticed, say, some limp seagull on the roadside. He'd want to turn the car around right then and there. God, the more Eamon thought about it, Bunko had a million of them. There was the matter of his shirt, his lucky shirt. This one was a beauty, a watermelon-colored silk Mafioso number that he refused to wash; a throwback to the old days, the kind of thing he wore with regularity before he decided to go upscale. Lucky clothes and lucky cloverleafs and lucky gum and lucky M&Ms. It just went on and on. Eamon wasn't even sure how his partner kept track of it all.

It didn't matter. The only thing that mattered was that Bunko loved Atlantic City more than almost any other place on the planet—and this was something Eamon could work to his full advantage. Nunn Bunce still ran his brother's old charter boat business out of Brigantine, which was only a mile or two north of AC. It had been over twenty years since the Coast Guard had fished what was left of Donnie Bunce out of the Atlantic. The propane explosion reduced his thirty-five-footer, the *Sand Crab*, to charred rubble, to mere flotsam. They'd already spoken to Elton Munk, who'd conducted the investigation. The retired police chief, living in Arizona now, remembered the case well and was more than convinced it was a freak accident, even if the investigation turned up an oddity or two. Nunn

Bunce wasn't so convinced. Nunn Bunce had what they call dark suspicions.

He wasn't very forthcoming on the phone. Kept hinting at the suppression of evidence. Kept saying something about the whole story not coming out. But when Eamon pressed him on it, Bunce got all agitated and paranoid and shit, telling him he wasn't getting into it on the goddamn telephone with somebody he didn't even know.

Just as well. Gave them an excuse to get out of the office for a day; it had been a long time coming. Bunko was clearly excited, racing the Bronco up over eighty miles per, which was fast even for him. He drove with a solitary pinkie on the wheel and hardly bothered to notice the road.

"Christ, we're almost there. Beautiful. Just beautiful. Just do me one fuckin' favor: Let's just do this Bunce thing in record time. That's all I ask. Nothin' there, believe me. 'Cause, Christ oh God, I feel lucky. I don't even know what I'm going to do with all the money I'm going to win. Christ, I always wanted to have my own bar. Naah, I'm not setting my sights high enough. Maybe like some kind of unbelievable entertainment complex, with drinks and pool tables and like some kind of movie theater that shows only horse racing. You know, like twenty-four hours of track action from all over the world. Something like that maybe. But classy, you know what I mean. No riffraff."

"Yeah, right, Bunk. No bums need apply. Nobody with a gambling problem or anything. We'll screen everybody. Make sure they have jobs and everything. Ahead of your time, that's what you are."

"Damn straight, kid," he said, ignoring the sarcasm. "You know, forget the entertainment complex. Too small-time. Why not my own casino? Give me one good reason why I couldn't—"

"You're a middle-aged postal inspector whose total net worth could fit neatly on the head of a pin."

Like he didn't hear a word: "Yeah, it'll be great. My name up in lights, just like Trump's. Call it something like Bunk's Place. No, no, you're right. Not snappy enough. Needs zing. Wait. I've got it. Bunko World. Like with that Disney World, you know. A casino for the whole family. Sure, sure, that's it. We'll cater to kids. But in a good way. We'll run clinics to get them off on the right foot. If only someone had taught me how to gamble when I was little. It's like with swimming or languages or ..."

Eamon just let it go right past him. Years of being together. Years of knowing when to tune in and tune out. Sinatra crooned on about an unforgettable girl under an unforgettable harvest moon. He tried to concentrate on that. They were nearly there anyway. The Atlantic City Expressway ran right through the marshland, just flatness and tall grass and the crying of gulls and the smell of low tide. You could see the casinos in the miragelike distance, great monoliths that stood defiantly on a fragile sandbar facing the rugged Atlantic. Actually, they looked like a row of grim, unyielding dominoes, ones that would never fall into place, no matter what Bunko might think.

Hundreds of billboards lined the straight-as-an-arrow highway. Giant winning couples smiled back at them. They were pictured eating in lavish casino restaurants. They had cordials in romantic casino lounges. They were massaged and pampered in casino saunas. And they never lost. They hit blackjack everytime. They threw magical dice and never crapped out. They pulled slot machine handles with coin-jangling success. They lived in billboards, these giant, fraudulent people. Eamon had been to AC enough times to know what the people in a casino really looked like. One needn't look further than the line at the credit card advance machines; the sickness held in those tired, hapless faces was not something you were likely to see on a billboard anytime soon.

And yet the buses came from everywhere. It was the land of buses. Of every type and persuasion. Sleek Greyhounds sprinted alongside chartered vans and old backfiring school buses. But mostly they were buses emblazoned with casino names, expensive new double-deckers filled to the rim with low-rollers, with average Joes and Joleens, their coupons safely tucked away in their vinyl wallets. Of course, there were also plenty of those long white limousines, and it wasn't hard to imagine the fleshy, satiated men behind the blackened windows.

The traffic slowed, suddenly a great flash of red taillight.

"What the fuck?" Bunko blurted. "Christ, we're behind schedule as it is. What the hell's going on around here?"

"I thought we hit all the tolls," Eamon said, somewhat less concerned. "Could be a fender-bender or something."

They crawled forward, stop and start. "This is unbelievable. Costing me money every minute. Jesus, wait'll I get hold of the guy responsible for this."

Sinatra sang a little song about taking it nice and easy while Bunko continued to sputter and moan.

"Oh, my God!" he suddenly exclaimed. "Not that. Anything but that."

"What, Bunk? What is it, what do you see?"

Bunko had gone mute. And up ahead Eamon could see the reason why. There'd been a little accident. Nothing to write home about. No need for ambulances or tow trucks. It was an odd little thing, really. What had apparently happened was that a Ford Taurus had slammed into a couple of big birds as they were trying to cross the highway. Closer inspection of the feathery disaster site revealed the victims to be a mother crane and her two babies.

"Anything but that," Bunko repeated numbly, as if his world had suddenly ended.

Brigantine was just over the bridge from Harrah's. A quiet, sandy peninsula, some older motels and newer condos, seafood restaurants and gas stations, a sense of just passing through.

It was warm and humid for mid-October, and the sky remained a sagging, dopey gray. The dock was hushed and still, and they didn't see anyone about. They walked past a friendly flock of sailboats first, Hobie Cats and Sailstars and Newports. Then the Boston Whalers and those phallic-looking high-speed jobs. Eamon would've taken a varnished, sprightly sailboat over one of those expensive speedsters any day. The big, impressive cruisers with their double outboards, the Bayliners and Hatterases and Vikings, were parked at the end of the dock, in front of shacks the size of outhouses. The names of the boats and the kinds of fish they went after were posted outside the shacks. Most of them departed at six in the morning and returned around noon. It was a little after two, which explained the absence of people. Still, Bunce had said he'd be about.

"He's obviously not here," Bunko complained. "I say we just forget about the whole stupid thing. I'm not kidding."

"You're just in a hurry to lose all your money."

"Yeah, well, at least I'm in a hurry to do something."

It wasn't long before they found the *Sand Crab IV*, a thirty-some-odd-foot Bertram with twin Mercury engines. Bunce was on the stern, watching TV. He was a rangy, knotty-looking fellow with a scraggly mustache and ponytail. He was in cutoff jeans and a T-shirt. The shirt said Fuck the Dolphins/Save the Fishermen. He took another swig from a can of Bud Dry. His face was empty of expression, but there was something angry and inarticulate there nonetheless. Eamon could feel it, just feel it.

"Hi, Nunn? I'm Lieutenant Wearie. My partner, Lieutenant Ryan. Spoke on the phone, remember?"

He seemed to take a long time answering. "Yeah, so?" His voice was as gnarled and belligerent as the rest of his features.

"So fuck you," Bunko interjected. "Federal fuckin' agents, pal. Working on an A-Number-One-priority case. So don't fuck with us, know what I mean? Now just answer my friend's questions. Then we can all get the fuck out of here, okay?"

Eamon didn't much care for Bunko's approach. But he knew it was an approach with a very big success rate. And Bunce did get real contrite in a hurry. He even mumbled something about being sorry before asking them aboard. There was fish blood all over the deck, and it didn't smell too great on a still and tepid day.

"Nunn, you told me something about things not being right about your brother's death. What did you mean?"

"I still don't get it. Who are you guys? What's this got to do with my Dono?"

Bunko took out his badge and shoved it in Bunce's face. "I'm going to have you arrested for obstructing justice in about one fuckin' second if you don't get mighty fuckin' cooperative. We don't have the time for this bullshit."

"I never even heard of, like, whatever you guys

87

are," he uttered meekly. "Something to do with the post office, right?"

Eamon took over. Time to play good cop. "Listen, Nunn, we're not even sure what we're after. We're just checking all the angles. For all I know, we're barking up the totally wrong tree here. We just want to know if there was anything weird about Donnie's death. Anything at all."

"Yeah, if you count being murdered as weird," he spit out, refusing even to look at them. He leaned back in his deck chair with his Bud and stared ahead at the battery-operated television. A baseball game was on. National League playoffs.

"Give me a break." Bunko had had about enough. "That's not what Elton Munk says. And he should fuckin' know. He was the sheriff who led the investigation, in case you forgot."

"I didn't forget nothin'. You ask Elton about the beer cans? Did you? You know about those? Or the cigarette butts?"

"Talk English, pal. You got something to say, just say it."

"Dono didn't smoke, man. And Dono didn't drink. But they found all these beer cans and cigarette butts in the water near what was left of the *Crab*. Elton and the Coast Guard came up with this bulldink that there was a leak in the propane stove, and that the whole thing went kaboom when Dono had a cigarette. That's what they put in their official report. But Dono didn't smoke. Explain that shit, man."

"Well," Bunko said, considering it, "there's probably a dozen possible explanations. Didn't your brother run a fishing boat, for Christ's sake? The beer and the cigarettes could have been left over from some fishing party or something, right?"

Now Bunce turned and gave Bunko the once-over, like he was wondering how far he could go.

Bunce was a hard one, all right, and there was something out of whack about him besides. His bloodshot eyes were always darting away from you, and he was missing a bunch of teeth. The ones that were left were a distasteful lot, stained and yellow and crumbly. It didn't look like the guy gave a shit about much. Like it'd been a million years since he'd been there for anyone. Eamon kind of felt sorry for him, and he wasn't really sure why.

"Could have been, maybe," Bunce said under his breath, his timing way off.

His eyes went back to the game. Mister Hard Nut to Crack. And just as they started to turn away from him, tired of the whole business, he lashed out:

"Except for one thing. I cleaned out the boat the night before. Don't you think I'd remember that? Sure I did. That was my job. I worked with Dono. He gave me a job. Nobody else would. Just my younger brother. I was older than him and shit, but in some ways he was older than me, know what I'm saying? He was just like always more mature and shit. He was just better than me, that's the truth.

"It was Sunday night, end of the working week. We didn't do Mondays. That was right after them astronauts landed on the moon, and ol' Dono was just bursting with American pride. Think I'd forget that? He just loved that moon shit. But it was Sunday night, and I emptied out the cooler and all that. Believe me, I'm sure I did. Because I used to always take the leftover beer for myself. That's not something I'd forget to do, you read me?

"It's just my feeling and all, but I think somebody was out there with him that day. I swear to fucking God I do. And let me tell you something else while we're on the subject and all: If there was some propane leak in the goddamn stove, don't you think

Dono or me would've smelt it? Sure we would've. We practically lived on that boat. Knew it inside out. And, besides all that shit, we never even used that freakin' stove, like never. So that's another damn thing that don't jibe.

"I don't think I'll ever know what Dono was doing out there in the first place. He sure as hell wasn't fishing. He left all the rods and shit, and he didn't even have much fuel. And believe me, him going out there without me, without telling me, totally unlike him. I was his brother. Don't you think I know shit like that? So when I tell you it don't make no sense, you should believe me, fellas. But when a little man dies in the big world nobody's going to go to too much trouble, know what I'm saying? That's the way it was and the way it is and the way it always will be."

Bunko and Eamon didn't say anything for a long moment, reassessing. They let their eyes wander over the life preservers and buoys and buckets of rotting bait and other crap that was just littered about. The day was a black and white photograph, the water like dirty glass. The TV announcer described a long fly ball to the warning track. Three up, three down. End of four, still zero-zero.

"Nunn, you mind if I have one of those beers?" Bunko asked casually, like you could discount everything that had gone before. He helped himself to one and then planted his butt down on Bunce's mega-size Igloo cooler. "Okay, let's say your brother was killed. Who'd want to do it? Who'd have a reason? Know what I'm saying?"

"That's just it," Bunce said, shaking his head. "Don't you think I've been over it a couple zillion times? The man had no enemies. One of the most liked son of a bitches who ever lived. That's why Elton never went after it properly. 'Cause he couldn't find no motivation. The only suspect in the whole thing was me anyway. Can you believe that shit? Like I'm gonna do 'way my own bro."

"Why'd Elton think that?" Bunko asked it carefully, in a tone far away from accusing.

"'Cause who do you think got the business? But the thing Elton didn't know was we were up to our ears in goddamn debt. 'Cause we bought the business from our old man. But Dono was trying to improve it and make it into something top shelf. Just like Dono to do that. So he borrowed all sorts of dough and got the first *Crab* and all, which was one sweet, beautiful tub, man. So there was no bread to score, nothing like that. We didn't even have insurance, we were such losers. I had to go bankrupt, and it took some time, man, to get it back together. But I vowed to Dono's memory that I'd bring it all the way back. Shit, yeah. It's not like I did much in my life, but I came through there, know what I'm saying?"

"You sure there was nobody out there who wanted to do your brother harm? Okay. What about just before he died? Do you remember anything about his behavior or anything else that seemed a little out of the ordinary?"

"It's like twenty-something years ago, but you don't forget, man. I been through it. Nothing. Nothing stands out. Just like always the night before. Sunday night. Had pizza together from Alberto's. I got shitfaced as per usual. He went through the books. Had the radio on. 1969. Music from 1969. Lot of Stones, just like today. Doesn't seem that long ago to me, I'll tell you. Jesus, some mornings I still get up and look around for Dono, like none of it ever happened. Pretty fucked up, huh?"

"Not so fucked up," Bunko said softly.

"You know, I'm forty-nine, man. Getting up there. But it's like I was left back there, like everything stopped moving after he took it."

"Did he ever talk about Vietnam?" Eamon asked.

"Naah. That was a closed subject. Said it was some shit over there. But wouldn't get into it nohow."

"Nothing? Talk about his buddies? Not ever? No specific incidents? No? Are you sure? Try to think back."

"Shit, I'd remember it if there was anything to remember."

"Ever hear of a place called Phuoc Linh?"

"Fuck what?"

"Never mind."

"It's funny, though, because he got a call from one of his Nam buddies not long before all the shit went down."

"What?"

"Yeah, see, I remember that. Just a couple days before. Maybe the day before, now that I think about it. I'm not really too sure. I answered the phone, and the man says he wants to talk to Dono, and I ask him who's calling and shit, and he says that he's somebody Dono knew over there, and he wants to surprise him and shit."

"You remember that?"

"I remember that."

"No name?"

"Like I told you, it was a surprise and shit."

"You don't remember your brother's reaction, do you?"

"What, are you kidding? It was a private call. I respected that."

"Are you sure this call happened just before the boat blew?"

"Yeah, but what's the big deal? What's going on here?"

"Nothing," Eamon said.

"Nothing that can't be explained reasonably," Bunko added.

The boardwalk was as dismal as their moods. Bunko was down a grand, and Eamon was down half that. It was drizzling, but they didn't seem to notice. They just walked through it. The concession stands were all but empty. The ocean was a flat, uninspired expanse of brown. The only people about were the panhandlers and those guys with the rickshaws. "Need a ride?" they kept calling out. A woman with no hands and no feet played a harmonica. Eamon threw her a buck.

"You're such a sucker," Bunko said.

"What do you mean? That lady's pretty bad off, even you can see that."

"I read an article about her, in the *Sun,* of all places. They showed how much these bums in AC cleared in a year. That one there makes over a hundred big ones a year. Declares it to the IRS, she does."

"Bullshit."

"God's honest truth."

"She makes more than I do."

"Well, at least she has a talent, Wearie."

Some scruffy characters held signs in front of Bally's declaring that the world was going to end tomorrow. GOD WILL DEMAND SOME ANSWERS, one sign dripped in red paint. DOOMSDAY IS COMING, another said.

"I got news for all of you," Bunko shouted at them. "Doomsday already went down. It happened to me at Caesars a little over an hour ago."

They went into Bally's. They had a good oyster bar, and it was relatively cheap, not a small consideration at this point. They opted for big bowls of creamy chowder and peel-and-eat shrimp and imported beers.

"So you're not buying any of it, are you?"

It was the first time Eamon had brought up the Bunce business. He knew Bunko was reluctant to get involved.

"I got news for you, Wearie," he said, dipping one of the icy shrimp into cocktail sauce. "You think you got me pegged, don't you? Think you know my reaction before I give it, right? Think maybe like I don't buy none of this murder-conspiracy bullshit? Right? Tell me the fuckin' truth now."

"I just think you need some hard evidence, and—"

"Bullshit. Hear me. Bullshit. I think something's happening here, okay? How do you like them apples? Yeah, I do. Three vets from the same fuckin' platoon dying within a few months of each other is a bit fuckin' much, if you ask me. And something smells about today, too. We're obviously going to have to go a little further with this shit. We got to do a lot more checking on those other guys. Christ Almighty.

"And there's some other stuff I haven't even told you yet. I just didn't want you to get all worked up the way you always do. But yeah, I heard from Flapper about a couple other things. Turns out Ford did testify on the day he died. Some fuckin' official army commission. I forget what they called it. Some internal affairs bureau. Anyway, here's the deal. The whole thing's sealed, no way in hell anybody can get a copy of it. Not even fuckin' Flapper. Imagine that. Two-star general, and they won't let him near it. Mighty fuckin' unusual, said so himself. Flapper also said that as far as he and his staff could determine, there were no major battles in Fuck City. Just a little nothin' hamlet near the Cambodian border. Which pretty much convinces me that Mister Postage Due and this whole Ford thing are related somehow. So what do you think about that, smartass?"

"I'm completely stunned," Eamon declared. "I can't believe you've actually come around on this. This isn't like you at all. You're usually the last person to arrive at an obvious conclusion."

"Very fuckin' funny. There's a lot of shit you don't know, Wearie. I read Ford's letters. I was moved by them. Yeah, *moved*. I got feelings, pal. I was over there once upon a time. Just a kid, you know. A scared kid who'd made the mistake of enlisting. Believing in God, the American way, and Superman, the whole enchilada. You just wouldn't know anything about that, would you? You and your fucking generation. All of you cynical know-nothing bastards, not believing in shit. I know all about believing in something and wanting to believe in something. There was a time, pal, not so long ago either, when the good guys wore white hats and John Wayne wasn't some cynical fucking joke. We believed in that shit, me and Lieutenant William Ford. We believed in things. Which is a hell of a lot more than you can say."

Eamon knew enough to keep his mouth shut. He watched as Bunko tilted the chowder bowl back to his mouth and slurped up the last remaining bit.

"Good soup," he said, dabbing a napkin at himself. "Whatayasay we hit the Castle going out of town? It's the only casino I haven't made a little donation to. Let's face it, I owe them a couple of hundred."

They walked out of Jib's Oyster Bar and made a path through the crowded casino. It was the usual mad swirl of bordello color and flashing light, all accompanied by the usual shrieks and groans of the dice tables and the usual frenetic slot machine noise. The machines whirred and clanged and buzzed and dinged whenever a few quarters dribbled out. It was all to make you think that lots of people were winning and that all you had to do was dig a little deeper. Women with blackened hands brought the handles down with numbing constancy in sad, endless pursuit. They were of a sort, these women. These women with their pink and blue hair. Dangling cigarettes from their mouths like a forgotten addiction. These big-bottomed women in their fuchsia velour jogging suits. Dreaming of triple cherries and wild sevens and the golden fruit salad. These possessed-looking women who at least knew how to dream.

They went from the Slot People to the Bus People. The Bus People were a most forlorn group, moping about the cavernous waiting room, sipping colas and contemplating the agony of defeat. They were old men in straw hats and shabby alpaca coats with faces etched by the deep, granite sadness of time. Their unforgiving wives, on the far side of those worn benches, eyed them with supreme distaste, as if they were lepers besides having lost the grocery money. One after the other the huge, beastly buses pulled up to the curb, growling and snorting, pausing only long enough to gobble up these small people.

"Jesus, look at all those losers, willya," Bunko said with his own special brand of empathy. "So I think we parked on three, right? Yeah, level three, I'm sure of it."

Eamon merely smiled. On another day—and there would certainly be other days at this tacky shore town—he might have seen it all differently. He probably would have felt like those losers in the bus terminal, down all that money and feeling like there was nothing on earth left to smile about. Losing money could do that, make you feel all tapped out in the soul. He'd been there. Who hadn't? But today he saw it for what it was, a vast and tired carnival of penny-ante people and spinning wheels and colored lights. You could take it or you could leave it. You could do anything you wanted with it. It didn't matter to him.

Of course, he had his reasons for not caring. He had the luxury of thinking about her. And she'd been on his mind the entire day, just sticking there. He kept trying to imagine everything through her eyes, always wondering what she would think and dumb shit like that. He was probably in love. He didn't know for sure. Love wasn't something he was any expert in. But just the same he kept saying her name to himself, like some damn mantra. Justine, Justine, Justine. Three times like that. God, it was so damn stupid. He had to be in love. No other explanation fit.

chapter fifteen

So I says to Lorna to shut up. "Shut up, bitch, I've had enough of your whining whimpering bullshit. Now pay attention to what I have to say."

It was tough, real tough. We had some times, me and Lorna. She was a piece of work, this one was. That Mona Lisa face of hers. Those melons she had, ripe and firm and juicy. And she was a good lay, no one could take that away from her. In fact, we'd just done it in the one bed, and now we'd moved over to the other bed, the clean bed. They always put two big queen-size beds in those rooms over at the Ramada, which I could never really figure unless it was exactly for times like this. We were in our regular room, number twelve. Let's just say we were sentimental about things like that. Anyway, to get on with it, I didn't want to break the news right away and all. So like I said, we'd done it and all, and then we were smoking cigarettes and having hits of Wild Turkey and stroking each other in that affectionate post-orgasm way.

"Listen up, babe," I said again, cutting through all the man-woman bullshit stuff. "I gotta dump you, I'm sorry to say and all."

Of course Lorna was hurt and probably surprised as well and started yelling and screaming and spitting at me and all that woman stuff. But I explained it to her. I told her our affair had to end. That it wasn't right. I had to be tough, show some resolve. And it wasn't easy, I'll tell you. There she was all naked and looking good the way she could. And of course I would probably be missing out on my normal blowjob and all.

But Lorna finally calmed down, and then she said something like, "It's your wife, isn't it, Bunko? She's found out about us, that's it, isn't it?"

I said, "Babe, it's not that. My wife, that fucking ogre, doesn't know a thing."

"Then what is it, my big teddy bear?"

That's what she liked to call me because she said I was all furry and cuddly and other stuff that I don't feel like going into here.

Anyway, I had to tell her. "No, babe, it's not my wife, that Loch Ness monster. No, the thing is this, I'm seeing somebody on the side. I gotta be honest here, babe."

"But Bunko, you're seeing me on the side."

"Yeah, Lorna. But there's someone else, too. Her name's Bunny. I'm sure you'd like Bunny if you ever had the occasion to meet and all."

Bunko looked over what he'd just written and wasn't nearly satisfied. He'd struggled over it all morning and a good part of the afternoon. It wasn't nearly tender enough. He just wasn't good with love scenes and mushy stuff like that. It was too bad. Because he'd felt something deep and profound for Lorna, and it just wasn't coming through. When he had first started doing the book he thought it would just write itself, nothing to it. But the more he'd been at it, he wondered if he was up to the job. It wasn't as easy as it looked, that was all.

Christ, writing was hard work. And lonely, too. He hadn't realized how much time writers spent doing nothing. There were these great lapses where you just stared at that stupid machine and tried to think something up. It had always looked like such a cinch when he'd read his favorite authors like Ludlum and Clancy and Deighton. Boy, he loved that kind of shit, that thriller stuff with all the spies and new secret military weapons and the fate of the world hanging in the balance. Even more than detective novels. Probably because he'd been a detective and knew what a boring bunch of crap it really was. But boy, give him a fat new Ludlum and he was in hog heaven.

Maybe he was just going about it wrong. Maybe he was making a mistake writing about himself. Maybe he ought to write a novel, something big, really big. Something with like a hundred different plots going off in a hundred different directions and everything building and coming together with great unmitigated suspense. Sure, that was the ticket. How hard could it be?

Bunko went right back to work, more determined than ever. His fingers fidgeted anxiously on the keys as he stared into that flickering gray energy field. He waited for it to hit him. That first sentence that would take him there. He kept waiting and staring and waiting. Now if he only had an idea of some sort.

Bunko was actually relieved when Percy and his Harvard cronies finally returned from lunch.

Wearie had taken the afternoon off, so it was his job to get Percy to sign the expense vouchers. Not that it was a big deal or anything. Percy couldn't have given a shit one way or the other. But he was taking no chances, just in case. Because the last thing he was going to do was pay for Detroit out of his own pocket.

Percy was standing in front of his secretary's desk with his assistants, Huntington Kissup and Howel Brownnoser IV and Linton Asswipe. Jesus, he hated these fucks. There they were, smartly dressed in their shiny double-breasted suits and five-hundred-dollar loafers and those plutonium Swiss watches that cost about a year's salary. He still couldn't figure how these guys did it. Must have been from rich families, no other way.

"Excuse me, Mr. Sedgewick," Bunko said, as politely as he could muster. "I need you to—"

"Wait your turn, will you, Ryan?" he said imperiously. "Can't you see I'm busy? *Really* now."

Percy turned his attention back to Ada Frompner, his executive secretary:

"Listen, make that reservation for eight sharp. I'm serious about that. I won't have time to dawdle at the bar tonight. And make sure you tell Frederick that I want the back table, he'll know what I mean. Oh, one more thing. Have you verified my Virginia weekend? Well, get on it, then. I mean, that should have been taken care of eons ago. *Really* now. Do I have to do everything around here?"

Then Percy brought his unfriendly gaze back to Bunko: "Now, then, what is it?"

"Well, sir, Lieutenant Wearie and I are working on a particular case that requires we go to Detroit tomorrow, and it's a rather expensive proposition, since we weren't able to give the airlines much advance notice, and—"

"Enough. I don't want to hear another word

about it. These details are of no interest to me. Where do you want me to sign now? Hurry. Let's just get this bit of unpleasantness out of the way."

Bunko didn't know what to make of it. He had never had an uninterested boss before. Quite the opposite, actually. He'd always worked for small-minded bullies and tyrants who demanded to know his whereabouts every single second of the day. This was definitely a new experience. But as he watched Percy's gold pen race across the triplicate, he couldn't decide if it was a good thing or a bad thing, oddly enough.

Eamon arrived home in the early evening, packages in hand. It had been some time since he'd had reason to go shopping for clothes. He would not brave mall oblivion for just anyone. She had inspired him, though, to push his Visa card to its limit. He bought for her, wondering all along if his choices would be her choices. There were the Bostonian shoes, wingtips that were colored like fine wine. He also picked out a pair of tan oxfords, for preppy weekends together. It was not a day for knowing when to stop. He found a wonderful little place for shirts, and no one stopped him from buying as many of the beautifully striped shirts as he liked. He sorted through dozens of Italian silk ties in the most up-to-date drips and spatters, choosing without regard to price. He paid extra to have his gray flannel trousers cuffed and ready for tonight. Actually, it was fun spending money. There was nothing quite like it, really.

He also bought her a large box of assorted chocolates, splurging for the Perugina. He stopped in Little Italy to see Antony, his eighty-two-year-old barber. Antony still offered up hot shaves and still only charged three dollars for a haircut. Eamon always got a special feeling in the cozy old-fashioned shop with its spiraling candy stripes—all part of a vanishing world—and he never failed to tip the kindly old man extravagantly.

It had been a pleasant, breezy autumn day, and he had wandered about the city in the haphazard, unhurried way of a man of leisure. He relished his freedom, stopping here and there, innocently flirting with the salesgirls, treating himself to lunch at that English pub on Redwood, that little Tudor building he'd passed so many times before, where he indulged himself with the sherried steak and the cottage fries and Watney's from the tap, all of it as wonderful as could be.

"Doing your Christmas shopping a little early, aren't you?"

It was Pinkus. His tone sour. He was in a ragged old bathrobe standing in the doorway of the kitchen eating Campbell's alphabet soup right out of the can. Those two pesky raccoons were at his feet, looking up at him with something akin to admiration.

"Decided it was about time I spruced up my wardrobe. So where's the Muffin tonight? Searching out video shops all across our fair city for some minor and forgotten Streisand classic? Or is it going to be the action-packed *Yentl* yet again?"

No response. He just stood there in the dim light. With those tortured eyes of his and the long flowing hair and that biblical beard. He looked like Jesus in a ratty bathrobe.

"What, Dan? I say something wrong?"

"She's had a relapse. She's back at Smather's."

"Oh. I'm sorry." Eamon didn't know what else to say. Pinkus looked like he was on the verge of tears.

"Yes, it was all very tragic, not that you would care much. She went to the supermarket unescorted. Usually she goes with someone from her outpatient group. It's basically a buddy system. Well, you can imagine what happened. Alone in the supermarket, all those aisles. She was like a walking time bomb. She started in the candy section and worked her way to baked goods, and it was all over before she even made it to frozen foods. They had her pinned down at that point."

"What the hell are you talking about?"

"The good news is that they won't be pressing charges."

"I don't get it. What was she doing? Shopping without a license?"

"I suppose that was meant as something funny," Pinkus said, shaking his head in disgust. "That's just like him, isn't it?" Pinkus said, addressing those two overstuffed rodents now. "Turning everything into a big dumb joke. What did I tell you about him? That's right, he's callous. Callous, that's a good human word, isn't it?"

"Very cute, Dan," Eamon said, figuring Pinkus was just pulling his leg with this shit. "I'm sorry, I didn't mean it that way. I just don't understand why Muffie was arrested in the IGA."

"Well, she was out of control of course. Helpless, as it were. Banana cakes, coffee cakes, those Ding Dongs and Yodels and Twinkies and God knows what else. I mean, this was all right there in the open for her. She just went wild and started devouring everything in sight. No way she could hold off until the cashier. I still don't understand why they don't keep all of these hideous temptations behind a locked counter, like with pharmacies and that kind of thing. Food can be a dangerous drug, too, you know."

"Yeah, right, Daniel." Eamon was looking at him as if he was wearing a straitjacket instead of a bathrobe. "Well, it's been swell, but—"

"Oh, incidentally, some girl has been calling you all day."

Oh, don't tell him that. If she cancelled ...

"Yes, somebody called Sanchez or something."

"Oh," he said, relieved. "Thanks. Listen, I've got to get ready. Big date tonight."

As he hurried away, up the stairs to the sanity of his own bedroom, he could hear Pinkus trying to explain the concept of a date to those two big furry things.

But nothing could deter his mood tonight. He put Tom Petty's "Full Moon Fever" into his CD player and turned it all the way up. Then he started running the bathwater. He hadn't taken a bath in ages. He was a shower person. Every morning he shocked himself into consciousness with a cold one. But tonight he felt like the whole shebang, warm bubbles and rubber duckies and special fruity soaps. Tonight was for baby powder and expensive new cologne. Tonight was for getting all duded up.

"I almost called to cancel," she said in that little-girl voice, drawing circles in his chest hair. "I was so nervous today, you wouldn't believe. I bought new perfume and a whole new outfit. Everytime I thought about you it was almost like too much. I started getting ... I don't know. I guess I just didn't believe it was all really true. And the funny part was I didn't even want to pick up the phone today. I was so afraid you'd cancel on me."

They were tangled in the sheets of her bed. It was a big brass bed, and Eamon kept thinking of that Dylan song. Their clothes, their new clothes, were still at the bottom of the staircase. They never made it out the door.

"I'm sorry about dinner," she said, not really apologizing. "I hope you didn't go to any trouble making reservations."

"Yeah, I'm really going to hold it against you," he said in good spirits. "Ruined my whole fucking evening. Having to make love to you when we could have been eating at McDonald's. Actually, it's too bad, though."

She looked at him with expectant eyes, waiting for the punch line. She was getting to know him real well.

"Yeah, tonight I was going to fly you to New York. Yeah, no big deal. But I'd read about this Lutèce joint being like the best in the country, and I just thought it might've made for a good change of pace. What do you think?"

"Well, I don't know. Remember last week when you took me to Paris on the Concorde? Of course you do, don't be silly. We were going to have a little dinner at Maxim's and then fly to London for a show. You remember now, don't you? But the problem was we wound up eating all that airline food on the way."

"Oh, yeah," he said, happy that they could play this way. "It's all coming back to me now. Chicken à la king in first class. We were sick as dogs for days. How could I forget something like that?"

"Eamon, I have something to tell you."

Her face had gone all serious, and she was gripping his arm. She took a deep breath. "Here goes nothing," she said, inches from him. "I'm in love with you, Eamon. I love you."

Just three itty-bitty words. Three words he hadn't been able to utter in years. He'd heard them a few times, but even so, not for a while, and not from anybody like her. He fell back into her eyes, into her eternal blueness. "I love you, Justine," he returned, easily.

"I love you," she said again.

There they were in the dark saying over and over the three little words. Words that always wound up meaning too much or not enough at all. It seemed like he was in the middle of this great unreality, in shadows and half light, in a place of sweet distortion. He didn't have to think, and he didn't have to know in the unreality. All he had to do was say the three little words, and as long as he kept saying them everything would be all right.

They didn't seem to tire, not of the words nor of each other. Bodies in the dark. Approaching. Responding. Doing it again. She swayed on top of him in the great unreality. Naked, white flashes of her. Losing himself to feeling, to just feeling. The way she smelled, her very breath. The way she felt, the way she felt. He floated through memory and time, thinking of other women he'd known, lewd snapshots that were just as easily discarded. He could fall back into her eyes anytime he desired, and that was a power over all things.

Then it was over and they were lighting cigarettes and retreating back into their own tiny unshakable worlds. He could only guess at what she was thinking. He was spent, and it would have been nothing now to drift off to sleep; how little it would take. But he knew better than to do that. He stroked her hair, caressed her. Just wanted her to know he was there for her. Actually, it took a long minute before he realized something was wrong, to see that she was crying. The thing was, she did it without making a sound.

"Did I do something wrong?"

"Oh, no, just hold me. Hold me close."

He brought her in to him, covered her in the darkness.

"Oh, Eamon, will you protect me? I need someone to protect me."

"Protect you from what?"

"From myself. From that."

"What are you talking about? I want to help you."

"I'm always looking. Can't you see that? I'm always looking. I don't know any other way, don't you see?"

"But Justine, what are you looking for?"

"I wish ... I wish I knew."

Then they were quiet again, just glowing cigarette tips in the lonely darkness.

When she finally snapped on the lights he felt more than a little disoriented. He experienced a sudden, almost indefinable sense of loss, and he didn't know why. She said she had a surprise for him. She got out of bed, unabashed, and he followed her with his eyes, with his pornographic eyes, as she disappeared into the closet, the walk-in closet. It was that kind of bedroom, like a suite in a fancy hotel with a couch and chairs and rich draperies.

"I'm sorry I didn't wrap it," she said.

It was that painting he'd liked, the one from that artsy-fartsy café. The still life, autumn squash on a windowsill. He was taken aback. It was really lovely, and he couldn't remember anyone ever doing anything like that for him before. He couldn't help thinking of the box of candy he'd given her, how it paled. She stood there, in all her naked, brazen glory, remarkably at ease.

"It's too much," he managed. "Way too much."

"I wanted to give you something to remember me by."

"What do you mean remember you by? Are you going somewhere?"

"Don't be silly, Eamon. It's just a way of saying something. So you like it?"

He went over to her and kissed her as tenderly as he knew how. "Justine, it's the nicest thing anyone ever gave me," he said, holding her, meaning it. "Now I've got to go. Which I wish I didn't have to. But I've got an early flight. You don't have to see me out. I'll find my way."

"When will I see you again?" It rushed out, in a lover's panic.

"Not tomorrow—"

"You'll be back from Detroit by the weekend, right? Oh, let's spend it together, Eamon. Doesn't that sound wonderful and romantic? We could go away somewhere, just you and me."

"Of course, I'll have to cancel my date with Princess Stephanie. It was my Monte Carlo weekend, but she can be such a royal pain in the ass, as you've probably heard."

"Oh, I love you!" she exclaimed, looking enthralled.

It worried him. It just fucking worried him. Things were going way too well. A flaming asteroid was probably going to slam right through the roof at any moment.

He began collecting his clothes at the bottom of the stairs, starting with his underwear, silk boxers bought that afternoon with dreams of a night like this. He marveled at the sheer lust and determination that would cause such debris.

He was almost dressed when he noticed the large, silver-framed photograph. It was in a lonely corner of the marble foyer, practically hidden behind a potted palm. Still, it was strange how he hadn't noticed it before. It was a picture from her wedding day. Justine was in white satin and as beautiful a bride as there ever was. But that's not what grabbed his attention. It was her choice of grooms, the heavyset, middle-aged gentleman who wore morning gray beside her. He could have been her father, if you didn't know better. He was not a young man, that much was clear. Nor was he much to look at. And while it was true that he might have made up for it with loads of personality, Eamon somehow doubted it. There was something smug and unholy about his countenance. Something obscene about seeing him there with that flower of a girl.

Eamon Wearie figured the obvious. That she had married him for his money. Here he couldn't have been more wrong.

They enjoyed eggs Benedict and Bloody Marys in the extra-wide comfort of first class. Bunko wasted no time upgrading them. The old master ravished the plumpish ticket agent, indicated dismay that she wasn't a professional model or actress. When she asked if it was a business trip, Bunko had to tell her sadly no. Eamon almost gasped when the big guy explained about the liver transplant he was to undergo in a renowned Detroit hospital. He only hoped he would be able to use his return ticket. The man had no shame, no concept of it.

Even though their every whim was being met, he was already busy complaining.

"Christ, I can remember a time, buddy boy, when the stewardesses were actually good-looking. Now I'm going back, way back. And then, you know, they wanted to be called air hostesses or some such shit, and then it was the whole flight attendant thing. Christ, I think they just ought to call themselves airborne construction workers. Did you get a load of the broad who's been serving us? I mean a good look. Christ, I'm not positive, but I think she used to be a linebacker with the fuckin' Bears. She sure as hell looks like him. What's that guy's name? You know who I mean. The Fridge. Refrigerator Perry. Yeah, sure, that's him. Great human interest story. Probably already been in *USA Today*.

"Christ, I can remember when flying was a big deal, kid. Not like today with deregulation and all. You take a look back there in steerage? Just take a peek behind that fuckin' curtain back there, and you'll see about two hundred fuckin' refugees eating Spam on toast. Hell, riding Greyhound is more glamorous than air travel these days."

He was a funny picture, really, deep in the soft plush leather, downing his third Bloody Mary, with his headset on and the shoes off. He was wearing those sock-slippers they hand out in first class, and he was half listening to the country music channel and still going a mile a minute.

"Christ, Detroit. Just where I always dreamed of going. Fuck California! Right? No, we couldn't go there and meet that actress with the big zoombas and soak up some good, cancerous rays. Naah. We couldn't do that. Couldn't make your old best buddy Bunko happy for one fucking moment in his entire lousy miserable existence. No, we had to go to Murder City. A dream come true, Wearie. I'm not fucking kidding."

Eamon decided it was about time to set the record straight. "Bunk, this was your idea. Not mine. You wanted to find out what happened to Robinson for yourself."

"Damn straight I did, kid. Jackie Jay Robinson. Unfuckingbelievable. I don't even know how I got involved in all of this. Kid dies in a fire. That's what the army says. But nobody knows any details. No obituary in any fuckin' newspapers. Nobody's left from his goddamn family. Two brothers gunned down in the streets in what looks to be drug-related matters. But nobody ever took the time to figure it out. No arrests, no nothing. His mother dies a few years ago, and the father was long gone before the kid was even born. Beautiful. Even the fire department doesn't have records. Listed the fucking thing as suspicious, but nobody ever took it any further. Like Jackie Jay never existed. I'll tell you, that's being black in America, my friend. Like nobody could give a fuck. You don't have to be awake too long to know that.

"So that's why we're putting off our trip to California. Because right now I'm going to get to the fucking bottom of this. But I blame you just the same, Wearie. Make no mistake about it. You're the one got us involved in the first place."

Eamon was glad to have his partner back on the case. In fact, this little trip was not something he would have undertaken without him. Neither of them had ever even been to Detroit before. They just had an address, 1276 Friendswood, which was off Jefferson Avenue. Where Jefferson Avenue was was another matter. They had a map, sure. Jefferson ran alongside the Detroit River. This is what they were going in with. A street number. The fucking number of a house that no longer existed. Jackie Jay Robinson's house. Bunko was satisfied that this would be enough. Eamon didn't doubt him.

They wanted to know a whole lot more about how Robinson had died. Neighbors might surely remember something. They'd searched for family members through the telephone book, sifting through several dozen Robinson listings before they finally gave up.

Their interest was renewed by two things in particular. Number one was the fire's official status as suspicious. Ironically, the complete files on the matter had been destroyed in a municipal fire in the early seventies. This was about par for the course when you were dealing with twenty-year time lapses.

The second thing in particular was Chick Hurly.

Chick Hurly was the last member of Ford's platoon to die in the States. They'd only just learned that he'd lost his life in a car crash outside of San Francisco in 1972, three years after Donnie Bunce and Earl Shad and Robinson. It was not your average accident, though. Not by a long shot. Hurly was blown to smithereens in a Ford Pinto that, according to court testimony by on-the-scene witnesses, was merely tapped from behind by another car. The Ford Motor Company's lawyers tried to prove that the Pinto's rear-mount fuel tank had been tampered with. The Hurly family, after a bitter eight-year legal battle, was finally awarded $1.3 million in a jury trial.

Official court documents could have filled a dozen or so shopping carts. The fun reading was on its way. In the meantime, it was more than interesting to note that both Donnie Bunce and Chick Hurly had been blown to bits in circumstances that might best be described as ambiguous.

They were beginning their descent. Eamon could see the blue water of the Detroit River through his window. It made no difference if the river was polluted, which he guessed it was. All water looked blue from a mile up. Even the city, its downtown spires and sheet glass brilliant with morning sun, seemed unremarkable at this height, like any other metropolis. But Eamon knew about Detroit. Everybody knew about fucking Detroit.

They got into the lead cab in the queue. They were each carrying a small tote bag. In case they had to spend the night.

"So where can I take you two gentlemen this morning?" the cabbie asked genially.

"To 1276 Friendswood," Bunko said, lighting up a Marlboro.

"You guys must be from fucking out of town or something," he said, still smiling. "You don't want to go there. Nobody wants to go there. Not even the ones already there."

"Just move it," Bunko said.

"What if I don't want to take you?"

Bunko showed his badge. "See this? Federal agents. We have the right to commandeer this cab and throw you out on the curb. You want that? Or would you rather be paid today? Take your pick."

The cab pulled out. Bobo Warshawsky, Hack #8469, looked like that demented comedian. That guy that threw watermelons off buildings. Gallagher. Bobo was balding on top, but he kept what was left long and stringy and greasy.

"Youse aren't from around here. You just don't understand. I got nothing 'gainst them people. They just took our good city and run it into the ground, that's what they did. That's an indisputable fact. Grew up here, should know. Little house on the east side, not even there anymore. Moved to Macomb like everybody else with any sense in them. Let me tell you."

Eamon bummed a cigarette off Bunko, and they both sat there smoking and looking out the window and hoping the guy would shut up. It was a blustery cold morning with lots of sunshine, but in some parts of the world that good weather didn't mean a thing. Unfortunately, it hadn't taken long to see what the cabbie was talking about.

"Welcome to Motor City, boys. Should have seen it in the old days. Downtown was somethin', I'll tell you. Now big buildings all deserted. Big hotels all empty, weeds coming out of the sidewalk, I'm not kiddin'. When I was little my pop used to love to take us all down Woodward Avenue. All them

Grosse Pointe people and their kind of stores and museums. Hot shit back then. Old man worked for Chrysler for over thirty years. There's a story for you, now . . ."

It was bad, just what you'd think. But there were parts of Baltimore just as bad. They went through scenes of destruction, whole blocks that looked like they'd been lost to civil war. So many of the two-story houses looked like they'd been scorched by flamethrowers. Many had been burned to the ground. Windows were smashed out in house after house and replaced with tape and cardboard. There was so much crunched and broken glass in the streets that it seemed intentional, as if road crews had scattered it. Garbage cans overflowed, and there were ragged hills of Hefty bags everywhere, torn open and spilled about. It was too easy to imagine the prosperous rat population.

"See? That's what I been tellin' ya, if you'd only listen. Them people done this. This is their town now. Got a colored mayor and police chief, the works. This is what they do when they're put in charge."

Bunko answered him evenly: "Listen, pal, we all done this, all right. Old story. Scared white corporate tax base starts running for the green pastures of suburbia, leaving a town with no bucks to do the job. And let me tell you something else: It doesn't matter who the mayor or police chief is. Politics is politics. Politicians are all the same color."

"What are you, taking their side or something?"

"You just don't get it, do you? There are no sides in this, you dummy."

"Who you calling a dummy?"

"You're right, Bobo. I should be calling you an ignorant racist bigot, but what the hell. I just got carried away."

"I ain't no bigot. I got nothing 'gainst them people. Just dangerous here. Anyone tell you that. Guns and shit. Not safe to walk nowhere. Everybody getting popped."

Eamon stayed out of it. Bunko and Bobo kept at it, strangely civil, all things considered. He thought Bunk was probably wasting his time, that there was no educating some people. He thought there were too many Bobos in this world to take on one at a time. Besides, Bobo had a point. The Bobos of the world had eyes and could at least see two feet in front of them. Maybe they couldn't see the big picture, but they sure as hell could see those boarded-up stores and vacant lots, all those bleak reminders of what once was. There were no more dry cleaning shops or supermarkets or banks. There were only cinder-block churches and convenience stores, only liquor stores and bars.

"So what are youse packing anyway?" Bobo asked. "You're armed, ain't ya? C'mon, don't kid with me here."

Bobo, whether you liked him or not, Eamon thought, was making some excellent points. They went through neighborhoods that simply did not exist anymore, whole blocks of unoccupied houses, whole blocks overcome by wild, weedy growth. The hulls of big old American cars, former Impalas and LTDs and Supremes, sat in the overgrown yards, on sidewalks, even in the middle of streets. It seemed like each scorched shell had been left out on purpose, as intentional as any other No Trespassing sign.

There were few other cars—working cars, that is. Traffic lights were frequently darkened, and too many stop signs had been decapitated. There were no other taxis racing down the lonely, jagged streets. There were no squad cars, either, at least none that they could see, but there was a steady drone of sirens in the distance. There were some people up and about in the wasteland. They sat on porch stoops, drinking out of pint bottles. They gathered around oil drum fires, passing around thermoses.

"Here you are," Bobo said, pulling up to a god-forsaken corner, "1276 Friendswood. This is the best I can come up with. So now do you want to come to your senses or what?"

"This'll be fine. Wait here for us. I don't know how long we'll be."

"You gotta be kidding, mister."

Bunko stared him down. "Let's put it this way, Bobo. You take off and I will personally hunt you down and crush your skull in. Are we clear?"

"Right you are, chief."

They got out into the blustery day. They yawned, they stretched. They lit up some smokes. Eamon still had no idea what Bunko was up to. They wandered about the ruins. Just broken beer bottles and old butts. Eamon winced when he stepped near the skeletal remains of a cat. What were they doing here?

They both heard it and turned at once. Evidently Bobo wasn't waiting around for Godot. He hit the gas and squealed out.

"Great, Bunk. Got our bags in there, too."

"I must be losing my touch," he said, more surprised than anything.

"Yeah, you really intimidated the shit out of him. Great work. We can't even handle a guy named Bobo. This is going real well."

"It's over now. Let's get to work. Must be somebody around here that remembers Jackie. Remembers that fire. Something. The first thing we gotta do is canvas the neighborhood."

"What neighborhood? Every fucking house looks closed down."

"There's plenty of people here. You just gotta

look for them. Nobody leaves these kinds of places. They die here. But nobody goes anywhere on his own."

They started walking. The first person they met up with was a young mom and her two toddlers. She just shook her head when they mentioned Robinson. It went like that. People weren't exactly unfriendly, but they weren't exactly helpful, either. They knocked on doors when they saw lights on or heard a television going. There was a lot of shaking of heads. But Bunko was not one to give up easily.

"You see, kid, I spent half my life doing this. This is what's called being a detective. You ask people simple questions. See if they remember anything at all. You never know. You sit in your car and drink coffee and wait for people to come home or go out. You make repeated phone calls. A big day is going down to the library to look something up or down to the county clerk's office to check a deed or whatever. No fucking glamour whatsoever. Just legwork and instinct."

They passed a pickup game on one of the dead side streets. The kids were playing baseball without gloves. At least they didn't have to worry about traffic interruptions. Actually, it was probably the only thing they didn't have to worry about. Bunko talked to everybody. He talked to the kids. He talked to some winos in an abandoned station wagon. He had a word with the Arab shopkeeper at the All-American Grocery. You just never knew.

They went into O'Malley's, a saloon with an old name and a new clientele. It was your standard hole. The windows were long gone, and now it was just the plywood. A string of faded cloverleafs hung behind the scratchy old mahogany bar. There was a psychedelic plastic juke and an out-of-order cigarette machine. Some old posters of the Emerald Isle still survived. At ten in the morning there were three customers. Their tap beers were backed up by shots of something dark and whiskeylike.

When Eamon and Bunko came in they all looked up and kept on looking. Eamon couldn't remember feeling more aware of his skin color. It made him feel red and prickly, the way they were staring. Bunko went right over to the bar though and ordered Budweisers from the tall, lanky man in the apron. His face was speckled with white spots, and he took a long time deciding. Bunko peeled off a twenty and planted himself down. Eamon followed. This seemed to help the decision-making process.

"What you two cops want anyway?" he said, sliding the beers in front of them.

"We're looking for somebody who might know what happened to a young man named Jackie Jay Robinson."

Bunko said it loud enough so that everyone else in the bar could hear. He was getting tired of repeating himself. And he sure as hell wasn't going to discourage the notion that they were cops.

"He was a Vietnam veteran who died in a fire in August of 1969, not three blocks from here. Does anybody remember him?"

Silence. Stares.

"No one's going to get in any trouble," Bunko said, seeking to reassure those mistrusting faces. "I'm just looking to find out something about this young man. Anything at all."

The bartender leaned on the bar and said, "If you knowed the man died in a fire, what else you need to know?"

"I need to know if somebody killed him."

The bartender laughed at that. He went back to work. Cleaning glasses. Putting bottles on ice. He went down to the end of the bar with the others.

"Finish these and go?" Eamon asked.

"That's how much you know," he said.

Gloom of Night

Bunko wasn't going anywhere. He just felt it in the blood. He called down to the bartender and ordered two more Buds. He took out his cigarettes. It looked like they were going to be there a while.

The time passed the way it always passes in a bar, slowly. They put away three more beers. Bunko bought a round for the men at the other end. The bartender smiled slyly, like It's your nickel, do what you want. Bunko went to the juke and put in a couple of bucks. It was all early Motown: Smokey Robinson and the Miracles, Diana Ross and the Supremes, Little Stevie Wonder. He stood there in that crazy mixed-up psychedelic light, punching in numbers at random.

Eamon didn't like drinking this early in the day. It was only a week ago he was off the stuff forever. He wasn't getting buzzed at all, just felt sluggish and inside of himself. There was no way to create enough distance from this reality. It was hard to believe he had been in her ritzy Bolton Hill townhouse last night. He wondered if Justine knew such places as this existed. At least they'd all stopped staring and were going about their business as usual.

"I'm glad you're drinking again," Bunko said.

"Yeah, I'm touched you feel that way," he said grimly, tired of this whole assignment.

"Let's have a shot to celebrate. What do you want?"

It was all pretty much generic and bottom shelf. There didn't seem to be much of a market for your upscale cordials, your Grand Marniers and Frangelicos and so forth. They threw back some tumblers of Jack. This was probably a mistake. Eamon would've been the first to admit that. This just did not seem like the right place to get fucked up.

Stevie Wonder sang "My Cheri Amour" as three new customers entered. One was a woman in a Tina

Turner wig and red mini and fishnet stockings. She looked pretty gone and didn't seem to notice them as she passed. The two men wore flashy sharkskin suits and couldn't have been more than twenty years old. One of them had a terrible scar. Someone had evidently taken a knife and carved his face into a jack-o'-lantern smile. The wound extended out from the corners of his mouth to each ear.

They paused to examine the strangers in their midst. "I think these boys must be lost, that's the only thing I can come up with," the scar said.

"Yeah, they must be from Canada. They probably got lost doin' that duck huntin'. Yeah, that must be it."

They thought this was very funny. Knee-slappingly funny.

"Or else they just don't know how it works here. Don't know about the different sections. They probably don't know this is the motherfucker section. Where the motherfuckers live. Like us."

"I think you were right the first time. Dumb-ass duck hunters from Canada."

"Either that or CIA. Sure, secret agents, that's who they are. They got lost and think they're in a plenty bad section of Moscow."

Eamon and Bunko didn't say a word. They just waited it out. Waited for them to join their friends. Which they finally did. It was getting crowded down there. You could hear them going, *What the fuck?*

Bunko said quietly, "You get a load of that scar? Somebody must have used a machete on him."

"Let's just get the hell out of here, Bunk. What are we waiting for? For when they figure out we're not Detroit's finest and that we left our Uzis at home?"

"What, leave before the happy hour? That's not our style at all."

"Bunk, aren't you just a little bit scared? Tell

me the truth. Because I'll tell you, I don't like this at all."

"Sure I am, kid. But now we're here, and we're gonna see it through. Or else what was the point of coming in the first place? You always got to go the distance with whatever you do. Life isn't for quitters, pal."

There was a certainty about Bunko. Eamon had seen it before, where he just seemed to know things before they happened. He was in a place all his own. It was after three in the afternoon, and there was a steady stream of customers now. Without exception everyone gave them the once-over. It was sad to think that two white guys sitting in a bar was news.

There was only the one woman. Every once in a while Eamon would glance down at her. She was quite beautiful, really. It was in the large pained eyes, even if she was really wasted. You had to get past that violet mascara and dark crusted ruby lipstick and the rest of the whorish getup. That's what he guessed her to be. She'd given herself away, and now she was just barely there. That's what made you feel sorry for her. That she even knew the barest littlest bit what was happening to her. When he saw several drunk, laughing men lead her back into the restroom he didn't want to know any more. The sharkskins collected the money.

"So what you want with Jackie Jay? Dead forever now, you know."

He was in his forties, and he was wearing paint-spattered overalls and a painter's cap. His voice was flat. So were his eyes.

Bunko said, "You're just the guy I've been looking for."

"What are you talking about? You don't even know me."

"I've been waiting for you all day, my friend. I just knew you were out there."

"I don't get it. Jackie went down a hundred years ago, it must be."

"Suspicious fire. And that's what we're investigating."

"You can't be real, man. What are you, like fire marshals? What, you like behind in your caseload, and you finally taking the trouble to check it out? Get real."

"Sit down, have a drink," Bunko coaxed. "So what did you say your name was?"

He was backing away, shaking them off. Bunko had half expected something like this. He took the letter out of his sports coat. "Here, just take a look at this. Hey, it won't hurt you to look."

It was a letter Robinson had written to his mother. It had been in that army mailbag with all the rest of them. Except this one never went anywhere. There was no place for it to go. Jackie's mother was dead now, and so was everybody else.

It really took something to get that painter to accept the blue airgram. It wasn't much, just some words to reassure the family back home.

> *Dear Mama,*
>
> *I miss you and Lionel and Darnell and everybody else like crazy.*
>
> *You would not believe how hot it is here. Mama, please do not send anymore chocolate chip cookies. They are all melted before I even get them. Feel free to send more of the oatmeal kind anytime you like.*
>
> *Thank you for writing me so much. It means a lot. I am trying to be better. You know I was never good with words and paper. Just look at my school grades. I always liked playing ball more than sitting in*

*any old classroom. Which reminds me.
Thank Uncle Eddie for sending the baseball
stories from the* Free Press. *I think the Ti-
gers have a great shot this year. I'd like to
see that boy McClain pitch. I hear he has
the golden arm.*

*Mama, I just can't wait until they let me
out of here. I just want to come home and
eat barbecue until I fall down. I miss all the
faces in the neighborhood. That is the funny
part. I find myself thinking of people I never
gave a second thought to when I was there.
I miss everybody, just everybody.*

*Does Yolanda ever say anything to you
about me? She doesn't write anymore. Have
you seen her around with anyone? You can
tell me. I knew that would be the worst part.
No girl can wait for any man. I think I was
stupid to think she would.*

*I love you, Mama. You keep praying to
Jesus and I will be home before you know
it.*

J.J.

"Boy, that's just like Jackie," the painter said,
chuckling. "Keep it nice and clean for his poor
mama. You should have seen the letters he wrote
me. Totally different. Night and day. Tell me the
shit that was really going down. And I forgot all
about that Yolanda. Oh, he never got over that
one. Never did."

He sat down with them. It turned out he was
Jackie's cousin. Wilson Lincoln was the name.
Everybody shook hands. Bunko called over for another round of drinks. Wilson still couldn't understand what they were doing with one of Jackie's old
letters. They tried to keep it short and straight.
Postal inspectors working on one very weird case.

"Postal inspectors? Don't that beat all. Everybody thinks you're Homicide. Think you're investigating the Chile's thing. That's the man who got shot in here a few weeks ago. Just couldn't figure why you were bringing up Jackie's name. Thought it might be some kind of very odd smoke screen."

"Let's keep them thinking that," Bunko said.

"I think I see your point," Wilson said, still chuckling. "You know, it's the damndest thing, you wanting to know about Jackie. He was a great kid, and we were about the same age, so we were pretty tight. It broke me up something awful when he was killed. Hurt bad."

Wilson took off his cap and put it on the bar. He was suddenly staring off, just a reflection in the bottles. What was left of his hair was flecked with silver. He had a long face, the type of face that would always seem a trifle wistful.

"Like he never existed," he said. "That's the worst part. A man lives a life, and it's like nobody cared. Gone like that, you know."

Sometimes people said things that you just had to leave alone. Eamon and Bunko were smart enough to lay back and let it happen. Wilson took out a pack of Merit Lights, and Bunko held out his lighter. Wilson took a long drag. They had time. The bar was noisy with the juke and the late afternoon, but it was like they weren't aware of it. It was just the three of them now.

"You know, Jackie got killed on August fifteenth. I remember that. I was working for Ollie Taylor back then, before I went into business for myself. We were all starting up back then. Jackie was sort of a jack-of-all-trades, fixed everything. Air conditioners. Oil burners. Did plumbing, electrical work. You name it. Good, too. Boy knew what he was doing.

"He'd only been back a few months. But he was

already making a go of it. He got the house there on Friendswood. Didn't cost much, everything around here changing so fast. Moved his mama in from the old place on Twelfth Street. She was out when it happened. Middle of a Sunday afternoon. That's what was so unbelievable. Typical August day with the mercury up around ninety.

"See, that's the thing of it. It was no fire. It was a big boom. Could hear it a mile off. I heard it ten blocks away. Painting somebody's house, and I thought maybe one of them extremist groups had planted a bomb. A lot of that kind of thing going on back then. But nope, it was Jackie Jay's new place.

"There was nothing left of that boy. I don't even know what they buried, to tell the truth. His mama never the same after that. Just never came back to the way of the living. Just going through the motions, you know.

"I never did tell you what done it. The oil burner. Can you believe? That's right. It just went up and exploded on an August dog day when it hadn't been turned on in months. That's why they listed it suspicious. I would have personally listed it in that 'Ripley's Believe It or Not.' "

The inspectors just sat there in the gloom of late afternoon, letting it wash over them. They should have been excited to have their suspicions confirmed. But that wasn't the kind of thing that entered into it. Not if you were any good. Because if you were any good, you knew it was just the beginning of something else. Three explosions was not the stuff of coincidence, that was for sure. It was, like Wilson said, the stuff of Ripley's. Somebody had kaboomed Bunce and Robinson, and maybe Hurly, too. They had a killer out there. Or they used to have one; 1969 had happened a long time ago.

There was a dirty yellow haze of cigarette smoke hovering over the bar. It was like some miniature ozone layer. Marvin Gaye's deeply sensual voice swelled up over the din. The beautiful whore in the Tina Turner wig started dancing in front of that crazy jukebox. She swayed seductively in paisley shadows.

"Even Marvin's dead," said Wilson glumly. "There's nobody left."

They still had to ask about Vietnam and that little village and everything else. They just hoped he had a long memory.

"What was the name of that town again?" He was straining to remember. "No, I wish I could say it rang some bells. Don't recall the specifics much. You know, Jackie, he told me about some of it, guys' legs being blown off and that type of thing. I wish I still had the letters. But they're gone like everything else."

Wilson was as frustrated as they were. His brow was creased with effort, and he kept saying "damn" and "lemme think a minute."

"Wait. Wait a minute. There was something about this one time. Something with this girl. Named Angie or something. Angie, I think it was. Oh, this was something. Like that My Lai thing. Remember that shit? Except it was only this one wacko. Did her whole family or something. I don't know."

"Could it have been Angel Girl? Not Angie, but Angel Girl?"

"I don't know. I guess it's possible. Angel Girl. Angie. It's so long ago since Jackie told it. All I remember is that somebody went nuts in the hut. Just like in all those movies.

"I think, I don't know, Angie was pregnant. Pregnant Vietnamese girl. I don't know. Guy shot the baby in her belly. I think that's what it was. God. Does that help you?"

Then they were back in first class. Then they were thirty thousand feet up, away from it all.

They zoomed across the sky, across worlds.

Bunko said, "That sure was nice of Wilson giving us a ride to the airport. We won't be home too late. Just after dinner. I think I'll give Franny a call."

"Who the hell is Franny?"

"That's my main squeeze, buddy boy."

"How come you didn't tell me about her sooner? I mean, I knew there was someone new. The new clothes, putting that junk in your hair."

"Are you saying I'm touching up my hair?"

"Oh, no. It's just going from gray to jet black on its own, big guy. A fuckin' natural phenomenon."

"Franny likes it that way. Says it makes me look younger."

"Jesus, I've got to meet this Franny. The woman who tamed Bunko the Beast. I can't even imagine her."

"She's perfect. The absolutely perfect woman. You come down to the Marlin with me some night and I'll introduce you."

"So should we call Montrez tonight? Or can it wait till morning? The Bureau will want in on this."

"It can wait, kid. It's been waiting over twenty years. A few hours more ain't going to matter to anyone."

The flight attendant, an enthusiastic young man with serious blow-dried hair, passed out menus. Bunko scowled at him.

"Well, let's see here," the big guy said, flipping it open. "You got your basic stuffed Cornish game hen. A filet mignon with a freshly prepared béarnaise. Then you have your Norwegian salmon with a lovely Dijon. Hey, they even got South African lobster tails. Beautiful. I wonder what they're eating back in steerage. Let me guess. Meat loaf with a perfectly subtle brown sauce? Or could it be the freshly caught tuna casserole?"

There was no doubt about it. There was no comparison between first class and steerage. So much better to be drinking the free Moët and making the tough menu decisions than to be behind that curtain with the huddled masses. So much better to be a have than a have-not. But that was nothing new. Eamon knew there'd always been two Americas. One for the rich, one for the poor. And the rules remained in place, even at thirty thousand feet.

There were only two other people in this section of the plane. Across from them a Ralph Lauren woman had her briefcase open, and she went over figures on a calculator. Several rows forward a gentleman in a double-breasted blazer read a financial magazine. It was a subdued world, all right, seemingly removed from it all. They had their own private steward and their own private food. They even had their own private restroom. Strangely enough, though, a flimsy curtain was all that separated the two Americas.

8

Percy was more than a little upset. He was late for a lunch date, and now this. He had a zillion things to do. He was supposed to have a fitting for his new formal wear at Manny's. And then, if he had time, he was hoping to get in a quick nine holes at the club. But that was beginning to look more and more like a foregone conclusion. God, they'd spoiled his entire afternoon.

The field agents were such a loathsome, scabrous lot. He had never known such horrid people. They took absolutely no pride in their personal appearance. They looked no different, really, from those annoying street people the city was so full of. He wondered what they made. It couldn't be much. Certainly not enough to afford Hugo Boss or Armani. They were such peons in their Haggar double knits and Thom McAn Hush Puppies. If only his appointment at the State Department would come through.

This couldn't have come at a worse time. They were going to eat at La Scala, his favorite. They did absolute wonders with the veal there. Not that it was any secret. Reservations had to be made weeks in advance. It was so unfair. Everything had been spoiled because of them. Well, Wearie and

Ryan would not pull a stunt like this again, he could assure you of that. And things had been going so swimmingly. Then this Montrez had to enter the picture and make such a fuss. The FBI, really now. That was the last thing anyone needed.

Percy Sedgewick marched back into the bowels of the Command Post, determined to put an end to all of this nonsense.

Bunko and Eamon were at their desks, working the phones, when they caught the unlikely sight of their boss striding purposefully for them.

"Jesus, who is that guy?" Bunko said. "I don't think I've even seen him around before. Snappy dresser, I'll say that."

"Whoever he is, he's frothing at the mouth," Eamon commented, unconcerned.

Percy Sedgewick could hardly contain himself. "See here," he said, not knowing where to start. There were so many contrary thoughts running through him at once. His lunch at La Scala. His golf game. This Montrez pest. No one seemed to understand the many varied pressures of being the CEO around here.

"*Really* now," he began again. "Bringing in the FBI. What are you *crimebusters* trying to do? I've just had the most dizzying, disorienting conversation with some Montrez fellow. I suspect he thinks he's J. Edgar Hoover or Elliot Ness or something. Well, to get on with it, this dreadful chap expected me to know all about some big investigation with all sorts of dead people everywhere and these annoying old letters and Vietnam and God knows what else."

Bunko interjected, "I'd be more than happy to fill you in."

"Oh, *please!* Spare me that. I have more important things to occupy my time around this sinkhole. The last thing I want to do is play cops-and-robbers with a bunch of frustrated middle-aged mailmen. In case you haven't noticed, the day-to-day administration of this lunatic asylum keeps me very busy indeed. There are at least a thousand men under my charge. You cannot, I'm sure, realize the *enormous* responsibility that I assume here. You field agents are the least of my problems. Depot 349 is one of the largest intermediary processing stops on the entire eastern seaboard. And the last thing I need, the very last thing, is to have the Federal Bureau of Investigation breathing down my neck. Do you understand?"

They did not. They stared back at him in mute disbelief.

"Well, it's simple," Percy explained. "Do I have to spell it out for you? Very well, then. I want this Montrez character out of my hair. I want nothing at all to do with this whole squalid situation."

"You don't even know what we're working on," Bunko pointed out.

"And I don't want to know. Just leave me out."

"Mr. Sedgewick," Bunko said tightly, trying to keep his temper in check, "I'm sure Mister Tony just thought you'd want in on this. This is the big time. I think we've got a serial killer, and—"

"Enough! Not another word. I must be going. I'm late as usual," he said, dispensing with them.

"I didn't know one could be late for a four-hour lunch," Bunko mumbled.

Percy turned on his heels: "What was that, Ryan? Something amusing you'd like to share with everyone?"

"Nothing, sir. Bon appétit."

When he was out of earshot Eamon said to Bunko, "Can you believe him? What fuckin' planet is he from?"

"He's from fuckin' Planet Gucci, that's what I

think. Man has all the brainpower of shoelaces. But he has great taste in suits. You've got to give him that. Today's was nice. That bold, adventurous cut. And the color choice. Inspired. The guy dresses like fuckin' Arsenio Hall. Those outfits must go for a thousand a pop easy."

"So what's left to do?"

"Not much from this end. I think we should give Earl Shad's mother another call. I don't know why. I can't imagine his mother steering us wrong. Hard to see how a guy with a brain aneurysm could fit into this. It's not like the son of a bitch exploded or anything. But just the same. Nothing has been what it seems in this one. Why don't you take it, kid? Just give her another call. Maybe something's occurred to her since you last spoke."

He was getting tired of that phone. He'd been on it all day. Trying to explain the unexplainable. This was far from your everyday kind of case, but fortunately they had a good listener in Tony Montrez. They'd worked with him plenty of times in the past, and though no one had ever accused him of having a personality, he was a solid, dependable pro. They'd shipped him the Ford letters and everything else relating to them. Montrez, in turn, had already sent agents out to interview the last two remaining members of Ford's platoon, that hardware store guy out in Montauk and Cheeves Lundquist. They still couldn't find an address on Lundquist. The best they could figure was that he was homeless in New York City. The last address anyone had for him was a shelter in lower Manhattan. And Eamon had already spoken to Coleman Briggs himself. He didn't think there was anything there. Cole was okay, you could just tell.

It was complicated shit. And then you threw in the explosions. Montrez wanted to know all about Robinson and Detroit. Then it was Donnie Bunce and Brigantine. Not to mention Chick Hurly and his exploding Pinto three years later. It just got more and more confusing. Eamon and Montrez must have been cradling their receivers for three or four hours that morning, just sorting it out. And it was still anyone's guess how those psychotic threats on the president's life tied in. Who was Angel Girl, and what went down in Phuoc Linh? How many soldiers were involved? Who knew about it? Montrez kept ringing up the questions, and Eamon had to keep telling him he didn't know. This called for a certain finesse. You never said, "I don't know." You said, "That's not clear yet, sir." You said, "We'll know more on that later, sir." And of course, the standard refrain: "We're working on it."

After going back and forth with Montrez, Eamon spent time conferring with Widge Amis. He'd worked on the Chick Hurly lawsuit. In fact, Widge, a retired homicide detective, had been the Ford Motor Company's chief investigator. He'd worked on several of the Pinto suits in the mid-seventies and had total recall of the Hurly accident. Except, as Widge emphasized, it was no accident. He did not care what the court verdict was. It would never change the truth as far as he was concerned. There was no doubt, he said, that someone had tampered with the carburetor and fuel line. And if he had to hazard a guess, and it was just a stab now, it would not have surprised him in the least if plastic explosives had played a role. The explosion was so tremendous that they found pieces of Hurly's Pinto half a mile away.

Then Eamon had to call Montrez again to tell him about Widge Amis. Back and forth. Back and forth. He knew the more he told Montrez the less they'd have to do. The Bureau didn't just want in. They wanted it all for themselves. And Eamon could understand that. The murders of Bunce and

Robinson were way out of Postal's jurisdiction. Still, he couldn't help envying Montrez's boys, the way they were hopping on for the ride here. Postal had opened up this baby, and now they were being cut out. It didn't take a genius to see that. He knew they were in trouble the moment Montrez started expounding on the glories of teamwork.

He called Earl Shad's mother in Pittsburgh. Her name was Dorothy. She insisted that he call her Dot. It was all there in his notes. He'd spoken to her eight days ago. At two-fifteen in the afternoon. A lot could happen in eight days. Atlantic City. Detroit. Justine. He'd slept with her twice since then. Damn. Busy signal.

It'd been one hectic Friday. He was sure looking forward to his weekend with Justine. She had promised him a great surprise, said she was going to take care of everything. He had no problem with that. He'd follow her anywhere she wanted to go. Somehow it was strange to think that this had all started with her dad's letters. They still didn't know if he'd been murdered or what. Coleman Briggs had said it was Earl Shad's rifle that went off. They hadn't been able to get official confirmation on that yet. Who knew for sure? Earl Shad certainly wasn't talking. Earl Shad had been in the ground since 1969.

He tried Dorothy Shad again. This time it was ringing.

"Hi, Dot? Lieutenant Wearie again at Postal. I'm sorry to bother you, but I wonder if you wouldn't mind—"

"I told you already, I don't know anything about what went on over there."

She didn't even bother to say hello. Her sound was shrill and pointed. It was obvious she wanted nothing to do with Eamon Wearie.

"Listen, Mrs. Shad, I just have a question or two. Just take a minute of your time."

"I don't know why we have to dredge it all up again. Why can't you just leave me alone? I've already told what happened. My poor Earl died of a clot to the brain. It was all very sudden and all very tragic, and I don't even want to talk about it anymore. Do you understand?"

She was talking very rapidly, and she seemed just seconds away from hysterics.

"Mrs. Shad, I'm sorry. I really don't like intruding on your privacy at all. I just need you to answer a couple things for me, all right? Okay? Good. Listen, did Earl ever mention anything at all about his year in Vietnam? An accidental shooting, maybe?"

"I told you he never brought it up. Not once. I don't know what went on there. How many times do I have to tell you? It was not something he felt comfortable discussing with me. It wasn't because we didn't talk, though. No, we had a wonderful relationship. And he loved me. I know that. He loved me so very much. I know he did. My poor baby. He was a wonderful boy. A fine, decent young man ..."

Her voice trailed off. He could picture the tears streaming down her cheeks.

"Okay, thank you, Mrs. Shad. I just want to ask you one last thing. I know Earl was receiving disability payments. Could you tell me what kind of injury he was suffering from?"

"Why don't you just go away? Why can't you leave it alone? Can't you see how this hurts me? Can't you see anything? Who cares how he died anyway? He's dead! He's dead! For the love of God, just leave it alone!"

She hung up on him. He held the phone dumbly, in the dead zone of telecommunications. Her words were still reverberating in his skull: *Who cares how he died anyway?*

Bunko swiveled around: "Anything?"

"Bunk," he said, still dazed, "I'm afraid we have to go to Pittsburgh."

"What's wrong?"

"I don't know. I don't know."

"Well, as long as you got a good fuckin' reason, kid. Christ, you must be the world's fuckin' worst travel agent. First Detroit, now Pittsburgh. What next? Cleveland? Dubuque? Peoria? Christ. So when do we gotta leave? Right away?"

"I guess it can wait until Monday."

"Good. Because I'll tell you, me and Franny have a big weekend planned. And I've been looking forward to it like you can't believe. I haven't been laid in days."

"Don't get sentimental on me, big guy. You know how I hate that."

It was drizzling, but you'd never know it by the way he felt. The drabness came at them through the tinted windshield and intermittent wipers. Sade hit the high notes in the CD player, and although normally that wouldn't have been his thing, she sounded great to him today, that high-throated warble, sexy and sweet and sexy again.

They took Route 50 down through the ramshackle towns, passing those dilapidated postcard scenes, rundown service stations and closed-up farm stands and second-rate motels blinking VACANCY. Everything looked sad in the rain, like it would always be so, like it would always be raining and nobody would ever come to these lonely, forgotten places. But it was impossible to be sad. Everything was so right when he was with her. A three-hour car ride in the drizzle was somehow autumn magic.

He'd never been in love before, not like this. He'd loved Jenny. But that was different. That was just two high school kids groping under the bleachers. This was something else entirely. This was loving somebody who was real and there and who could love you back. Boy, that was the best, having it returned like that.

She did the driving, and that was fine by him, too. He didn't have to think, didn't have to do anything. Every once in a while she'd turn to look at him with this smile in her eyes, or else she'd touch him, just touch him, graze his shoulder or his hand or his cheek. You could say a lot with just a touch. You could tell the whole history of the world. Sure you could.

Sometimes, though, he'd get scared. It would just race through him, and in that second of cold doubt he'd wonder if he really knew her. Everything had happened so damn fast. It wasn't like he didn't know that. But he wanted to trust in his feelings, in himself, and especially in Justine. He had to trust her; he had no choice.

They sat on the big screened-in porch drinking Rolling Rocks and looking at the rain falling on the water. It was a hard, steady rain now, just long, solid needles, and you couldn't see much at all on the bay, just the fog and the rain and the occasional ghostly mast.

There he was on the old wicker couch with his arm around her, not thinking anything at all except the rain. It drummed down on the house and pelted the trees and sloshed through the gutters and filled the whole entire universe with its sound. Rain was all there was and all they knew. He was at ease with himself, and there was nothing he really needed or longed for. It was all here, all right now.

He was thinking about asking her to marry him.

He saw them together. Saw them eating dinners at home, nothing special. In the evenings they read by firelight, just part of the everyday. All there in the rain. He saw the two little girls they'd have. Girls, for some reason. In the rain. They took a train ride through French countryside. In the winters they flew to the islands. Their daughters grew

140

up, and they grew old together. It was all there in the haunting rain.

And their house, the one they'd have, if he had his way, would be just like this one. The modest cape, with its rustic brown shingling and white shutters and flower boxes and sturdy flagpole, was perched on a bluff overlooking the Chesapeake. It had been her grandparents', the house where she'd grown up with her mother and Bobby, the same house her father had known, too. It was hers now, and she'd chosen to leave it in its pristine state, wide plank floors and velvet-covered ottomans, lace curtains and countless knickknacks, cozy and warm with memories.

The rain kept falling. She cuddled up close, and again he was aware of how good she smelled. She was jasmine and cigarettes and lemon shampoo and Rolling Rocks and the sweet rain. She was the very perfume of life, and God knew there was something heartbreaking about that. It was possible to feel the greatest sadness in the most perfect and lovely moment. He knew it was just the nature of moments, the way they were always gone before you knew it, before the next rain.

He didn't trust his good fortune, that's what it was. There she was. There she was in her ponytail and her jeans and sneakers and Duke Blue Devils sweatshirt. The all–American girl. The girl for him. He liked her out of the fancy duds, liked it a lot. Sometimes she could just intimidate the hell out of him. That townhouse of hers. The big job on the twenty-first floor of Legg Mason. The Jag and all the rest of it. There was all of that, all right. But then there was that other side of her, the vulnerable and fragile Justine, that little girl lost. Sometimes it was like he felt there were two completely different Justines, and that you couldn't bring them together no matter how hard you tried.

He looked out at that rain, not so steady any-more, just off-and-on splatterings now, and tried to reconcile himself with the past. There were a lot of faces in that rain, including Trish's. Trish had been cocktail waitressing at Frankie's, and he had been just another faceless customer knocking back the beers. It had been no great love story, just two lonely people at the bar one night late. That's how those things sometimes happened, without a sober thought entering into it. Except instead of a one-night stand, he married the girl. Strangers, forever strangers. And it wasn't like they hated each other's guts or anything like that. No, it was far worse, far more normal. They were attractive, intelligent, impossibly reasonable people who managed to keep their voices insanely low and everything else buried inside of themselves. Every night they slept in the same bed, occupying the marital position, their backs to each other, the great lockout. When Trish left he was frankly relieved. She had the courage to do what he could only think of doing.

She was there, in those flashes of lightning, blue flickerings of the past. He wished Trish well, wher-ever the hell she was these days. It was all part of coming to terms somehow. In his life there'd been too many one-night stands and one-week encoun-ters and one-month relationships. There was shame in that. And hopelessness. He'd lost his dreams and his youth in that great and tawdry cavalcade of Sues and Lindas and Debbies and Alisons and Lauras and Jennifers. They came and they went, and each time he was left a little more diminished. It was his own fault, really. He couldn't seem to let go of the old dreams and the old lies, so that when he was confronted by the ordinary, the ordinary Lizes and Tracys and Lorraines, he was never satisfied and always found himself wanting and hungering. He just believed somehow that *she* was out there; he couldn't help it. It was such a stupid, ignorant, naïve thing to think, yet he thought it just the same.

The lost dreams seemed to end on the big screened-in porch with the ponytailed girl in the Duke sweatshirt. He was getting ready to pop the question. The time would probably never be more right. One of the most perfect days he had ever known—a timeless, uneventful day that made him feel, for once, like he belonged to something greater than himself—was coming to a close. They'd gone through family photo albums, and she had even shared portions of her teenage diary. They made love in her old bedroom, on that single canopied bed with the Winnie-the-Pooh–patterned sheets. He was on top of her, surrounded by sea-shells and teddy bears and posters of Peter Framp-ton and David Cassidy, in the middle of her lost dreams.

They went to Buddy's for dinner. They rolled up their sleeves and picked apart dozens of those messy steamed crabs on the newspaper tablecloth. They drank beer by the pitcher, which cooled off the hot bite in their mouths and loosened their tongues. They confessed and confided, coaxed and prompted. She told him something about what it was like to grow up without a father. Birthdays and Christmas were the worst. As a kid she was a scrawny little runt with braces. Eamon acted like he didn't believe her. There was the world's worst prom date with a boy named Irwin. Irwin's mother drove them in the family station wagon and waited outside the gym until it was over. Then there was her best friend Tina Mansini, who was always get-ting them into loads of trouble. They were fifteen when they faked their way into Jezebel's, a down-town bar. That was the night Justine lost her virgin-ity. With a handsome young clammer. He was rough and it hurt, but she still thought she was in love with the creep. She didn't know any better, and she couldn't understand it when he told her to go blow. She cried into her Winnie-the-Pooh pillow for months.

Eamon nodded and sighed and made all the proper and requisite uh-huhs and hmm-uhms. They stared into each other's eyes for long, unquestioning periods.

They came home and made love again, this time in one of the grownup bedrooms.

A softer rain fell on the Chesapeake.

She put her warm mouth on his neck and spread little kisses about.

Something was troubling him. He didn't know what it was. It was just a sudden thing, rushing through him like a cold, damp breeze.

"What are you thinking?" she asked, the voice hoarse and rusty.

"Nothing," he said, like all the men in the world before him.

"I wish you could meet my brother," she said, looking off. "I know you'd like Bobby."

"Bobby's out in Minnesota, right? What's he doing out there? You never got around to telling me."

"I didn't want to, that's why. He's had some problems, Eamon. He's at that clinic. It's kind of famous, the place. Hazelden? Have you ever heard of it? Well, it's not important. He's trying to clean himself up. He hasn't had it easy. I think it's especially hard for a boy to grow up without his daddy. And Bobby was so sensitive to begin with."

"I'll bet," Eamon said.

"What's wrong? There's something wrong, I can just feel it. What is it?"

"Nothing, nothing at all."

"Something's wrong. Your body has gone all

rigid and everything. Why don't you just talk to me?"

"Justine, why did you get married?" he suddenly asked, surprising even himself.

"Oh, you mean Sam?"

"I saw that picture of you and him. He looked quite a bit older."

"He was, actually."

"It's just that you haven't spoken about him at all. Nothing, not a word. I think it was bothering me, and I didn't even know it. You never told me why you got married. Or even why you got divorced."

"It's just that ... well, most men don't like to hear about that kind of thing."

"I want to hear."

It came out all wrong. Sounded harsh, almost mistrusting. But he was more than just interested now. Somehow everything was on the line. This was the girl he was about to ask to marry him.

"Well, there's not that much to tell. Sam was a very successful businessman. Still is, I guess. He owns Martinex, they make razor blades and shaving cream—"

"Jesus, that's huge. No wonder he was able to buy you a Renoir."

"Well, that's not why I married him, if that's what you're thinking."

"Why did you marry him then?"

"What's that supposed to mean?"

"What do you think?"

"I don't think I like your tone at all. And if you think I married him for the money, you're totally off base."

"What was it, then? I saw that picture of him—"

"What's that supposed to mean?"

"You know—"

"Yeah, I know. And I don't think I like what you're implying at all. Sam was just someone I re-

145

spected and looked up to and who knew how to take care of me. He was actually a wonderful person—"

"Then why did you get divorced?"

"It didn't work out, that's all. It was a very mutual thing. And to tell you the truth, I don't really think it's any of your business. Now I don't want to hear or say another word about it."

They were silent on the dark porch. All they could hear was the rain, the soft rain.

Years later, though, when they looked back on the evening, they would not remember the pitter of soft rain. Years later each would be sure that great zigzags of lightning had filled the night sky and that the earth had echoed with atomic thunder.

Berlin was twenty miles outside of Pittsburgh, on the Ohio-Pennsylvania border. They scooted off the interstate and entered a familiar landscape of mini malls and used-car lots and gas giants, the blink and wink of America. It didn't matter where you went in this vast and sprawling land; there would always be Burger King and Holiday Inn and Taco Bell and Blockbuster Video. You were never far from that twenty-four-hour brightness, never far from the turnpike. Yet Eamon felt there was a kind of comfort in that, somehow.

"America the beautiful," Bunko noted sullenly.

They stopped at a Dunkin' Donuts for coffee. He wasn't in a good mood at all. That he'd pass on those chocolate-frosted, cream-oozing things he loved so much was indication enough.

"Another fuckin' day, huh? They just keep on coming, don't they? No end in sight. One after the other. Somebody hand me a revolver. Let's get it over with. No use in prolonging the suspense."

"Had a good weekend, I see."

"The best."

Eamon thought he might just be upset about the rental car. The Hertz lady wouldn't upgrade them, and so they were stuck with the compact, a puny

147

Honda Civic that looked almost like a circus car with the big guy behind the wheel. It was eight-thirty-five on the blinking clock. Their flight had left BWI at six, and now they were out there with everybody else, in the concrete everyland, held hostage by traffic lights and drive-time radio.

Bunko kept fiddling with the dial, trying to find something halfway civilized. But it was just the usual happy-talk bullshit. The Sharkman and Doctor Doo-Doo and Steve the Boogie Man were ringing bells and sitting on whoopee cushions and screaming out that they were number one and all sorts of other full-throttle idiocy. Right now he was trying to make sense of some interview.

Deejay: Snake, man, how you hangin' there, huh?
Snake: You know.
Deejay: Right, right, of course. Listen, that latest album—
Snake: Yeah. Tell me about it.
Deejay: Wow, what can I say? It's hot hot hot—sizzle, sizzle, baby.
Snake: Yeah, we keep hearing that, man.
Deejay: I'll bet you do, man. I mean this, man, you guys are breaking new, important ground. This is like renaissance heavy metal, man. Powerful, powerful stuff.
Snake: Uh, yeah. Well, we were, like, trying to, you know, like, make a statement. That's, like, the way we operate, man.
Deejay: You guys are God. And, man, I'm not just saying that.

Bunko said, "Are you listening to this garbage? Who lets this shit get on the air? *Some retard*

148

named Snake is God? What the fuck is happening to our country?"

"It's only some radio program. Don't take it so seriously."

"It's not just some goddamn radio program. It's everything, everywhere. Don't you see, Wearie? We live in some goddamn Loony Tunes hamburger land. Just look around you, pal. Garbage everywhere. We eat it, drink it, buy it, watch it, and shit it out for breakfast."

"What's got you so wound up, big guy?"

"Ah, it's weird," he said, letting out a sigh.

He rolled down the window and lit up a Marlboro. It was another cool, wet, unfriendly day. The skies were a dark, billowy gray.

"Ah, you're not going to believe this," Bunko continued. "It's crazy shit. I think it has to do with all this Vietnam crap. Christ, we were so stupid. Just fucking dumb kids. Eighteen fucking years old. What did we know? We didn't know shit, that's what we knew. But everybody thinks they know somethin' anyway. Just fuckin' words now. Freedom. Democracy. Protecting the American way of life. Christ, imagine believing that bullshit. And then there you are all the way on the other side of the planet hauling your fuckin' pack through mosquitoes and rice paddies and shooting at anything that moves and scared out of your mind all the time. But still, there you are going through all this shit, somehow believing that it's important, that you're doing it for your country.

"What a joke. Look out at this ridiculous, insane K-mart world we live in. Nobody giving a shit about nobody else. Everybody in it for himself. Greed and money and more greed. Not to mention all these dodo-brained deejays running off at the mouth and proclaiming some guy named Snake as the second coming. It's too fucking much. Don't you get it? That's the crap we were protecting. We went over to that little piece of hell and put it all on the line, and for what? We protected everybody's freedom to eat Big Macs and fill up their tanks with super unleaded."

"I think you exaggerate, big guy."

"Maybe so, Wearie. But I ain't eighteen anymore. And I know some things. I know there ain't too many things worth dying for. In fact, there ain't hardly anything worth dying for."

"You're forgetting the World Series and the Super Bowl. Ain't that worth dying for, Bunk? Or how about cold beer? What if some foreign army tried to come over here and destroy all the breweries and—"

"For once could we just do without the comedy? I was trying to be serious back there—"

"Or what if terrorists from the Middle East came over here and kidnapped Vanna White? Of course, I don't have to tell you that this would just decimate 'Wheel of Fortune.' Isn't this worth putting your life on the line for? Big guy, don't tell me you'd sit this one out."

"Kid, this is just what I was talking about—"

"The cancellation of 'Wheel of Fortune' might even lead indirectly to the cancellation of 'Jeopardy.' Both shows, as I'm sure you're aware, are Merv Griffin productions. God, I just thought of something else. Alex Trebek would be without a job. Bunk, are you telling me you'd just sit idly by in the face of this catastrophic chain of events?"

"Kid, you're part of it. I mean it. You're as bad as everybody else. It's the whole degeneration of American life. That's what it is."

The town of Berlin, with its limestone German Lutheran church and indestructible clock tower, was a heavy, brooding presence on the Beaver

River. It was a town made entirely out of stone and brick and the sweat of masons, a stronghold of yesteryear. It was an impersonal town, a town of banks and insurance offices and fussy old lawyers, a place of no return. There were no video stores or pizzerias or even bars on Main Street. The one soda fountain looked like something out of the 1930s, and so did the big five-and-dime, all of it calling back the spare, lonely lines of an Edward Hopper painting.

They drove through the silent, empty town. The maples, which lined the wide avenue, were a deep, defiant red. In just a few days the magnificent trees would be totally bare, in keeping with the rest of Berlin. Dorothy Shad's house was not far from here, according to her own directions. They drove up Frederick, up through the hilly, rocky country that surrounded the little town, through occasional clusters of gold and crimson.

Eamon was grateful for the brightness of the remaining foliage; otherwise it would have been too depressing. The houses were mostly big three-story clapboards on narrow lots. Everyone had laundry hanging out, and there were too many old cars gathering rust in too many unkempt yards. And there weren't any dog catchers, judging by the packs roaming freely about. He noticed, too, that even though people didn't seem to have the money to afford clothes dryers, many had put up the most sophisticated and up-to-date satellite dishes on their rooftops.

They parked the circus car in front of 553 Frederick, a freshly painted white house with a small, neatly raked yard. It stood out from its neighbors by its sheer tidyness.

They rang the doorbell, an odd, surreal moment if ever there was one. You never knew what to expect.

151

For example, they didn't expect Dorothy Shad to look like Wilford Brimley. The man who answered the door looked just like the character actor. He was a stout, white-haired, granny-spectacled gentleman with a memorable walrus mustache. In his plaid woolen shirt and extra-thick khakis he had a homey, grandfatherly air about him.

"It's the right thing to do," Bunko said, mimicking that commercial Brimley did for Quaker Oats.

"Oh, right, very funny," he said, chuckling. "I get it all the time. Never fail to get a kick out of it. You must be those postal inspectors. I'll tell you right now we don't want to be disturbing Dottie with this anymore. I'll handle any questions you have. I'm her brother, Howard Landis. Come on in. Make yourself at home."

The living room would have had Betsy Ross rolling over in her grave. There was dark walnut cabinetry and a giant carved bald eagle that spread its wings over the doorway. There was a mounted deer above the brick fireplace and a hand-woven rug in colonial stars and stripes. There was early American bric-a-brac, copper kettles and hanging china, a proudly displayed musket and a framed copy of the Declaration of Independence. It wasn't that Eamon had any problem with these Ethan Allen artifacts, only with what superseded them: the Mitsubishi television with a screen that was more in keeping with a multiplex theater; the huge contemporary sectional with a floral design that might have passed in Florida; the big recliners in crushed orange; the new track lighting; the modern ceiling fans that revolved lazily on a cool autumn day.

All of the furniture looked like something from *Land of the Giants*. Eamon sank uneasily into a pillowy couch section. Bunko, on the other hand, looked right at home. "Nice place you have here," he said.

"Well, I'm not much on the decorating end," the folksy Landis said. "That's more Dottie's department."

"Well, Howard," Bunko said, trying to seem convivial, "what can you tell me about your nephew—"

"Listen, boys. I think there are some things you oughta know from the outset. Earl didn't die of some brain attack or whatever Dottie told you. I never thought it would matter, or I wouldn't have done it. But she's my sister, and she hasn't had it easy, let me tell you that. Lou Shad died over there in Korea. That was her husband. First-rate guy, too. Aces in my book, I'll tell you. And then to see what happened to Earl, well, you can imagine . . ."

His voice just trailed off. He was in one of the velour recliners, to the side of them, facing the mega-set. He took off his spectacles and started polishing them with a handkerchief. It was like he'd just forgotten all about his visitors. They waited, hoping he'd rally.

Finally Bunko said, "Howard? I think we're totally lost here. What happened to Earl? What did you mean when you said you didn't think it would matter?"

"Boys," he said, resuming, like there was nothing odd about his behavior at all, "you see, Earl killed himself. That's right. Stuck a Colt .45 into his mouth and blew his brains out. In this very house. I cleaned it up. Some mess. Poor little Dottie found the body. Just a terrible thing all the way around."

"I don't understand at all," Bunko said, looking completely mystified. "We had a copy of the death certificate sent to us. Says nothing about suicide. Natural causes, that's what they got down."

"Boys, I don't even know why you're digging this thing up anyway. This ain't important to anyone but us. Family business is what it is. The boy was never right, really. Even before he went over there.

153

Okay, he was worse when he come back, but he was never exactly a stable individual, take my word on it."

"Wait, wait. I still don't understand why the coroner didn't classify it as a suicide."

"Oh, that. Boys, I don't want to go around getting people in trouble. Peachtree is a friend of mine. He just did it because I asked him. We hunt together, do some fishing, you know how it is. Course, he's retired now, too. See, I was the sheriff. Thirty-two years I was. So Peachtree, that's Doc Edwards, done me a little favor. That's how it was. Now I hope you're not going to get us in trouble for that after all these years. I depend on my pension. So does little Dottie."

"Dottie's the right word, all right," Bunko mumbled from the sectional.

"What's that? You got to speak up. I'm not a young man anymore. Hey, you boys mind if I put on the TV? It's almost time for the 'The Price Is Right.' Boy, I love that show. Bob Barker is a prince, ain't that the truth."

Eamon, sinking deeper into sofa obscurity, felt they were letting this one get away from them. "I still don't understand why you went to all the trouble," he said over the din of the television. "What was the point of changing the death certificate?"

"Oh, that. This is a small town, you've got to understand that, fellas. You don't know how these things play around here. Oh, look. There's Bob. He's looking swell. His skin color wasn't so good yesterday. But today he looks tiptop. I think it's that green jacket. Brings out the glow in the man."

Bunko got up and took the remote away from Landis and aimed it at the television like it was a gun. A life-size contestant was jumping up and down and squealing for joy. Bunko clicked it, and she imploded.

"That's not very nice," Landis said.

"Howard, I don't think you get it. This is a murder investigation. We're investigating whether your nephew Earl Shad was murdered. Now if you'll just help me out with a few details, I'll let you get back to your regularly scheduled program."

"I hate missing the first bid. A lot of times that's when they bring out the car. Or sometimes, of course, it's just a Kenmore washer-dryer combo or the Amana range or something boring like that."

"Howard, why are you so sure Earl killed himself? Why couldn't someone have killed him instead? Did he leave a note?"

"No, he didn't, actually. But I was in law enforcement thirty-two years, like I told you, and I should think I can tell the difference between suicide and murder."

"Howard, in your thirty-two years of law enforcement, how many suicides did you come across?"

"Two, including Earl's. Leonore Shanker locked herself in the Olds in the garage. Never forget it. Leonore was quite the looker. No one could figure it out. And let me just add, Mister Smarty, she didn't leave a note, either."

"Can you tell me how you found Earl? Do you remember what the room was like? Was there any sign of struggle? Was the Colt Earl's gun? Was there anything unusual at all?"

"Just blew his brains out. My gun. Since sold it. A bottle of tequila nearby. Been drinking, must have been. Did it in front of Dot's dressing room mirror. Just brought it into the room for some reason. I'd read about that. One of the reasons I knew it was a suicide. Mirrors, something about mirrors. People like to just get a last look at themselves. I guess I can understand that."

"Anything else? Think hard. Had he been depressed before this?"

"Boys, that's just it. He was always depressed. On all sorts of medication. Went to the VA Hospital twice a week. Never right, I'm telling you. Bit of a sissy, really. I don't like saying it, him being family and all, but he was a little light in his loafers, if you know what I'm saying here. I once came home—God, I hate like hell to say this—and found him in one of Dot's dresses. I swear to God. Just glad that Dottie never saw that. Would've broken her poor little heart."

"Did anyone do a proper autopsy? Did you check his blood alcohol? How do you know for sure he was drinking? Did you check at least for carbon residue. How do you know he fired the gun?"

"No need for any of those things, boys. It's like I told you, all cut and dried. And who in the world would've wanted Earl dead anyway? Gosh, the boy didn't have any friends, or even know anyone, for that matter. That's why we were so happy when that nice friend of his from the war came to visit. Yup, one of Earl's army buddies. Thought it might cheer the boy up."

The two inspectors exchanged a look, a dead certain look. In that quarter of a second they had a little dialogue that went something like this: Buddy kills Earl. Yeah, the guy's a depressive to begin with. Of course everyone's going to think suicide, the obvious. Maybe the buddy's the same fuck that nailed Bunce and Robinson and Hurly. Maybe. But that's probably too much to hope for. All we need is a name, just a fucking name.

"Howard, do you remember the friend's name? Try and think now."

"Can't say I do. Nice fellow, though. Was here a couple days. Helped me clean out the garage. Not like I could ever get Earl to help around the house, no, sir. Boy was plain lazy—"

"Howard, can you describe this friend to me? How long was this before Earl killed himself? Are you sure he was in Vietnam with Earl?"

"Sure I'm sure. Oh, he was here just a couple days before. Nice boy. Big strong fellow. Sure, sure. I remember that."

"Howard, we need that name."

"Maybe Dottie would remember. She was always very good with names. A schoolteacher, you know. Oh, only for a short while, and—"

"Where can we find her?"

"Well, if I tell you, will you let me watch 'The Price'? I think it's getting close to the showcase. That's my specialty. The trick is not to overbid. Of course, you've got to study it. I'm always checking the prices in the *Sunday Shopper*. You wouldn't believe how many people walk in there blind. Totally unprepared. Just a crying shame. Why, the whole country is falling apart. Have you boys happened to notice that lately?"

Eamon had never liked cemeteries. As a little boy he always averted his eyes when they drove past the one in Flushing, that square mile of crosses and granite slabs and tombs. It gave him the willies seeing those endless rolling hills of the dead. To think that it all wound up under a few shovelfuls of dirt. Everything we did and thought and spoke and touched and loved. That we just rotted away in the great forgetfulness of eternity. Ashes to ashes, dust to dust. Then everybody got into cars with the headlights on and drove away. So yeah, Eamon averted his eyes. After all, who the hell wanted to think about things like that?

"Jesus, look at that one, willya!" Bunko exclaimed, pointing out a huge Greek Revival number, its columns better suited to the Parthenon.

"Now that guy knew how to go out in style. Beautiful, just beautiful. You got to admire that."

The weather was perfect for walking through a cemetery, drippy black skies, and except for the diggers there wasn't anybody about. They were looking for section 38, row 257. Greatlawn just went on and on, acres of dead people. Eamon tried not to think about it.

"Oh, that's a nice one, yes, indeed," Bunko said. "Look at that tomb, huh. Probably cost a fortune. Look at all them angels and shit they got carved in there. Awfully nice work, don't you think?"

"Let's just find her. We don't have time for tombstone browsing."

"Hey, what's eating you, Wearie? Let me tell you, as far as cemeteries go, this is right up there. Lawns and gardens are nicely pruned. Lots of pleasing white statues. Beautiful. I'm telling you, this is the kind of place I've been envisioning."

"Oh, don't tell me you've been thinking about your final resting place. Just don't tell me that. It's almost too much to bear. Next thing you'll tell me is you wrote out a will. Of course, that would probably be a very wise thing to do. Knowing how everybody's going to be fighting over that stack of old *Playboys* and the award-winning beer-can collection. This is not even to mention Frank, your blind and deaf fifteen-year-old Saint Bernard. Probably be in probate for years."

"Ha, ha. Very fucking funny. I'm not kidding, Wearie, you oughta be a fuckin' stand-up comedian. I know what your problem is, though. You're scared of dying. You just don't want to deal with the messy little details. I, on the other hand, do not want to leave these details to ex-wives and other freeloading relatives. If it was left up to them, they'd just pour lighter fluid on my body and toss it into some ravine."

"Why does it matter, Bunk? Dead is dead. Doesn't matter how they bury you."

"Kid, you got a lot to learn. No way I'm gonna be cremated, that's for damn fuckin' sure. I want it to be big, elaborate. You know, maybe a mosque or something. Or maybe one of those pyramids. Yeah, that's it. I'm telling you, those Egyptians had the right idea. See, that's the thing. Nobody gives a fuck when you die, so you got to force them to remember you."

They saw Dorothy Shad then. Hard to miss her, really. She was sitting in a folding lawn chair, apparently engaged in conversation with the two rose-colored headstones in front of her. "No, no, that's not right at all," they heard her saying adamantly.

Introductions were made. It seemed strange showing badges to a woman in a lawn chair in the cemetery. Dorothy had obviously made a day of it, judging by the picnic basket and big thermos at her feet. She was a frail, dour-faced woman in her sixties. She was also losing her hair in a very noticeable way. Eamon wondered if she was undergoing chemotherapy. It wasn't just those sad white patches—as if it had all come out in recent clumps—it was the color of her skin, too, which appeared greenish.

"Oh, that's very nice," she said, examining the official blue and gold.

"Mrs. Shad," Eamon said, "we're sorry to be intruding—"

"You look so different from what I pictured on the telephone. I didn't think you'd be a nice-looking young man at all."

"I'm not sure that's a compliment, but—"

"I figured you'd show up sooner or later. My poor Howard. You should have seen him in the old days. You wouldn't know it now to look at him, but he was one sharp cookie back then. I don't know what happened. Ever since he stopped working. At least it's not Alzheimer's. Just a little daft, that's all. He's gotten so peculiar lately. I keep catching him going to the bathroom in the yard. I have no idea what that's about—and I don't want to know."

"Yes, ma'am."

"Well, I guess he told you some of it. Poor Howard. Always thinks he's protecting me, but of course it's the other way around. He'd simply be lost without me. So what can I do for you? It must be mighty important for you government men to come all this way and find little ol' me."

They did the best they could with the explanation. Told her they knew all about the suicide. Told her they were investigating something to do with Earl's unit in Vietnam. Did she remember the name of his army buddy, the one who visited just before he died?

"Oh, of course I do. I would never forget such a thing as that. One of the nicest young men I ever met."

The inspectors were relieved by this piece of good luck. Bunko said, "Oh, that's great, Mrs. Shad. Just great. You don't know what a help this is. So who was he?"

"Why should I tell you?" she said, suddenly petulant. "What has the United States of America ever done for me? You people just show up one day at my door and expect me to jump up and salute and give a damn. Why should I? Why in the hell should I? Can you tell me that?"

The inspectors contemplated this while looking down at their shoes. They did not know what to make of Mrs. Shad. But the one thing they didn't want to do was alienate her any further. She was withholding one unbelievably important piece of information.

"You people. You just don't know. You just don't care. Look. Just look. That was my husband. And that was my son. They gave their lives to this country. Not that it really matters. Just look. It's right in front of your noses."

They were average polished headstones. There wasn't anything elaborate about them. Just the names and the dates. Some engraved flowers. She started to sob. The two inspectors went back down to their shoes again.

"You don't know," she said, bringing out the Kleenex. "Oh, God. There was a time when it was all different. Lou went to Korea. He thought it was right. We never questioned it. We thought it was a real threat. You just don't know. Who even remembers Korea now? Sure, you hear about Vietnam, plenty. But does anyone ever talk about the thirty-eighth parallel anymore? Maybe people hear about it in 'M*A*S*H' reruns, I don't know. God, we thought the whole world was hanging in the balance. Worried about the Chinese like you couldn't believe. All those boys. All those handsome young boys. Dead, dead, dead.

"I was still young, still had my looks. I remember kissing Lou good-bye. He said, 'See ya.' Like we'd see each other the day after tomorrow. The last words I ever heard him say. He was just a boy himself. I got old, but Lou, he just stayed the same. Just this tall, funny-looking boy with this goofy smile. Sometimes I can hardly remember him. Isn't that horrible? We were only married a couple of years, you know. Earl was just about two, I think. It was a snowy Christmas Eve, like in some kind of faded home movie. I had a turkey in the oven—my parents, God bless their eternal souls, were over—and little Earl was watching the tree twinkle when I saw him through the window, that man in the uniform they always send. I started to scream be-

161

fore he even reached the door. I just knew, the way you always know.

"I still don't even know how he died. The army doesn't tell you things like that. They just leave you to wonder. Then it's funeral time. The neighbors make food. Everybody calls you and writes a little note saying if there's anything they can do. The army sends a color guard. It lasts all of five minutes. Then you're left to go about your life. As if you could just resume it like nothing's happened."

She stopped talking for a minute, but the inspectors were in no rush to jump in. They knew better than that. Let it run its course. Let the woman have her say. Didn't she at least deserve that?

"Oh, you just don't know," she said again. "When they brought Lou's body back I was beside myself, of course. But I thought my husband had made the ultimate sacrifice. I was almost proud. Can you believe it? Oh, it was a different world. It took years for me to get bitter and resentful. Years of living without him, all the hard, lonely decisions. How often I wished for someone to lean on. My friends had their husbands. Someone to take them out to dinner, someone to admire them.

"What did I have? A few memories. Not even many of those. I had Earl. But then to see it happen to him, just like with his father. I should've done something. We should've moved to Canada together. We could've done that. Because Earl died in Vietnam. As surely as anything. The person who came home was not somebody I recognized. He was an empty space. I don't know how else to describe it. There wasn't anything behind the eyes anymore. And he had such beautiful eyes. He was always such a beautiful boy. Everyone said so."

What a useless, senseless world, Eamon thought. He could only feel pity for the damaged woman before him. There was no fairness. No justice. No anything that could ever make it right. Eamon loved his country. America was his kind of town, lit up for business twenty-four hours a day. It was not like any other place on the planet. There were so many things he liked. You walked into a saloon at two in the morning and there was always someone there, somebody to talk to. You flicked on the TV and there were like a million things to choose from. You felt like a pizza or some Chinese, you just dialed a number. Whatever you wanted. Whenever you wanted it. The gas was always cheap, and the great American highway stretched in every direction. He loved getting into his Pontiac and cruising the night. Roll the windows down and turn the sound up. It was a rock 'n' roll country—loud, fast, here today, gone tomorrow. He knew it wasn't for everybody—it could be terrifying as hell—but he could not imagine living anywhere else, nor wanting to. But he wondered now, perhaps for the first time, about what he would have been willing to give up for this privilege.

Giving up your life seemed a little extreme. You only had one of those.

"Would you like a sandwich?" she asked. "I made too many. Sometimes I give some to the men who work here."

"What kind?" Bunko asked.

"Tuna. Light on the mayo. With lettuce and tomato."

It was odd. There they were, eating tuna fish sandwiches in the cemetery, everything suddenly normal as could be.

"His name was Donnie," she said between bitefuls. "That's what you wanted, isn't it? Donnie Bunce. He was a very delightful person, I still remember that. Helpful and concerned. From New Jersey, you know."

Eamon and Bunko exchanged startled glances.

This was not the revelation the inspectors had eagerly anticipated. For one thing, Donnie Bunce and his boat had already been blown to smithereens by this time. Bunce had gotten it in July, and Shad had left this world in September. Now either Bunce's ghost had materialized and paid a visit to Earl and his family, which would have definitely complicated things plenty, or something just normal screwy was going on.

Eamon said, "Mrs. Shad, we're going to need a detailed description of Donnie. Whatever you can remember."

"He had beautiful blue eyes. Paul Newman eyes. But he didn't look anything like Paul. He was tall, robust. Ruddy kind of complexion. He had nice, curly brown hair. Very nice hair. I remember that, too. And he had some tattoos on his arms. I don't really approve of that, but he was such a nice boy anyway."

"Can you recall what the tattoos were?"

"Oh, no. I don't pay much mind to such things. May I ask why you need to know? Did Donnie do something he wasn't supposed to?"

They told her that they didn't really know yet and thanked her for the sandwiches.

"Well, if you need anything else, this is usually where you'll find me. I come here most every day. You probably think I'm crazy. But I don't really care. These were the people who meant the most to me. And it wouldn't be right to let them just be forgotten like that, would it? You know, I didn't always come here so often, just every couple of months to pull out the weeds and check the flowers and things like that. But lately, for reasons of my own, it's become more important. And I think they appreciate it, I really do. I come here and I talk to them. Sometimes I read the paper to them. They always liked the sports section—they both did—so I try to keep up for them. Do you think I'm crazy? Well, it really doesn't matter. Everyone has to do what makes sense to them."

They left her there, in her lawn chair, alone with her memories.

"So what about this Bunce deal?" Bunko asked when they were out of earshot.

"Either somebody was just using Bunce's name, which is odd, because then Earl Shad had to go along with it, and that doesn't make any real sense, or maybe Bunce didn't go down in the Atlantic like we all think."

"First we get a description or a photo from Nunn Bunce. Check to see if it matches the Dotster. That ought to eliminate some things right off. In the meantime, let's get out of here. Catch an early flight home."

"Yeah. Too bad about Dot, huh? I feel pretty sorry for the lady. She looked like she was on her way out. My guess some kind of cancer."

"Yeah," Bunko said, tired to his very soul. "She's already gone. Believe me, kid. She's been gone for a long time. Just shows, you don't have to be in the ground to be dead."

Then Eamon was in downtown Baltimore. Like that. Across worlds. Across weather patterns. One minute it's raining. The next it's the beginnings of a clear, cold night. It threw him. One minute he's in Berlin, Pennsylvania. The next he's standing at a busy crosswalk on Pratt, waiting for a light to change.

The great corporate towers were emptying, spilling their cogs and cogettes out into the cool, delicious thrill of early evening. They came out—these smart, impeccably dressed men and women of ambition; these sad, tired, worn, lackluster participants in the modern tragedy—and looked up into the night sky, into sterling blackness, unbelieving. Another day had passed, another night descended. Where did all the time go? Where did it all go? It ticked away in the tiny glass cubicles, hooked up to artificial life support; ticked away while they kept track of other people's money, punching the numbing figures into their computer-calculators; ticked away while their unseen customers and bosses barked out orders on the otherworldly telephone; ticked away in the pursuit of finite dreams. They watched the sun come up and go down through their tiny portal on the world. They missed everything, these people.

They brushed past Eamon with strident purpose, heading either to the parking garages or the neon bars. The bars were alive with their kinetic frustration, three-deep with their anger and their sorrow and their helplessness. These men—and they were mostly men—drank with determination and discipline, downing their two or three double-whatevers on a rigid schedule. They kept glancing at their slick designer watches as they pushed their one free and shining moment—in a day otherwise devoid of personal pleasure—to its absolute limit.

Eamon was glad not to be among them this evening. It was just after five, and he hoped he hadn't missed her. He'd come straight from the airport, stopping only long enough to purchase the dozen long-stemmed roses. He wanted to surprise her. He wanted to take her out to dinner, to some great place somewhere. That is, if she didn't have to work late or have some other kind of plans. He wanted to make it up to her, that's what it was. It was his fault, the way the weekend had ended. He'd been thinking about it, and he decided that he was probably being too pushy. If she didn't want to talk about something, that was her right. Her marriage really wasn't any of his business, whatever the hell happened.

He couldn't get her out of his mind. Everything was different because of Justine. Things didn't matter in the same way they used to—the same way they mattered a mere two weeks ago. He just wanted to be with her, that was the single overwhelming truth of his existence. He couldn't seem to keep his mind on the work. Even if the work had everything to do with her father. It all went back to that young lieutenant and the summer of '67. Eamon was eight years old and telling anyone who would listen that he was going to be a fireman. That was how long ago that was. It all starts with a letter. A letter that had been sitting undisturbed in Holding for a quarter of a century. A day before Ford died in a so-called accident he wrote to tell his wife not to believe in accidents. That was the starting point. No, that was not really true either. The starting point was a blue-eyed blond stunner named Justine Ford. That was the real reason it had gone any further. If Joe Blow or Irene Nobody had walked into the Command Post, it was his guess that the mystery would have kept on gathering dust for another twenty-five years. After all, they were postal inspectors, not military police, not homicide detectives, not Schwarzenegger and Stallone. They were in the exacting business of going after mail fraud and kiddie porn, which mostly meant working their way through tedious and baffling paper mazes. Let's face it, he thought, they knew more about going after the perpetrator of a chain letter than they did about going after a fucking killer.

And that wasn't the worst part. The worst part was that Eamon was not at the top of his game, no way. He finally had one of the all-time great cases—it had everything, explosions, suicides, murders, threats on the president's life, you name it—and he was in love with the dead lieutenant's daughter. He couldn't concentrate. Everything was going right past him. He was busy thinking about some girl. He was no help to anyone. He had realized it in Berlin. It was a good thing Bunko was able to step right in and take charge. He was in dreamland, lost to the world. Thank God Montrez and the Bureau wanted in. They could use all the help they could get.

He just wanted to be with her. He drifted through a world that was illusory and ephemeral, that seemed put there only for him. The buildings were just facades, like Hollywood sets propped up by two-by-fours, and the hydrants and the hot dog carts and everything else belonged to the prop department. The early moon was big and round and made of Day-Glo. The people were extras, just the underpaid and faceless, all of them brought together for the requisite crowd scenes. They pretended to be in a hurry to get somewhere, but he knew that once he was past them, once the camera left them, they simply went back to their coffee and their waiting. Everyone was just a minor character in the drama that was love. The only thing that was vivid and real was the two of them.

He came in through the revolving door and took a place behind one of the tall papier-mâché trees in the impressive lobby of the Legg Mason building. The six elevators—packed with hair-teased secretaries and smug young turks and world-weary vice presidents—came down continuously, unloading their cargo, shooting up for more. He watched the numbers light up and down, all the while wishing for her.

He waited fifteen minutes, waited as the crowds thinned and the elevators arrived with less urgency. He was thinking about going up, but he certainly didn't want to embarrass her. He knew that could be a delicate situation, with co-workers and everything. He didn't know if she wanted to go public with their little romance. He'd give it another five minutes or so.

Just as he was about to go up he saw her emerging. His heart immediately leapt at the sight of her.

She was animated.

She was talking to one of those distinguished vice presidents.

They looked into each other's eyes. A momentary pause.

They kissed. It was gentle and lasted more than a moment.

They pulled back.

They smiled at each other in that knowing way.

She saw him, finally.

It was all in slow-mo.

He dropped the roses and ran.

She called after him, "Eamon! Eamon! It's not what you think!"

He ran, he didn't care.

He felt only blind, burning rage.

Everything was suddenly real again, ugly and very real.

11

He couldn't get drunk fast enough. Boxcar kept sliding the cold ones over, and he kept gulping them back. Every other Rolling Rock, he'd do a shot of Jack and buy a round for everyone else. He didn't feel a thing, just the harsh wetness of the beer going down.

He stood there at the end of the bar, at the waitresses' station, in their way. He just didn't feel like talking to anyone. McCleary was down at the other end with his latest, a bimbo in a spandex jumpsuit and stiletto heels. Jack and Timmy were up with the darts. Larry, an insurance adjuster with a wife and two kids at home, was interrupting the conversation of two annoyed-looking women. They obviously wanted to keep to themselves, but Larry just didn't get it. He was Willy Loman tonight, and he kept on jabbering, trying to initiate something, anything, from the weather to off-color jokes to desperate card tricks, while they continued to stare at him like he was a carrier of the bubonic plague. Eamon felt for the guy, even if he was making an asshole of himself. Before Larry had made his move he'd thought about giving it a wing himself.

It was just another night at the Blue Marlin. The small dining room was packed as always, and Gena

170

and Carrie were running back and forth from the service bar to the tables to the kitchen. The food was great, besides being inexpensive. They knew how to charbroil a steak, and they put enough Tabasco in the gumbo, and the homemade fries were legendary. He was thinking about ordering a bacon cheeseburger with onion rings and maybe a blue cheese salad. He hadn't eaten a thing, and although it was his plan to become shitfaced and incoherent—if that, indeed, qualified as a plan—it was always better to do that with something in your belly. Because, unfortunately, you still had to wake up the next morning. Long, hard experience was his guide here.

Gena said, "You okay, Eamon?"

Gena wasn't just some waitress. She was someone he used to go with, a month of his life somewhere along the line. She was looking very fine tonight, he had to give her that. He couldn't even really remember why he'd dumped her.

"Sure, sure, couldn't be fucking better. Why you ask?"

He was close to slurring his words, everything just a little beyond him now.

"You look a little unsteady, that's all. Maybe you should slow it down a bit."

"I got my reasons."

"What, somebody finally give you a dose of your own medicine?" she said, edging on malicious. "If so, it's about time."

He tried to bring her into better focus. Gena was just someone from long ago that he'd gone to the movies with a couple of times. She didn't have the right. She didn't know him. She didn't know anything.

"How 'bout we do without the fuckin' sarcasm and you get me something to eat? Deluxe special.

Tell Bobby it's for me. That way it won't take so long."

"I'd like to meet this woman," Gena said, the smile as evil as anything he'd ever seen.

Maybe she was right. Maybe it was that what goes around comes around. Maybe it was his turn to get fucked. He thought of Sanchez suddenly. That night he stood her up. For that stinking bitch, for that stinking bitch. He never wanted to hear her fucking name again. She could just go rot in hell for all he cared.

Chris Isaak's haunting "Wicked Game" came on the juke again. There was a sexy redhead punching in the numbers, swaying in that tainted glow. There were a few more babes in the joint since he'd last looked. Some of them were looking back at him. They didn't know how drunk he was. They didn't know what they were messing with. People never did.

The redhead had a friend; he liked her. She was drinking a tall icy daiquiri and tapping her unlit cigarette on the bar in time to the music. She was the three Bs, blond, beautiful, and bored. She thought she was something special, and she acted like she could give a shit, but you knew it had to be otherwise. Otherwise why was she even there? It was cheaper and easier to drink at home. Everybody was lonely. Everybody was trying to make a connection. Everybody was fucked up. Everybody. He didn't care who you were. He knew. It was all clear when you were in the place he was in. He was thinking about going over to Blondie and giving her a hard time. Okay, maybe he had something to prove. Maybe he needed somebody to make him feel good. So what? Didn't you ever feel that way? Didn't you ever want something just because it was there?

No, you were different. You didn't need nothing. Tell him about it.

Boxcar cut him off. "You're fucked. Go home."

"Yeah, thanks for the memories. What we had together will always be very special to me."

Boxcar saw this kind of thing every night. She looked into his eyes for signs of life. When she failed to make contact she said, "I'm going to pour you some coffee, all right? And I want you to drink it, okay?"

"Did I ever tell you about the time I was on safari in Africa?" he said, his head wagging. "Yeah, that was right after I had the sex-change operation. Or maybe it happened after I married Zsa Zsa Gabor for the second time. I forget now. It all jumbles together at my age. Yeah, sixty-two. I know, I know. Look great for sixty-two. Everyone tells me."

She shook her head in wonder. Then went down to McCleary, who was doing his own clamoring. Once her back was turned he grabbed the closest reachable bottle—Johnnie Black—and sent his coffee into orbit. Moments later he held onto the bar as its bottles and human contents did a slow waltz around him. Drunk people weren't kidding when they said that thing about the room spinning.

He made it stop. Sheer force of will. He needed another drink. That's what he needed. He was still standing. He wanted to be knocked down to the canvas, not to feel, not to know, not to think. He stared at Blondie, and she scowled at him. He took that as an invitation and staggered over.

"Eamon Wearie at your service," he said on some kind of automatic pilot.

"Go 'way. You're drunk."

"And you're rude. Why are you so rude?"

She didn't answer him. She sure was hot-looking. She was all in skin-tight lacy black. All the girls went out in their underwear these days; it was the latest thing. She wasn't even in a blouse or anything, just this bra, like something Madonna would go out in.

"I'll buy you a drink," he said.

"I already have one."

"What, someone steal your shirt or something?"

"What?" she said, annoyed and confused.

He turned away. Went over to the jukebox. Put in some Roy Orbison and Elvis and Tom Petty. Old reliables. Wouldn't let him down. "Don't Be Cruel" was the first one out. That redhead came over and joined him in the pale light. Awfully nice of her. He could use someone to talk to tonight.

"Hi, I'm Andrea."

"And I'm Elvis. I've lost some weight since I died. Changed my hairstyle, too."

She laughed; that was a good sign. Her hair was cut like a boy's, short and severe, but the rest of her was curves in all the right places. In fact, all the girls looked awesome tonight. He didn't know what it was.

"Hey," he said, pulling out some crumpled bills, "do me a favor, all right? Get me a drink. Just don't tell the witch behind the bar who it's for. Get yourself one, too."

"So what do you want?"

"Don't matter. Whatever you're doing."

Then they were putting away White Russians. Tasted just like coffee milkshakes and went down just as easy.

"Good choice," he said. "So what did you say your name was?"

"It's Andrea. I have to tell you something. I was watching you before. You just looked so lonely, do you know that? And I was like so surprised. Because you just don't look the type."

'So you know your friend," he said, not keeping

track of anything at this point, "is one very rude young lady."

"Don't worry about her. She's just got her problems. You know Dean that comes in here? He just tested positive. She didn't know he was swinging both ways. She has to wait for hers to come back now. Two weeks not knowing, that's some rough shit."

"I don't know about any of that, but she's real rude. Let's have another drink."

Then Bunko and this woman appeared.

"Hey, kid! How you doing? Why didn't you tell me you were heading down here this evening?"

"Am I glad to see you," he said, not really knowing if it was real anymore.

"Listen, I want to introduce you to Franny. Remember me telling you about her? She's a crime reporter for the *Sun*. Finest broad I ever knew."

Franny was this big blowzy woman who smoked cigars and drank scotch. She was like some female version of Bunko. Which struck him as kind of funny. He started to laugh hysterically, but for some reason it was like he wasn't making any sound. Nobody could hear him in the place he was.

"Christ, Bunky," she said, "your friend's looped."

He couldn't really see them now. They were talking about him, but it was like coming from far away. "Maybe I should drive him home or something," he heard Bunko saying in the abyss. "I don't ever remember seeing him like this."

Red came back with the drinks and led him to one of the small tables. He kissed Red, and she kissed him back. They were colliding tongues in a bad dream.

"I just knew this would happen," Red said. "I just had a feeling. There was something about you and something about me, and I just knew we were going to wind up together. Isn't that something?"

"My name's Eamon. What's yours?"

"Don't fool around with me like that. It's Andrea, you know that."

"So what are you doing here, Andrea?"

"It's kind of a long story. I just came back here again. I'm looking for my father—"

"Yeah, that seems to be going around."

"What? Well, anyway, I haven't seen him in a few years. Last I heard he was living in Fells Point. Did you ever hear of Jerry Reno? He works on the tugs and things like that. Big drinker, always was. So I've been checking the usual places. Because I need a place to crash. I sure hope I find him."

"Where you living now?"

"Last couple nights I've been in the car. I've got a good car. Thank God."

"Well, that's good. What kind?"

"It's only a couple of years old. It's a Ford Tempo. My husband gave it to me."

"That's weird."

"What's weird? That I've got a husband? Well, that's still up in the air. Because I left him. He's back there in Morgantown. I don't think he's coming after me, either. I don't think he really cares."

"Sure he cares," he said, things just coming out of his mouth. "How long you guys married?"

"Not long. Eight days. See, it's not as bad as it sounds. We lived with each other for a few months first. Then, you know, I caught him cheating. And I just put everything in the trunk, 'cause I'm not going to sit around waiting for explanations. Everybody lies, don't you think?"

Red started staring into his eyes again, and then they were back to their sloppy antics.

At some point he pulled back and thought to ask her age.

"Around twenty," she said.

That she was eighteen did not matter. That she was there did not really matter. What did matter was that he'd achieved his purpose. He'd been able to banish that other woman from his head for a few crazy, fucked-up hours.

Then Boxcar snapped on the lights and ordered everyone out. It was way too bright, and he had trouble adjusting his eyes. There was no more juke music, and all the other people had gone. The Marlin looked sad and dirty with all the lights on. The hardwood floor was messed with peanut shells and cigarette butts. The walls needed to be painted. All that Colt memorabilia, the team photos and pennants, looked faded and yellow. It was just another old, tired, shabby bar, and he was just another customer that should have known better but didn't.

"Come on," she said again, dragging him by the hand. She was just a girl, some girl with ruined makeup and dyed hair.

"Just tell me your name again," he said. "This time I'll get it for sure."

Daniel P. Pinkus was beside himself. He just didn't know what to do. The strange girl with the red hair told him not to disturb Eamon under any circumstances. But he didn't know. Everybody sounded so urgent. You had that Justine person, who must've called twenty times already, and then that horrible Bunko person. He was getting downright nasty. Threatening him and all sorts of horrible things. He really didn't know what to do. He was getting afraid to answer the phone. But Muffin was supposed to call this afternoon, and he didn't want her to worry needlessly. Because that's just what would happen if he didn't pick up. Oh, it was just one of the most horrible days he could remember. It was making him crazy thinking of that strange girl in the kitchen making breakfast. And she was using food from his side of the refrigerator. She hadn't even asked permission. He thought she must be crazy, really. He didn't know where Eamon found these horrible people. She just looked like someone who might carry diseases and things like that. And she just walks into the kitchen in her panties, nothing else. And does she bother to apologize? Of course not. Not an ounce of self-respect. And not only was she using his food, she wasn't cleaning up after herself.

She was that kind of person. The kind that just lets the pans and dishes pile up. He couldn't stand that. It was important to do them as you went along. That way you never fell too far behind. He didn't like her at all.

He was just going to stay in his room until she left or something. Even Pacino and Brando didn't like her. Cats were very intuitive about things like that. Oh, no, he could hear the phone ringing again. Well, he was not going to get it this time. But what if it was Muff? Oh, God, this was terrible, a nightmare.

He tried to think of something positive. Oh, God, he'd used that word again. He would have to stop thinking that word. Negative was the good word now. Negative, like in testing negative for something. It was hard to keep up. And he was still so worried besides. It could have been just a rash, but there was no way to be sure. And it was in a bad place, on the thigh region, which was certainly near places of sexual contact. Oh, God. It was all too horrible to think about. It was all Muffin's fault, the way she started in with that French kissing stuff, even though they knew very well that it was a high-risk activity. Although there had been no documented cases of getting the disease this way, one could not be sure. One could never be sure of anything. Life was just one hellish, agonizing moment after another.

Oh, God, how he wanted to live. He tried to think of pleasant things, the way they told him at Smather's. Oh, it was no use, it just wasn't working. He wanted to pray like he had in the old days before the hospital. He knew he shouldn't, but he couldn't help himself. He started praying for redemption. He wanted to be redeemed and forgiven. He prayed to God to go easy on him. He and Muffin would not engage in heavy petting again. Then

179

he began praying for the souls of all the dead people, for all his dead relatives and dead friends. He prayed for dead neighbors and famous dead people he didn't even know. It was just like the old days.

Dr. Elliot told Daniel that this might happen. The doctor said it was because obsessive compulsives felt responsible for everything and everybody. They thought that their every action and thought could have dire effects if not done in just the right way. The doctor told Daniel that he had to learn to let go, to realize that it wasn't all in his hands, no matter what he thought. Well, Dr. Elliot was a moron. Daniel P. Pinkus knew what worked—and it certainly wasn't letting go. What worked was praying. And he started to recite that litany of dead people again, just because he thought he might have missed a name or two.

Midway through, the phone rang again. Oh, no, he would have to do it all over again. Then he wondered if it was Muffin. What if it was something important? She could worry so. He counted fifteen rings. What if something had happened to her? What if she needed him? What if she killed herself because he refused to answer the phone? She could get so depressed. Finally Daniel P. Pinkus could stand it no longer and answered it.

"Listen, Pinkie, or whatever the fuck your stupid name is, if you don't get Wearie on the fucking phone in about ten seconds, I'm going to come over there and give you a fucking colostomy. Are we clear on this?"

Eamon didn't even dream. It was just the blackness. He had not just overdone it. He'd been closer to death than he ever realized.

He didn't know where he was at first.

Actually, he didn't know *who* he was at first.

There was just Pinkus screaming something about

colostomies and shoving the portable phone into his face. That was his wake-up call.

"Hello?" he said in the bad dream.

"Kid, get your fucking ass down here right away! You picked some fucking day to oversleep. All hell is breaking loose around here. Just get the fuck down here."

"Bunko?"

"Of course it's fucking Bunko, who the fuck do you think it would be? Just get out of fucking bed, kid. You gotta move it. You don't know what's going on down here. Make sure you shower and shave. Don't skip the essentials this morning. Put on a fucking nice suit even. Do what you can, kid. Everything depends on it. And do it in about fifteen fucking minutes. Do you read me, little buddy?"

"What's happened, Bunk?"

"It went down this morning. Sedgewick and his bozos have all been suspended. Looks like they're even going to be indicted. It was all Sanchez's doing. She's one smart cookie, let me tell you. But listen, let's not get into it now. Just get your ass in gear."

"Who's in charge?"

"Oh, that's the thing. They brought in FBI. Went inter-agency on us. And you're not gonna believe who's down here right now. Mister Tony. Get a move on it. Or you might just find yourself out of a job."

"Bunk, one last thing—"

"What, kid?"

"What's a good cure for a hangover?"

"Cure? You want a cure, you got to go to fucking Lourdes. Otherwise just put two Tylenol in some Coca-Cola and take your lumps like a man. Now get a move on. The fucking world awaits."

Good morning, Eamon Wearie. Good morning, you stupid fuck.

He wasn't ready. For any of it. He was having difficulty just getting out of bed. The brain signals just didn't seem to be reaching essential body parts. He felt hot and feverish. The sheets were in fact soaked. His head throbbed, and he could still hear the distant echo of last night's music. Summoning all of his available willpower, he got up. He was in trouble. He tottered between feelings of nausea and vertigo. Every simple act demanded powers of concentration. He rummaged around for his wallet. This was the first thing. He was relieved to find it in his pants, even if there was not a single dollar in it. He had had several hundred when the evening started. He attempted to put it together, piece by piece. He'd lost his watch somewhere along the line. Perhaps his corduroy jacket, too. They were both gone. There were strange clothes on the floor. Female clothes. He drew a blank. The last thing he remembered was Boxcar cutting him off. His memory was Felliniesque, full of dwarfs and wicked laughter and lascivious strangers. After she cut him off, what did he do? Where did he go? How had he gotten home? How had he survived?

It was terrifying to have such a gap.

He hoped all the usual things. He hoped he hadn't hurt anyone. He hoped nothing had happened with the girl, whoever she was. And if something had, he hoped she'd been tolerable.

He popped the little magic capsules first thing. He forced himself into a cold shower. Then he shaved. Then he shaved again. He dressed with care, choosing a navy blue blazer and a staid, out-of-date burgundy tie. Montrez was a straight arrow. It was something to work with, at least.

The portable was bleeping. He picked up, thinking it was Bunko again.

"Eamon? Is that you? Please talk to me. I'm in a panic about everything. It wasn't what you thought. You have to believe me. Please. Please talk to me."

His heart kind of stopped. Her voice. What she had done. She kissed that gray-templed vice president in slow-mo again. That was the image that lingered.

"Eamon, I love you. I love you like no one else I've ever loved before. You have to believe that."

"Yeah, right."

"Eamon, I wanted to tell you. But everything happened so fast. Phil's history. I was telling him good-bye. That's what you saw."

"Yeah, right."

"I'd been seeing him before I knew you. I know I should have told you. But I thought I could handle it. I told him it was over. I told him that. That's what you saw. I love you. You're the person I love."

"Fuck you. I don't have time for your bullshit."

He clicked off. The words didn't even sound like his. They came from the coldest hollows of his heart. He started to cry. He forced himself to stop. He saw his father, his towering father. It went right through him. Eight years old. "Crying's for crybabies," the man said, angry as anything. He'd just gotten his butt kicked in by the neighborhood bully. Stevie Delray. Just proved nobody forgot nothing. A couple of decades from now that phone call would probably sneak up on him, too. His words—"I don't have time for your bullshit"—would reverberate through the years and turn his blood to ice once again.

He was late. He didn't have time for his emotions.

He saw his mistake at the foot of the stairs.

"Oh, I'm glad you're up," she said. "I've got some breakfast ready for you."

A young redhead wearing his robe. He wondered what her name was. He wondered if anything had happened. He couldn't see how it could have, given the shape he was in.

"No, thanks. I'm in a hurry. But help yourself to anything."

"Oh, that's no good. We have a lot to talk about. And you know, I was kinda hoping we'd ... you know."

"I don't think I follow you."

"You know. Sex. I was hoping we'd be able to consummate our relationship. That's why I didn't mind last night. I thought we'd have today."

"Look, I don't think this is going to work out. As far as I'm concerned, last night didn't happen. No offense. I'm sure you're a real nice person and everything, but—"

She opened up the robe. "Look what you'll be missing. Maybe you should think it over."

She was white, chalk white. Her breasts were impressive. He felt weird viewing her, like he was on a surreal shopping trip.

"You're quite beautiful," he said, not wanting to hurt her feelings. "It's not that—"

"When will you be back? I'll make dinner."

"Look, I don't think that's a good idea."

"Look," she said in a new voice, "I'm in trouble. I need a place to be. Can't you understand that?"

It was the one thing he could understand. "A day, two at the most," he said, surprising himself. "I mean it. On the couch, okay? Look, I got to run."

He stepped out the door into an unforgivably sunny day.

"You'll be in New York by seven tomorrow morning," Montrez said in his somber, all-too-quiet way. "I don't care how you get there. You just have the Department of Human Services staked out before it opens. Is that understood? If there are any screw-ups, I don't want to hear about it. You can hand in your badges and collect early retirement for all I care. Are there any questions? This is the time for it."

The inspectors knew better than that. Asking questions just made you look dumb in the eyes of higher-ups. You didn't have to be around long to know that.

"Very well, then. You're dismissed, Agent Ryan. I would like a word with you, though, Agent Wearie. In my office."

Montrez was still in his FBI mode, addressing them as agents. Eamon was nervous, even if they did go way back. He'd been in Montrez's document identification class at Quantico. In fact, back then when he was busy preparing to become a special agent—before he was unceremoniously shipped off to Postal at the end of a lean recruitment year—Montrez had been one of his role models. He had consciously tried to imitate the man's personal style, his habit of dressing and talking in low-key shades of gray. Even his hair was a thick, unworried gray; it was easy to admire the fact that he didn't opt for Grecian Formula, the common artificial choice.

Montrez led him to what until late yesterday had been Percy Sedgewick's office. It was the only one not cordoned off with that yellow police tape. Eamon hardly recognized the Command Post, the way it looked like a murder scene or something.

"Have a seat," the gray man said.

The office was almost entirely bare, just the executive desk and the two black leather swivels. All of its contents had been seized.

"Your boss was not only corrupt, he was incompetent," he said without rancor. "Left a lot of work for us to do. It's catch-up ball all the way. That young Sanchez lady did quite a little job of ferreting this out. What's your opinion of her?"

"First rate," Eamon replied. "Promote her if you can."

"Very well. I guess you have some idea why I want to talk to you."

He was inexcusably late and he looked like green shit. That was just for beginners. Not to mention that he was having undue difficulty with such fundamental motor skills as walking and talking. So, yeah, he guessed he had some faint idea.

"It's just that you've been on top of this from the beginning. Agent Wearie, I'm counting on you in this situation. I'm getting some severe heat from above, I don't mind telling you. I'm sure you've seen the latest missive from Mister Postage Due. The president's wife opened it up by accident. She thought it was a personal invitation, of all things. She was quite distressed by it all. And this, of course, quite distressed the president. And this, in turn, quite distressed my boss's boss. I think you can fill in the rest of the chain of command."

The gray man said all of this very calmly, the very eye of the storm. It was amazing to Eamon that you could know someone for over ten years and not know a single intimate detail about his personal life. For example, he could only guess if Montrez was married. He wasn't wearing a ring, but that didn't prove anything. He wondered where he was from, what part of the country. He possessed a slight drawl, not deep south by any means, but top of North Carolina south. But he didn't know for sure, didn't have any idea. The gray man just didn't invite the normal give-and-take banter. The gray man knew how to keep the world at a professional distance, knew how to hold on to his advantage. It almost qualified in our confessional society—that swirling toilet bowl of gush and flush, where intimacy and personal dignity were pissed away without heed or thought—as a defiant act of genius.

"Of course, we have high hopes that Lundquist might be the key to unlocking a portion of this," he said. "I don't want you to take any chances tomorrow. I want this man arrested on the slightest suspicion or provocation. We cannot afford to err on the side of caution. We may not get a second chance."

Cheeves Lundquist, one of two remaining members of Lieutenant Ford's platoon—the other being Coleman Briggs out in Montauk—had been impossible to find. Even Montrez's agents had not been able to locate the homeless man. But Cheeves Lundquist was going to pick up his monthly social security check tomorrow at New York City's Department of Human Services. This was practically a given. Lundquist had gone to their Upper Broadway offices on the third Wednesday of the month for two years running, according to Human Services' records. Montrez was throwing the postal inspectors a bone, an awfully big bone.

"If Lundquist doesn't pan out," the gray man continued, "I want you to do me a favor. I want you to go out to Montauk."

"Sir, we'd only be retracing steps. You had one of your own men already look into it. I've seen the report. Briggs seemed to check out just fine."

"That's just it. It was all too pat, as far as I'm concerned. Doesn't make sense that Briggs doesn't know anything."

"I spoke to him myself on the phone, and—"

"I know. He's a nice man. I saw *your* report. Still. I want you on this. I must tell you in all candor that the man we assigned to Briggs has, I think, the beginnings of a problem. Bit of a drinker, I understand. Of course, it can happen to the best of them. Shame, though. Hal was someone I could depend on in the old days. I guess that's all, Agent Wearie. Good luck in the Big Apple tomorrow."

Eamon wondered if there really was an Agent Hal with a drinking problem. He wondered if Montrez was being cagey. You couldn't tell with the gray man.

He popped two more Tylenol at the water cooler. He felt shame at his behavior. He demanded to himself that he change. He wanted no more lost nights of the soul. He never again wanted to feel like he did right now. He made a vow to himself. That's it, he said. That's it.

And thus it was done.

It had been weeks since he'd last been at the wheel of the Bob Hope Special. So much had happened. So much was still happening. He didn't feel quite in control. No, he didn't feel like he was there at all. He felt capable of most anything. He hit the gas on the garish cart and drove recklessly down the cramped, spottily lit aisles of cardboard boxes. He brushed up against those cardboard mountains, in that game of seeing how close you could come to something without actually touching it, leaving in his wake great collapsing havoc.

The sickness churned inside of him, percolating up the body's acids and bile, sending up the geysers of heartache. Every time he thought of Justine he winced from the absolute unbearable pain of it. He had never hurt like this before. And so he was unprepared for it.

It took ten minutes to reach the Catacombs, where they kept the air-regulated vaults, which in turn held the earliest-dated mail, undeliverable letters that went back to the 1840s. To Eamon it was an almost sacred part of Dead Letters. There was great beauty in those vaults, in those brittle slips of paper that had been sent out and returned by horseback and steamship; such marvelous strokes of penmanship, such dramatic flourishes of the quill pen, the rich clot and drip of American history.

Sanchez was there, directing traffic. Montrez's agents were going about the chore of ascertaining damage. Sedgewick had been one smart rascal. Everyone knew he'd been up to something, but they hadn't figured anything like this. They figured he was taking from the obvious places, the unused credit cards and uncashed IRS checks that fluttered about all over the place, or maybe even the bigger goods, the crates of televisions and VCRs and CD players that routinely washed up in Holding, the obvious riches.

Nobody figured on Percy being a philatelist. The ardent stamp collector had gone back into the vaults and walked off with those very first prepaid envelopes and adhesive stamps. Many of them were priceless, of course, and it was a wonder, really, that no one had thought of it before.

Eamon wanted to congratulate Sanchez himself. She'd done everyone a favor getting rid of that slimeball. There was also something else on his mind, the matter of a long-owed apology. It had taken this Justine thing for him to finally realize what a prick he'd been.

"Oh, I know why you're here," she said, seeing him. "You probably want to ask me out again. Yeah, that's it, isn't it? You decided that I was probably just about over the last time—so it was about time to ruin my life again. It's an ego thing, right? You probably want me to go out of my way to make you another real nice dinner, right? And then when everything is burned and I'm in tears again, you're going to call and say, 'Gee, I'm sorry. I crashed into a Mack truck, and I won't be able to make it tonight.' "

"Lita, let me explain—"

"Oh, this is going to be good. You're going to explain about some accident in your spaceship, and you had to go to this hospital on Mars, and—"

"That's not fair—"

"I'll tell you what's not fair: You don't even call me back. You stupid fucking shit. I don't even care if you are this really good-looking guy. I don't care. I don't care if I thought maybe once like a long time ago that maybe something could happen between us. I just don't care, and I don't want to hear it. You're the one missing out, you stupid shit."

No question it was time to change tack. She was on a full boil. "Look, I just came down to congratulate you. Good work down here."

She narrowed her eyes and viewed him suspiciously, not sure what he was after. "I didn't do anything. I just knew the creep was up to something, and I followed him."

"Well, I was just up with Montrez, and—"

"Oh, and you were probably telling him that I was just this silly girl you went to bed with once, and—"

"You don't know what you're talking about. Let's just leave it at that. I'm sorry I came down. Really."

"You should be," she said, simmering now.

She was a beautiful, spirited little fighter, he thought. He'd taken her for granted, and now he couldn't have her anymore. Her dark, knowing face. Her large, sad green eyes. That long, sexy black hair. He'd really blown it. What had he been thinking? Where had he been? What was he doing now?

"Stop that," she said, unnerved.

"What?" he said, staring into her green depths.

"The way you're looking at me. Don't do that anymore. I don't want you to."

He went right up to her and took her into his

arms and hugged her. "I'm sorry," he said. "I'm really sorry."

"Don't do this," she said, hugging him back, regretting it all the while.

Then he did something really stupid. He tried to kiss her. She pushed him away with real force. She was angry. She was close to tears. He was just messed up. Really messed up.

"Stop it! Don't do things you don't mean. You don't know the trouble you're causing. You don't know what you're doing to me."

"I didn't mean to—"

"I don't want to hear it. I don't want anything to do with you. Just go away. I don't ever want to see you again. Do you understand?"

He backed off. Shaking his head. Close to tears himself. He didn't even bother getting back into that ridiculous-looking cart. No, he just turned and started to run. He ran as hard as he could, ran because it was the only alternative.

When he finally stopped running, when he'd finally run out of gas and when he was sure that no one else was around, he did what he had wanted to do in the first place. He cried. He wept. He let it all come out of him, let that lifetime of heartache and hurt flow down his hot cheeks. His father be damned.

13

DEAR BUTT FUCKER,

I BELONG TO HISTORY NOW.

I AIN'T EVEN GOING TO HAVE PROBLEMS GETTING CLOSE TO YOU. THAT'S THE REALLY PERFECT PART. NO FUCKING BELL TOWERS FOR ME, OR BOOK DEPOSITORIES.

I'M GOING TO COME RIGHT UP TO YOU, LBJ. AND NO ONE IS GOING TO THINK TWICE.

I'M GOING TO BLOW YOUR FUCK-ING HEAD OFF, LYNDON.

IT IS MY DESTINY.

IT IS THE ONLY WAY THAT I CAN POSSIBLY GIVE MEANING TO MY LIFE. EVERYTHING ELSE WAS LOST IN GOOKLAND.

NOW GOD WILL ALLOW ME TO JOIN MY ANGEL GIRL, THE WAY IT WAS MEANT TO BE.

ME AND ANGEL GIRL.

"I don't get it, Bunk," Eamon said, looking up from Mister Postage Due's latest, dated not four days ago. "Why is the son of a bitch confusing presidents? What's all this shit with LBJ?"

The bolted-in RCA was having vertical hold problems. David Letterman was giving the top ten reasons for living in France. They were in a drab, musty, hundred-dollar-a-night fleabag on the Upper West Side. They were exhausted and wired at the same time. The five-hour drive had taken it out of them. But coffee and thoughts of their big day tomorrow kept them on edge.

Bunko said, "Yeah, that LBJ reference throws me, too. Maybe the fuck just doesn't keep up with politics. Who the fuck knows? Or maybe he's genuinely psychotic. And in that case, we got something to worry about. Did you notice that this one was all in caps? More urgency to it, somehow. Before I thought it was just a lot of hooey, but I'm not so sure anymore. This banana could be the real thing."

Bunko was sitting on the edge of his queen bed in an undershirt and boxer shorts. He poured some more Dewar's into his glass. He was trying to come down.

"You sure you don't want any, kid? It'll help you get some sleep. We're only gonna grab a few hours as it is."

"My drinking's history," Eamon said with some finality.

"The hell it is. You're a fuckin' Irishman like me. You'll be back. You'll see. Don't you think I've been there? Sure, who hasn't tried to quit? Christ, in the old fucking days, every time I'd make an asshole of myself, which was often enough, I'd get all self-righteous the next morning and vow to abstain forever. Let me tell you, forever always lasted about two days. You get older, you wise up. You stop making promises you can't keep."

"I'm serious this time, I mean it. I've been out of control, you just don't know."

"Yeah, I saw you last night. One for the record books. Christ, you were beautiful. Drinking everything in sight. Hitting on everything that moved. You made passes at some of the ugliest women in bar history. Women who hadn't been looked at that way since the Nixon administration. Christ, you struck a blow for shitfaced men everywhere. I'm mighty proud of you."

"Thanks. You've made me feel a whole lot better."

"Kid, you just don't get it. You don't got a drinking problem. I known you, what, ten years or something. You usually have your couple beers and then you call it a night. You're no fucking alcoholic. You go to an AA meeting and you listen to the stories there, and then you'll know what I'm saying. People losing their houses and their marriages and their jobs and everything else that matters. You should sit in sometime, give you some idea of how the world works. Be good for you. You're too fucking sheltered. You just don't know the shit going on out there."

Bunko poured out some more Dewar's. There was something bold and preposterous about that.

"See," he continued, "drinking's not your problem. You got a problem, all right, but that's not it. What you got is a woman problem. Which you just happen to be taking out on the bottle. Believe me, I know the difference."

What Bunko said made him feel better. But on the other hand, he wondered if it wasn't more self-deception. No one wanted to believe he had a problem.

"You should've stuck with Sanchez," Bunko said. "Now that's my idea of a woman. Got it all. Brains. Great pair of melons. A good-paying job. Christ, what's not to like?"

"She says she never wants to see me again."

"What's your secret, Wearie? Christ, you oughta write a book, I mean it. Be the opposite of those ones on how to pick up chicks. Yours would be all about how to get rid of babes who are crazy about you. Call it like *Wearie's Guide to Loneliness*. Or how 'bout *Ten Steps to Celibacy*? Naah, you're right, not catchy enough. Wait. I've got it: *Choosing the Masturbation Life-style*. I think that just about says it all right there."

"Thanks. I knew you'd be there for me when I needed you. It's your particular brand of sensitivity that I count on."

"Listen, kid, I tried to warn ya, didn't I? I told you about that crazy Justine broad. Didn't I?"

"I still don't understand it, though. I mean, I thought she loved me. That's the weird part. Then I see her with that old suit. I just don't get it."

"What's not to get? It's got everything to do with what we're working on. That's right, old buddy. She don't got no father, and so she's out there looking for substitutes. Don't you know nothing? She needs a daddy, that's what she needs. Get with the program, kid."

It was what he'd suspected, too. It's what made sense.

Still. It was hard to get over. The way he felt. What he remembered. The things they had said in the darkness. Bunko was right, he'd lived a sheltered life.

He crawled into his bed and hoped sleep would come easily. The trick was not to think of anything, not Justine, not Sanchez, not Montrez, not Cheeves Lundquist, not anybody. The sounds of the city drifted up to him—long fading sirens and whizzing cabs and isolated shouts and even snippets of sidewalk conversation—the sounds of any city, the sounds of New York. He lost himself in that, in that discordant symphony of life that went on right outside his window.

Upper Broadway was quiet in the early morning. Actually, those first hours of pallid light were the nicest and the gentlest. The addicts and the whores and the homeless and the rest of the city's angry and disenfranchised were just going to sleep, leaving everybody else alone for a short, merciful while.

They strolled up through the eighties, passing such Manhattan landmarks as Zabar's and Shakespeare and Company, passing all-too-familiar scenes of the nineties, shoeless men and women sprawled on park benches, covered with newspaper blankets. But New York would always be New York, no matter the economic downturns. There were still plenty of double-breasted suits hurrying to catch cabs for the commerce of midtown. There were still those buildings of privilege and pedigree that looked askance at the wide, dirty avenue. Doormen in Prussian uniforms still hailed cabs and stood sentry, just as they always had and always would.

Eamon loved New York. He'd lived in Baltimore a long time, but this was the town that brought back memories. New York was where his dad had been a cop. New York was his backyard. New York was where they'd gone for Knick and Ranger games. New York was home to the St. Patrick's Day Parade. He'd done that a few times, and everything else besides. He just felt at home here, instantly at home.

"Crazy city, huh," Bunko said, more a complaint than anything else. "Christ, it's a wonder they don't charge ten bucks for a paper."

Bunko was upset about breakfast. They'd had eggs and spicy sausage and coffee at a Greek diner, and the bill came out over twenty bucks.

"Christ, you go to the best restaurant in Charm

City for dinner, including wine, dessert, tip, everything, and it don't come out to that. Jesus. No wonder everyone's fuckin' homeless."

"I think you exaggerate, big guy."

"Fuckin' highway robbery. I shoulda shot the cashier on the spot."

"That's a good attitude. Sort of makes me wish we'd left the guns at home."

That was what was different this time. They were armed. This time they had brought their Smith and Wesson thirty-eights. Eamon wasn't used to it, the way it felt so snug and heavy under his jacket.

He could count on one hand the times they'd worn them. He'd never fired it in the line of duty, not once. They were still required to go to the indoor range once a month, which he rather looked forward to. It was a relaxing afternoon away from the office, more than anything.

Actually, the inspectors had so little cause to carry their guns that the main problem was finding them. Eamon had some real trouble remembering where he'd put his. He finally found it at the bottom of his underwear drawer. Bunko just kept his in the glove compartment of the Bronco. They both should have been smarter about it.

But something had happened that morning that was kind of weird. When Eamon was strapping his Smith and Wesson on, he had had a premonition of sorts. Things like that didn't usually happen to him. But this morning he had seen he was going to use the gun, seen himself pulling it out of the holster and taking aim at some blank unspecified someone. Just like that, a flash on the brain. It was probably nothing—most things turned out to be—but it had discomfited him nonetheless.

The Department of Human Services was located on the thirty-fourth floor of a brand-new skyrise on

West Ninety-first. It was crazy, really. Here was this forty-story glass and granite tower that was otherwise completely empty. There were no other tenants listed in the ground-floor directory.

The elevators kept opening to reveal the destitute and unfortunate. They were men and women of every color and persuasion. It wasn't so much the quality of their clothes—although it should be said that a good many were in rags—or any other material manifestation that bound them to one another. It was the expression on their faces that gave this wildly assorted group its spiritual cohesion and unity. It was a look of deadened acceptance, a common face that went beyond mere humility and tacit defeat. These were people who would not, or could not, complain. People who waited hour after dreary hour for their turn at the cashier windows without so much as a half-stifled groan.

Human Services seemed to combine the charm of a large, sterile bank with the efficiency of the Department of Motor Vehicles. Lines stretched into eternity. Tellers worked behind bulletproof glass. Velvet ropes were stretched in daunting, incomprehensible patterns. A large booth was set up in the center of the airport-terminal-size room, where information officers handed out forms and directed traffic. Unalert-looking security guards slumped in place, which was entirely understandable in this gray, somnolent world. Eamon and Bunko had positioned themselves near the tellers—who were to cue them at the first sighting of Lundquist—and had waited, and waited, and waited, and waited.

Cheeves Lundquist made them wait until nearly three o'clock. The pretty Puerto Rican girl in charge of line eight, Disabilities & Deceased, signaled to one of the guards to retrieve the inspectors, who were by this time snoring away on a beige plastic bench.

They came up behind him, allowing him to collect his welfare check first. When the slight, meek-looking, horn-rimmed Lundquist turned from the girl into their badges, he didn't hesitate. He bolted. The two startled inspectors would certainly have lost him if he hadn't managed to tangle himself immediately in those velvet ropes. He tried to leap over them but caught one of his black Reeboks and came down hard, forehead first.

It was quite a gash, and the blood flowed freely down his grizzled face. Bunko couldn't have cared less. He had his gun drawn, and he was talking tough:

"Okay, prick, nice and fuckin' easy. Oh, and Cheeves, just for your fuckin' information and enjoyment, I should tell you that I will blow you apart if you attempt to run again."

Amazingly, hardly anybody in line paid attention to the scene. Some pointed, some even laughed. But mostly the reaction was profound indifference, just the shuffling quiet, as if this was a snapshot from the everyday, guns drawn and a guy bleeding, like tell me something new. It was the opposite of those TV shows and action movies. If someone pulled a gun on TV, everybody started screaming and scrambling for cover. Here, it was business as usual.

Eamon gave the vulnerable-looking Cheeves a handkerchief and collected his tortoiseshell glasses for him. Cheeves had tried wiping at the wound with his hands, and now there was blood all over his chinos and baby blue oxford shirt. The preppy clothes had been frayed and stained to begin with, like they hadn't seen a rinse cycle in years.

"I'm ... I'm ... sorry ... officers," he stammered. "I should ... have guessed ... you'd find me eventually. But I don't have any money for her, I just don't. I'm sorry."

"What the fuck are you talking about?" Bunko barked.

"Louise, right? My wife, Louise. The alimony payments. Isn't that what this is about?"

The inspectors didn't know what to think. They didn't make a move for a long, calculating moment. This was high-stakes poker. Either he was bluffing like crazy or he wasn't. And either they played it straight or they tried bluffing themselves. Cheeves sure didn't look like he had any hole cards. He was a bloody mess, and he was scared and trembling besides. He was fucking shaking.

"Listen, ace," Bunko said, "we're not police. We're postal inspectors working in conjunction with the FBI. Now we know you were in Vietnam under the command of Lieutenant William Ford, and ... What the fuck now?"

At the mention of Ford's name Cheeves began sobbing. He collapsed to the floor in great sobs of anguish, all at once baffling them. Bunko and Eamon shrugged their shoulders, absolutely chagrined, not sure what to do next. Someone in a nearby line yelled, "Police brutality!" Someone else said, "Leave the poor man alone, you big bully."

Bunko was thoroughly disgusted: "Christ, get up, Cheeves. Just get up. Act like a fuckin' man. Christ, this is embarrassing. And if there's one thing I don't like, it's a public scene. So let's get up off the floor, and we'll take it from there."

And he did. He was that pliable. He was a terrible, pitiful sight. It was all that blood, wet and teary on the face, matting his hair, turning dark on the clothes. Somehow his delicate eyeglasses only added to the pathetic picture.

"Maybe we should begin by taking him to the hospital," Eamon suggested. "Get him stitched up."

"No, let's just get him in the men's room first

and see how it is," Bunko said. "These things are usually not as bad as they look."

Then he turned to Cheeves: "C'mon. Let's clean you up. No trouble now. Nobody's going to hurt you. Not unless you give us reason."

Cheeves did as he was told. But Bunko wasn't taking any chances. He kept his gun on him all the way. He'd already made up his mind to shoot him in the leg if he tried to make a run for it. There was no use in being unprepared. You had to know what you were going to do before it happened. That was the only way.

In the washroom they tried cleaning him up with pink industrial soap and sandpaper towels. The cut was deep, but they might have been able to get away with just a bandage.

"What do you want to do?" Bunko asked Lundquist. "You want the hospital, or what?"

"I want to go home. That's where I want to go. I can treat it best there, I know I can."

"We got it on reliable sources that you don't got no home. So what's the story? You got some plan or something? Because, so help me God, I'll squeeze the trigger if you try anything at all."

He didn't look like a threat. He had a high, intelligent forehead with thin, receding blond hair. He was small, about five-seven, one-thirty, with pale, watery blue eyes. He hadn't shaved in a few days; the stubble was hard and gray, and the skin was bad enough to make you guess he was a hard-core drinker. At least that's what Eamon guessed. He wasn't shaking only because he was scared, although he was that, too.

"I live on a boat, that's where I live. Over by Riverside Park. At the boat basin. I'll answer your questions if you let me go back."

"The first thing I want to know, and I want to know it right now, is why the hell did you burst into tears at the mention of Ford? What the fuck was that all about?"

"He was a good man. I hadn't heard his name in a while. I was there, you know."

"You saw who killed Ford?"

"No. But everybody knew."

"Was it Earl Shad?"

"Who told you that?"

"Never mind who," Bunko said impatiently, "just tell me if it's true."

"I'll bet he told you," Cheeves said, almost to himself, that softly.

"Well, is that the fucking truth? Was it an accident?"

"Yes," Cheeves said, almost like a zombie. "It was an accident. Earl Shad's gun went off by accident. Isn't that what you want to hear?"

Eamon knew he was lying. He just didn't know why. "What really happened that day?"

"Just like I told you."

"What did you mean when you said, 'I'll bet he told you'?"

"I'm just dizzy. Can't you see that? It's my head. I need to go home, pull myself together. I'll be happy to answer all your questions there. Really. And you know, I have a few for you, too. I really don't understand what this has to do with the FBI and everything. Because I didn't do anything wrong. You'll see. I wasn't the one who did anything wrong. I didn't do anything. That's the truth of my life. You'll see."

Cheeves lived on a battered houseboat, a leaky one-room affair without electricity or running water that bobbed on the foul, slick Hudson. The black water, moving like poured molasses, full of half-drowned cans and paper wrappers, glistened with oil rainbows.

They were immersed in a deep, haunting autumn twilight, the sky like a frightful new bruise, orange and violet, yellow and purplish, in brutal flux. Across from them they could see the soft red glow of New Jersey, the light of refineries and stacks, the poisonous glow of night. Behind them they could hear the rush of traffic, see the headlights and taillights of the Henry Hudson Parkway. Beyond the cars was the deep primeval green of Riverside Park. Beyond that the great skyline, city of silver dreams and blue dread, at once luminous and foreboding.

They waited on deck for Cheeves as he changed inside. There was no way out; they checked. His boat had to be the worst in the basin. All around them were yachts and schooners of all shapes and sizes. There were private ships that came with helicopter landing pads. There were real houseboats, four-bedroom, four-bath jobs. It was a strange, removed world, a floating real estate empire in the shadow of the city, in the savage gloaming.

They watched the silhouette of a man casting off one of the piers. Fishing in that sick slop; it was hard to believe.

"You can come in now," Cheeves said, emerging from the cabin.

There were piles of books and magazines, books on every subject, zoology, nuclear physics, presidential politics, world geography, tons of them; magazines from *National Geographic* to *Time* to *Esquire* to *National Review,* as diverse as could be, as if he was preparing to be a contestant on "Jeopardy" or something. There were books and magazines, and there were gin bottles. At least a dozen empty Bombays.

"Care for a drink?" he asked, sounding like the genial host. "I have this delicious thing for gin and pineapple. Have you ever tried it? Oh, God, you don't know what you're missing. I practically live on the stuff. Of course, Bombay is just fine on its own. Splendidly aromatic."

He got up and went to the bottles, which were on a makeshift table, just some plywood and stolen sawhorses that were clearly marked as Property of the New York City Police Department, undoubtedly used for crowd control. There was also an oil lantern on the table, the only light, in fact. It colored them in warm, burnished shades and allowed them to cast those giant shadows.

"Have a seat, please," he said, directing them to the only piece of usable furniture, an eviction leftover, a moldy, cat-clawed thing that had once been sold as a couch.

Here he was, this perfectly amiable, obviously educated person with a large piece of gauze on his forehead. He'd put on another old, frayed buttondown and another pair of splotchy chinos.

"Oh, feeling better already," he said, downing the first one. "Are you sure? Well, okay, let me know if you change your collective mind. So what do you think? All the comforts of home, I should say. Not bad for two hundred dollars a month. That's the docking fee; nothing else to worry about. You see, this is quite a step up for me. For several undignified years I shared lodgings with a rather odd and unpleasant fellow by the name of Natalie. Well, I don't think it was his given name, but that's what he demanded people call him. Man wanted to be called Natalie—and believe me, no one was going to argue with him. Natalie needed very little provocation to cut a man's throat, or even a woman's, for that matter."

"What did you do—advertise for a roommate in *The Psycho Times?*" Bunko cracked.

"You see, it wasn't really up to me. Natalie just sort of moved in—and I was in no position to refuse. At the time I was living in the railyards, in an old Amtrak dining car. It was lovely, really; I'd even managed to run some electricity into it. We were the envy of the neighborhood. And then, without much fanfare, Natalie asked me to leave. It was hell after that for a while. I tried it down in the subway, but there were some real cretins down there. And then I did the Central Park thing. But then doesn't everyone?"

"What the hell happened to you, man?" Eamon said, astonished. "You obviously have brains. You had a wife, probably a place to live somewhere. What went wrong?"

"Oh, yes. Even had children. Lived in Greenwich. Very lovely. Light commute into Gotham. Worked over at Dreyfus. Evaluating municipal portfolios. Not too demanding, really. Nothing that would lead to this, I should say."

"I don't get it, then."

"There's nothing to get," he suddenly said with some steeliness. He knocked back another pineapple gin surprise. "I'm a perfect example of solipsism. Do you know what that is? Well, it doesn't matter. Suffice it to say that the only pertinent reality is taking place inside my own head."

Bunko was getting a little tired of all this crap. He was anxious to get some answers. "All right, enough philosophical bullshit. I want to know about Phuoc Linh and what went down with this Angel Girl. What the hell do you know about it, Cheeves?"

"I need another drink," he said, getting up for a refill. He poured an even ratio of gin and juice into his jelly-jar glass. He didn't even have ice.

"Well, you see," he said, sitting back down, "Phuoc Linh was a tiny hamlet, a dot on the map, really. Some thatched huts, some water buffalo, just like a thousand other dots. Except for Angel Girl. That's what was different about it. This lovely beauty of a girl. I think she must have been four-teen or something, no older, I'm sure. You really would have had to see her to know how exquisite she was. You really can't imagine her—"

"I can imagine just fine, Cheeves," Bunko said, testy as hell. "Just get on with it. What the hell happened?"

"He got her pregnant, the damn fool. He be-trayed God and his church and his family and the whole false cathedral of his existence."

"Who the fuck are you talking about? Who? Who? Who?"

"He murdered her, you know. He made us watch. He used a bayonet on her and the unborn child. We had to live with that. The only one with any courage was Ford. He had the soul of a hero, that man."

Bunko said, "Forget all that. We want to know who fuckin' did this."

"See," Cheeves said, "it would be meaningless if I didn't tell you something about the cast of charac-ters. I was the greenhorn. Just arrived, already a bit of an outcast. I'd blown my deferment by flunk-ing out of Princeton. Which had to be the bonehead play of the year. The only one of them to treat me like a human was the lieutenant. The poor son of a bitch was being tested, going through it. He was honorable. Honorable in a dishonorable war. He wanted to believe in us, in his country, in the funda-mental rightness and decentness of—"

"I don't give a fuck what he wanted to believe. Who did Angel Girl? Who shot Ford? Was it you, Cheeves? Is that what this is all about?"

"No, of course not. I'm guilty in my own way. Just like the rest of them, of course. Guilty of the insufferable silence. So long ago, of course. The mind is sometimes fooled into thinking it didn't happen. See, I don't really believe in it anymore.

Just as I don't really believe I lived in Greenwich, Connecticut and got on that Conrail train every morning. I had a beautiful topcoat in those days, camel's hair, you know. Such nice things. A collie named Shaw. An MG in the garage, for weekends. Children with cherubic faces. And on Saturday and Tuesday nights, that version of me, that man with the unknowing face, reached over for that woman next to him, that version of Louise. Just tired images in a tired memory, just the lies of the mind. That wasn't me at all. Just something wrong with it all, something."

"I don't know what the fuck you're talking about, pal. What do you know about your platoon mates? Bunce and Robinson? Hurly and Shad? You know what happened to them? Do you?"

"I have some idea," he said, looking vacant and absentminded.

"Why don't you share it with us? I'm sure this is going to be mighty illuminating."

"Dead, I suppose. All of them."

"You killed them, didn't you? The same way you took care of that little Vietnamese girl, right?"

"I'm not even sure you're all that real, to tell you the truth. In fact, I think I need another drink. I'll be with you in a moment. I need sustenance."

He got up and went over to the bottles again. "Are you quite sure?" he said in the flickering orange light, picking up the gin.

And that's when Eamon saw it. He'd been scanning the room, checking out the books again, making note of titles, using his powers of observation, when he came across the curious volume. *A Practical Guide to Plastic Explosives.* Which was clumped together with another anarchist's bestseller: *Making Your Own Pipe Bombs.*

Eamon said, "I notice you're interested in all

kinds of eclectic subjects. Russian history. Exotic birds. Homemade bombs . . ."

Before he could say another word Cheeves launched the lantern in their general direction and made a run for it, out the door before they could even react. They caught a break, though. Cheeves tripped on the deck of the houseboat. He got up, but in his half-crazed confusion he made another mistake, running the wrong way on the narrow wooden dock, toward the boats and the water, away from the park. They had him. There was no escape. Eamon was right behind Cheeves, almost on top of him. Bunko lagged behind, huffing and puffing.

He was trapped. Cheeves had made it to the dock's end, thinking desperate thoughts in the floodlights. There was only water, black water that way. Eamon stopped ten feet from him, his gun drawn and pointed. He was ready if Cheeves tried to charge him, tried to knock him off.

"C'mon Cheeves, make it easy on everyone."

He kept looking at that bad water, like it was even a possibility.

"Don't be nuts," Eamon said.

"I have to go now," Cheeves said, as surreal as anything, like he was sleepwalking.

Bunko screamed from behind Eamon: "Shoot him! Shoot the son of a bitch! It's the only way!"

Eamon froze, couldn't do it. By the time Bunko got there, a mere second or two later, Cheeves had slipped over. They didn't even hear a splash.

They hurried to the edge. It was at least a ten-foot fall into the river. They didn't see a damn thing. Just the swirling black water. When you got up close, like now, you saw there was real current to her, real danger. They kept their eyes on the surface, looking for bubbles, for any sign of life. It was hard to figure. Maybe he had somehow gotten alongside the pilings. They couldn't see anything.

No thrashing around, nothing. Maybe he'd just drowned.

"You're the swimmer, kid," Bunko said.

"Fuck that shit," Eamon said, unnerved by the thought.

"Well, you're the one who blew it," Bunko said accusingly. "You let that son of a bitch get away. I told you to shoot. I told you. You blew it. You just blew it."

Then they heard shouts in the background. Then they saw the flames. People were running for buckets and hoses. That stinking lantern. They didn't make a move. There was nothing much they could do anyway. They just watched Cheeves's boat burn, a wicked bonfire on the water. The old wreck crackled and popped, sending millions of glowing particles into the night sky. The sparks shot up in dizzying profusion, as pretty a fireworks display as you were likely to see.

It wasn't long, though, before they were engulfed in smoke. The wind shifted, and that eye-watering blackness swept over them. The light show was history, and now it was all just another lurid scene.

It was a long drive out to Montauk, and it seemed even longer with Bunko not talking to him. He let the tape of Johnny Cash's greatest hits play over and over, like he was in no mood to change it.

It was strange to be on the Long Island Expressway again, strange to be back. All those faces, all those years, all that history rushed through him on that boring stretch of concrete, the three lanes and the exit signs and the memories. It was a road without a view, missing the towns and the scenery altogether; paved through the Island's own silicon valley, through that high-tech sprawl of translucent glass; just the insipid flatness and more of the same.

But it was where he'd grown up, where it had all mattered. It was just an exit sign, after all. Northport, 51. In reflective green. But he could see his family's modest split-level—the sweet suburban pastures of Bittersweet Court and Starlit Drive— with its garage basketball hoop and backyard chestnuts, the unchanged terrain of memory. He had an undeniable urge to go back, to get off the highway. It was a glorious day, crisp and bracing, azure skies and golden splashes, and it would have been very fine to stroll Main Street one last time, down to the harbor and the town park, to sit on the steps of the bandstand and remember what once was. He had kissed Jenny there once, on the rotting steps just after dark.

He couldn't forget a thing, even if he tried. He was a stupid sentimental bastard. But Bunko wouldn't have pulled over anyway. Bunko blamed him for everything. Bunko thought he should have shot the son of a bitch and gotten it over with. As it was, they had no idea what had happened to Cheeves. Divers had searched the river all morning and were probably still at it, if Eamon knew Montrez.

Montrez had flown into New York and was leading the posse now. Bunko and Eamon were out. Montrez gave them the Montauk orders. Late last night agents had found a metal container on that smouldering houseboat, full of money and something else besides. Five thousand dollars in twenties and a piece of paper with Coleman Briggs's phone number and address. Montrez speculated he was going after Briggs next. Which struck Eamon as awfully odd. Because why hadn't he eliminated him with the others? Why had he waited all these years? It wasn't the only thing bugging him. He kept thinking of Dot Shad's description of the man who had visited her son, blue-eyed and tall with curly brown hair. That sure didn't sound like Cheeves Lundquist. Not to mention the tattoos. Because Cheeves didn't have any of those. Eamon had noticed that right off, when they cleaned him up at Human Services.

Montrez tried to make it sound like a real plum assignment, but they knew better. Keeping an eye on Briggs and his family in case Cheeves decided to strike was garbage work. Like they were private security guards or something. They'd fucked up, and this was their reward—ignominy. All the action was in Manhattan, going after the bad guy.

Eamon wished for redemption. It had been such a bad couple of days. He'd let everyone down, not to mention himself. He felt plain disgraced. At least he was getting some distance from Justine by the very nature of fucking up so much. It still hurt— sure, it hurt plenty—but right now he had other troubles to contend with. He had a partner who wouldn't talk to him and a boss who'd lost faith in him. As they came off the expressway Johnny Cash stirred the coals of "Ring of Fire" for about the fifth time.

On either side there was spectacular foliage, those last melancholy bursts, final shadings of the season, the deep, resolute permutation of all things. Let the poet describe the many reds and yellows and oranges and golds. Let the poet even begin to try. It was only a few days to Halloween. The farm stands were abundant with pumpkins and Indian corn and colorful, grotesquely-shaped squash. Route 27 carried them through the Hamptons, through those celebrity-infested villages, through those genuinely lovely towns that seemed to survive only as colonial outposts of Manhattan. The city's old money and nouveau riche summered here, arriving Memorial Day weekend and leaving by Labor Day. It did not matter how fine the fall or spring weather was. It did not matter a whit that the winters were, in their own right, just as extraordinary, traffic-free and marvelously lonely with the stark blues, perfect for the romantic getaway and sipping port by the fireplace. These things did not matter to people with money. Nothing mattered but to fit in.

The season was over. And the season was everything. The precious galleries and the gourmet delis and the saturnine dance clubs were all shut down until next Memorial Day. They came into Southampton and passed the huge Georgian mansions of

Gin Lane, receding back into their green dollars, tended to by their winter caretakers now. They made their way through Bridgehampton, and Eamon remembered a nice night at Bobby Van's when he was in college. It was Christmastime, and Jenny was home from Michigan State, and they drove out there on a whim, to forsake the world for a little while. They spent the evening at the old piano bar, staring into each other's eyes meaningfully. Eamon was tempted to say something, to let Bunko in on one of his old special memories, but he knew it would be wasted breath. So when they came into East Hampton, passing by the algae-stilled pond and the old cemetery, passing windmills and weeping willows, passing more memories, he didn't say a word either.

He knew all about this part of the world. He knew all about the great ocean beaches to the south of them. He knew about the oceanfront mansions that were hard to believe, Kennedy–like compounds with twenty bedrooms and tennis courts and all the rest of it, places that were worth a look. Ordinarily, he would have insisted on giving Bunko a tour, but fuck it today. Let the big guy stew, if that's what he wanted to do.

It wasn't his fault. He wasn't going to shoot anyone on the end of some fucking pier. Not when he wasn't convinced of anything.

They drove the last miles, the long, skinny stretch of sand between Amagansett and Montauk, that brought them right alongside the white-crested Atlantic and those monster dunes. It was a rough-hewn landscape, only partially marred by man. Of course, there were condos and sleek new motels nestled among the scrub pines and dune grass. But at least there weren't waves of billboards or the carnival atmosphere of Virginia Beach.

213

Bunko pulled off the road into the sandy lot of a clam shack.

"Hey," he said, breaking the silence, "can you forgive a guy? Sometimes I can be a big boob. I'm sorry, kid."

"No problem," Eamon said, brightened by this turn in the day.

It was that easy. And then they were talking and ribbing each other, just like always. They went in the shack and ordered up a storm. They started with baked clams and fried calamari. Then it was steamers with drawn butter. Plump mussels cooked in wine and garlic. Which they mopped up with their bread and ate with gusto. Then they said what the hell—oink! oink!—and went for the lobsters. Bunko washed his down with a couple of Molsons, while Eamon opted for plain tomato juice. He knew he might not last—that cold, golden beer sure looked good—but he was at least going to give it a try. He figured he owed himself that much.

Late on an off-season afternoon, fabled Montauk was just a windblown ghost town. It was an odd place, really, a tiny, idiosyncratic burg. The first thing to grab your attention was a seven-story red-brick building in the middle of the main traffic circle. It stood sentry to a thimble-size village, a touristy Main Street of gift shops and seafood restaurants, many of them closed now in the bleak twilight. They made their way to South Edison, which was just a few blocks away.

White's Hardware fit snugly between the post office and the blinking Neptune Motel. There were stacks of gleaming garbage cans and coils of new hose out front, along with an extensive collection of rakes and snow shovels. They opened the door and were greeted by the tinkle of bells and the strong, time-gone-by smell of linseed oil. Eamon immediately thought of his dad and those long-ago Saturday afternoons, the way they'd kill time in the dimly lit aisles of small treasures, searching out just the right primer or galvanized nail. Hardware stores were like that, calling back some musty, forgotten, lost world.

"So you must be them agents I was told about." He'd been expecting them.

They, on the other hand, were taken by surprise.

Coleman Briggs was a large, balding, red-faced fellow with twinkly blue eyes. He was also missing his legs.

"And you must be Mr. White," Bunko said.

"Oh, that." He was in a wheelchair, looking dwarfed behind a big, old-fashioned cash register. "See, I bought the place from old Whitey couple years ago. Never saw no point in changing something that was already working just fine."

"Amen to that, brother," Bunko said.

"So where you people been anyway?" he said heartily. "I'd almost given up hope on you. That Mr. Montrez told me you would be here hours ago. And with happy hour coming up, I was getting a mite anxious."

Bunko liked him already. "Happy hour, you say?"

"Oh, there's a dandy at Pearl's Oyster House, right up on Lake Montauk. Just the locals now, real comfortable over there, not pretentious at all. Oh, and the sunsets you get this time of year. Nothing like it. And I can tell you from experience that they never run out of Jameson. If you like that sort of thing."

Bunko liked that *exact* sort of thing. "Say no more, you've sold me. When's the damn train leaving?"

"Right now, if you want. Frank can close up for me. Not much to do around here these months.

Summer it gets crazy, though. Listen, you want me
to drive? Probably be quicker that way. Oh, I know
what you're thinking. Don't worry, I've got me a
specially-equipped van. Can do everything with my
hands. It's just great. Follow me."

Pearl's was all view. Every table in the restaurant
was placed strategically, either facing out over the
lake or facing in toward the three-thousand-gallon
shark tank that took center stage in the vast,
nautical-inspired dining room. Pearl's had all the
netting, buoys, and mounted sailfish that a tourist
could want.

The bar had a long, sensational picture window,
and on another evening Eamon might have really
enjoyed himself. As it was, though, there was nothing quite so humbling as drinking Virgin Marys in
the company of real drinkers. It was a boisterous
happy hour, filled with the raucous laughter of
fishermen and off-duty waitresses and retired folks.
It was the usual shit, too many jokes about female
orgasms and penis size, too many disparaging references to Italians and Poles and Jews, too much of
that. Carol, the fortysomething bartender, trying
hard in Jordache jeans and a low-cut blouse, moved
quickly to fill empty glasses. She did shots with the
customers and supplied her own punch lines, and
she lost interest in Eamon the moment he ordered
his nonalcoholic special. Drinkers just hated to be
reminded of that other religion, which they couldn't
help feeling was holier-than-thou.

He felt like he was all alone, especially the way
Bunko and Cole had hit it off. They'd been going
great guns since the first. Cole was real popular,
and it seemed like everyone was buying him drinks
and buying Bunko drinks just because he was with
him. Cole sat on a stool just like everybody else,
lifted up there by one of his cronies. He was a

strong-looking man, massive forearms and a footballer's neck, and even though he was heavy and slack in the middle now, you could tell that that hadn't always been the case. The legs had been blown off or amputated just above the knees. He was telling Bunko about it right now:

"That fuckin' war. Not much to tell, you know. One minute I'm walkin' and talkin', the next I'm in a white room in Tokyo. The mind's great that way. Just blanks out when something's too horrible. I swear to fuckin' God, I don't remember a second of it. Just stepped in the wrong place, should have looked where I was going, that's all."

"Christ, I don't think I could deal with something like that," Bunko said, softer than usual.

"You deal with it," Cole said. "You just reach down as far as you can go. For what you don't even think you have. What other choice is there? The tough part was Emmie. My wife. I didn't know how she'd react. Fortunately, I was rewarded by the good Lord with a fine, handsome woman who gave me seven wonderful children and not a moment's heartache. There's nobody like Emmie. She could have left me, she could have done a lot of things. God knows why she stuck by me so long. I'm just a lucky man, I guess."

"You got guts," Bunko said. "I mean it. I consider myself a good judge of people. And you, brother, have got courage."

"No more than anybody else. You know, the first year is the roughest, of course. You're just a kid—and they took your legs from you, those things that made you stand tall in the world. And you cry, my friend, like a fuckin' baby. They put you in VA hospital after VA hospital, and you hear all those horrible screams in the middle of the night, all those other boys who've been robbed of their birthright and manhood. Believe me, brother, there were lots worse off. There were boys who got it all blown off—and what you gonna tell them? You gonna tell them the lie that it's all going to be okay? No way. You just got to pump the morphine in them. Because that's the only way. Because you don't want them knowing, realizing, remembering."

"Fuckin' Christ, I know," Bunko said. "I know. I came home after my tour, and I literally kissed the ground. I made promises to my Maker over there that I was never going to be able to keep. Just so I could come home. And it was worth it. It's worth it to be fuckin' alive and drinking good Irish whisky in good company."

"Amen to that, brother."

They clinked glasses. They were like brothers in a way. They talked just like each other, all those f-words and all those sacrilegious references to their God, and to some extent they even looked like each other. They both had big bullish heads and florid faces, but Bunko had more hair. Cole was resorting to the technique of last resort, the neck-hair replacement system, lacing those slickened strands over his shiny pate.

"So," Bunko said, "what kind of work were you in before you got into the hardware biz?"

"Well, to tell you the truth, I never left South Edison. I worked right next door, in the damn fucking post office, of all places. Put in my fifteen years, then got the Christ out. Dreary, boring work. The guy in the back, just sorting and stamping, just waiting for quittin' time. Not like the kind of work you and your friend do. Nothing like that."

"Yeah, me and Wearie are in a real glamorous profession. Right up there next to fucking dog catcher. Yeah, just great. Just like I dreamed it would be."

"Christ, Bunko," he said. "I feel bad that you and your partner got to come all this way. I don't need no protecting. If a land mine didn't do it, I don't think no Cheeves Lundquist is going to be up to the job. I tell you truthfully, I never liked that guy. Not that I thought he was capable of this or anything. But an Ivy League prick, you know what I'm saying?"

"Boy, I hear you, friend," Bunko said. "Christ, what do you say we do another round?"

He called down to Carol. "Hey, beautiful. You want to come down here for a minute? I want to propose to you again. I'm not kidding. We could get married right away, right this second. We'll get one of these clammers down there to perform the ceremony. Sure, sure, they're just like ship captains. We tie the knot, and then we have a night of unspeakable romance and passion. All sanctified by God, of course. You'll love it. In the morning we get it annulled. How's that sound?"

"My, aren't you the sweet talker," she said, pouring liberally. "So, Prince Charming, are you going to be with us for any length of time?"

She asked it in that sly interested way, too flagrant to be missed.

"I've just moved here," Bunko replied. "Yeah, bought a great house on the ocean. You gotta come and see it. We'll drink champagne in the outdoor hot tub under the fucking stars."

She didn't seem to be sure if he was kidding or not. Maybe she just wanted it to be true or something. "If you're on the level," she said, "then you just got yourself a date."

When she left to tend to another customer Bunko turned back to Cole and said, "What do you say to lending me your house for the evening?"

Cole was laughing, saying, "Whatever you want, buddy. What's mine is yours. My house. My wife. Take your pick. After all, what are old friends for if not to help each other get laid?"

Bunko said, "Beats being in Nam, that's for fucking sure."

"Everything beats Gookland, my friend."

Gookland. Not something he'd forget too easily. After all, he'd just read it the other night. Mister Postage Due's latest mailgram. Maybe it was common enough slang over there, maybe a lot of things. Eamon couldn't be at all sure. And Bunko was no help. He was sloshed, everything going right past him. Eamon listened that much harder.

"You know, the funny thing is, I liked it there at first, no kidding," Cole continued confidentially. "It was my second tour, you know. I was older than the rest of them, even the lieutenant. The army was my life, my career. I was twenty-five, sergeant and radioman all in one. Had four of the kids already. We were in New Jersey in those days, out of Fort Dix. Emmie was a trooper, she understood what I was all about. She just let me have my way. She knew better than to interfere.

"Shit, I don't even know what it was. I just got this charge out of it, this crazy thrill, I mean it. Like my every nerve ending was kicking in, tingling with that scared-shit fear that at least made you know you were alive. Do you know what I'm saying here? Just getting down to the fucking essentials, to what makes a man a man."

"Yeah, you said it," Bunko rejoined.

"But then it's over, and you're in a goddamn wheelchair, and you've got that eternity to ponder everything. And then, believe me, it all starts to look different. Starts to look like you're the fucking horse's ass. That's what I was. Gave it all away for a few cheap thrills. And if you think anybody gives a shit now, you're sadly mistaken. People stare, that's what they do. They stare and they think, 'Poor, sad, stupid fuck.' That's what they think.

"And I don't blame them. They're right. I was

cannon fodder, that's about the size of it. Just another one. Just another young schmuck too eager to get his ass blown to fucking bits. Not that I deserved it, not anything like it. Nobody deserves what I've been through. Sometimes I think I already died and that I'm rotting in hell. Really, I ain't kidding. Sometimes I really think it. It wouldn't surprise me. 'Cause I don't think there's no way I'm getting into heaven anyway. Tell you the truth, I think even purgatory's a long shot. The things I've done. More than any man can live with, I tell you. Sometimes I wish there was a way to even the score, to make it right. But there probably ain't. You can't make fuckin' deals with God. He's just not interested. Got enough problems of His own.

"Christ, Bunko, it's good to talk to someone like you. Somebody who understands where I'm coming from. Christ, we must be about the same age even. You got any kids? I thought so. That's all the reason you ever need right there. Am I right? You know it. I'm just so proud of my boys and girls, each and every one of them. The oldest, Danny, is the chief petty officer on the *Kennedy*, big aircraft carrier. Got kids of his own already. Listen, I got eight grandchildren. No kidding. The last of my girls are in school now. Shannon's over at St. John's. And the youngest, the baby of the family, Maureen, is in her last year of high school. She's the only one still living with us. Damn, it all goes so fast. You know what I'm saying, Bunko? Of course you do. You're just good people."

They kept talking. They kept bonding. Eamon kept going back to Gookland. It bothered him; it wouldn't let go. And it bothered him somehow that Briggs had put in a stint at the post office. He didn't know why; it wasn't like any old postal employee would know that White House code. They called

Carol for another round. He went over to the free buffet, silver bins of Buffalo chicken wings and Texas chili over a blue flame. He went for the ground beef and red beans, sprinkling cheddar and onion over the slop.

At least Briggs was right about the CinemaScope view. He watched the sun's fiery descent into the placid water, watched as that gorgeous thing burned her remaining heat over the weathered dock and the comings and goings of motorized sailboats. When the sun had almost finished her daily death the burning embers mixed with the icy-blue gloaming to create a precious few moments of heaven on earth. Then it was night.

The chili didn't turn out to be so bad, a three-alarm version with plenty of jalepeño. It was all so out of whack. Monday he's in Berlin, Pennsylvania. By Tuesday he's lost the love of his life. Yesterday they're in New York watching some guy jump into the Hudson. Now all of a sudden it's Thursday night—and he's chowing down on the landlubber's special under the lobster traps and white Christmas lights blinking from the fish netting.

"Don't fill up on that shit," Coleman Briggs said, finally paying some mind to Eamon. "Emmie's expecting us for dinner. In fact, she's made up beds and everything. I insist you stay the night. And don't give me none of that motel shit, you hear me?"

Eamon watched as they ordered one more for the road. He watched as they laughed and flirted some more with Carol. He watched them with cold, unfeeling eyes, like they were the enemy.

Briggs's house was not the old-fashioned saltbox that Eamon had expected. It was a magnificent one-level cedar contemporary, nestled off Old Montauk

Highway, in the shrub-rooted hills, facing out over the moonlit ocean.

"Cole, this is fabulous!" Bunko exclaimed. "Absolutely state of the fuckin' art."

"Well, it does have its advantages," he said, wheeling himself in. "For one thing, no steps, no sunken living rooms, nothing to get in my way. We only moved in a year ago. Emmie's a real estate agent, does quite good, I might add. Anyway, with all the yuppie stockbroker scumbags going broke over the last couple of years, we were able to pick this baby up for a song. It's got five bedrooms, plenty of room for the grandkids and everyone else."

Cole got around pretty well, all things considered. Still, Eamon couldn't help but notice the inherent difficulties; he needed assistance getting in and out of the Voyager; every step and curb hindered him; even going to the bathroom posed unique problems. It just seemed to rule out what Eamon had been thinking. Yeah, he had to be crazy to even consider it. He was just getting paranoid, after everything that had happened the past week. It was just that that Gookland remark had set his mind in motion.

They waited in the living room as Cole went to find Emmie. It was impressive, with its high-vaulted cathedral ceiling and lustrous Norwegian wood floors. There was the pristine fireplace, a fireplace that had probably never seen a roaring fire. There were bookshelves, but no books. Just row after row of movie cassettes, alphabetized, no less. There was the requisite piano-size television with its VCR and cable attachments. The rest of it was cool and detached, the Plexiglas coffee table, the white leather sectional, the potted palms. Mauve walls were noticeably free of artwork—not a painting, not even a framed poster. There weren't any room-warming

Oriental rugs, either—nothing to hinder Cole's access. It was a thoroughly sensible and functional space, and if it hadn't been for the pictures, the dozens and dozens of photos from the Briggs family album, it might have seemed cold and heartless.

One whole wall was covered with them, pictures of Cole and Emmie, both before and after Vietnam, pictures of the children and the grandkids and the dogs and cats, pictures of a family seemingly in love with itself. It was all there, all documented, those first steps and first bicycle rides, the Christmas trees and birthday parties, the prom dates and wedding days, the christenings and other familial celebrations of selfhood.

Cole came back with Emmie. She was a tall, severe, unfriendly-looking woman. Right off Eamon didn't like her. There was something about her, the imperious gaze, the sharp, hawklike eyes, eyes that didn't miss a thing. She was dressed to go out, coat and purse draped over her arm.

"You can stay until Sunday," she said without introducing herself. "Not a day more. I'm expecting Constance and Jerry and the kids—and you'd only be in the way. And I'm sorry about dinner. But when my husband—a man who seems not to know the boundaries of time—did not call, I just assumed you were all eating out. Well, make yourself at home, then. Your bedrooms are all the way down the hall to the right. You can't miss them. There should be plenty of towels. Very well."

Then she turned to Cole and kissed him on the cheek. "We're playing at Muriel's tonight. Maureen is staying at the Gustavsons'. There's leftover casserole in the fridge, in case you're starving."

When she was gone Cole apologized. "She's not usually like this, fellas. Something's got her bugged. Damned if I know what it is."

Bunko said, "Don't worry about it, buddy. She's a woman. She's entitled not to make any sense."

"Don't you know it, friend. But if the cat's away, then the mice can go right back out and play. Emmie's bridge game usually goes to midnight. What do you say to living a little dangerously? The Reef has a pretty lively crowd about this hour. In fact, if I'm not mistaken, Carol usually heads over there after her shift."

"Let's roll," Bunko said, halfway out the door already.

Eamon said, "You know, I'm a little tired. Why don't you guys just head on out without me?"

They shrugged. Well, if he was sure and everything.

Success.

He watched them back down the driveway. He wasn't taking any chances. He wanted to be sure they were gone.

He felt like a cat burglar, the way he was creeping around the house. He started with the closets, the places big enough to hold what he was looking for. But he just kept finding the usual crap in them, the slide projector, the sewing machine, the vacuum cleaner, the tennis rackets. He checked behind towels and sheets in the linen closet, as thorough as could be. He went through the spare, unlived-in guest rooms in no time flat.

It wasn't long before he was in the master bedroom, their room. He opened bureau drawers and sorted through their private things. He had no business here, no business at all. He found their passports and mortgage papers. He went through their socks and underwear, just looking for clues. He peered into their closets, into their dark recesses. She shared Imelda Marcos's propensity for collecting shoes. Besides the neat row of dark suits, his closet contained two artificial legs and a strange-looking leather harness. He could only guess what the contraption was for; no, he couldn't even do that.

He opened the medicine cabinet in their oversize bathroom. All the usual stuff, the syrups and aspirins and cotton balls. She liked her Valium. He was on Prozac, the antidepressant.

He found a gun in the nightstand drawer, next to the Bible. A nickle-plated Beretta. But there was nothing so strange in that. Plenty of people kept guns next to their beds. It was fairly typical in America. He checked and found it was loaded.

He went back to looking for the one thing. The house didn't have a basement. He hadn't tried the kitchen yet, or the garage. Or their daughter's room. He'd poked his head in before but quickly retreated when he saw all those posters of Johnny Depp and Luke Perry. He thought about it some more and decided he'd better check it out.

Her room really made him feel like a snoop. There was an open diary on the desk, along with some pictures from a photo booth. The row showed a pretty girl mugging it up with some long-haired guy. He moved surreptitiously, quickly, in a hurry to get out of there. He looked under the bed, and then he opened the closet. It was weird, but he sort of knew it before it even happened, knew it was going to be there.

The Smith-Corona was on the floor, in its case. Model 206. A thirteen-year-old portable. What were the odds of its being a coincidence?

Zero.

Because it wasn't a coincidence.

Coleman Briggs was Mister Postage Due.

He'd been lying all along, about everything. He knew all about Angel Girl and what had gone down in Phuoc Linh.

Eamon wondered how far it went, what his connection was to Cheeves and the others. What the hell did he know? What the hell was his role in all of this?

All he knew was that Briggs had broken the law. You weren't allowed to go around threatening the president. Montrez would want him taken in tonight.

It was a tough one. Here you had this war hero, this guy who'd lost his legs over there, who'd given everything. And then he had seven kids and all the rest of it. Jesus. You had to feel for him. He'd probably go to jail. The embarrassment, the scandal.

Eamon needed some air, needed to sort things out. He stepped out through sliding glass doors, onto the redwood deck. Their bedrooms faced the swimming pool; how nice. It was a green tarp now, just a memory of summer. It was a cold, clear, starry night. He hadn't dressed warmly enough, only an old windbreaker, which he zipped up to his ears. He lay down on one of the chaise longues and stared up into the shining, piercing heavens. There were so many stars out tonight, points of sapphire and emerald and ruby, lights at the end of the world.

He was burned out, no question about it. Even solving the mystery behind Mister Postage Due did not get his blood pumping. It was like always, disappointment commingling with sadness. He was disappointed in Coleman Briggs, and sad that he was the one that had to catch him. The bad guys were never like the bad guys in movies; he had yet to come in contact with one of those psychotic-looking monsters with the diabolical laugh. Cole was all too human, a friendly, hearty sort who just happened to be confined to a wheelchair. That made it even harder somehow. God knew the man had all the reason in the world to hold a grudge.

He didn't want any part of it, really. But there

he was nonetheless, under the cold, glistening stars of Montauk. He waited for them, waited for the sound of the Voyager pulling up the drive.

He took Bunko aside first, explained it to him. Bunko was half drunk and unbelieving.

"I don't think we should wait on this," Eamon said. "I think we should arrest him, or call in Montrez."

"No fuckin' way," the big guy bellowed. "You got it confused. I'm sure there's a logical fuckin' explanation. You don't know him like I do. The man's aces. C'mon, I'll show you."

It was too late to stop him. Cole was in the gourmet kitchen, in the light of the refrigerator, taking things out.

"Oh, hey, fellas," he said. "Just making myself a little sandwich. Want one?"

Bunko said, "Cole, you ain't going to believe this. But my partner has one pretty bizarre idea. I don't even know where to begin. It's just way too ridiculous. You're gonna laugh, but he thinks you're this nut job who's been sending the president these nut job letters. He found this typewriter—"

"You were in Mo's room?" he threw out.

"That's right," Eamon said. "That's just where I found it. What do you think of that?"

He didn't answer. He didn't even try to. His face was a dark shadow in the fridge light.

"Cole, tell him it's not true," Bunko said, imploring him.

"You've been lying to us about everything, haven't you?" Eamon said, cocksure. "You know all about Angel Girl and all the rest of it. It was there in those letters."

"I didn't mean anybody no harm," he said. "You gotta believe me. I wasn't going to do nothing."

Bunko said, "You did it, Cole? You wrote them letters?"

"It's not as bad as it looks. Gotta see it from my point of view. It was all bullshit. I come home toasted, you know. I'm drunk off my ass, just like most nights. I don't got nothing. Just got my anger, my rage. Why the hell not? Look at me. Just look at me, willya? Fuckin' leave me a cripple for the rest of my fuckin' life. Look, Bunk, you think somebody like Carol, for example, ever gonna give me a second look? Afraid not, friend. I'm just this thing to most people. It gets lonely in this chair, believe it.

"So what if I put it down on paper, write a fuckin' letter. Sure, I know it's wrong. But I didn't kill nobody. I didn't go into no shopping mall with no M-16 and open fire. I just wrote some fuckin' anonymous letters. You gotta see it from my point of view. You gotta try."

"I don't know, Cole," Bunko said, suddenly subdued. "We got our own job to do."

"And how'd you know about that code?" Eamon demanded. "How'd you know how to send them out that way?"

"Oh, no big deal," he said, all the air let out of him. "Met one of the White House blue boys at a convention. In my old post office days. Drinking the Irish, got to talking, you know the rest."

"I got another question: How come the letters were so neatly typed? Not a mistake, not a whiteout. I mean, I don't get it. I mean, you just said you were drunk off your ass. What gives? What are you, some kind of professional typist or something?"

He didn't have an answer for that one.

"Fuck that shit," Bunko said, off and running. "Who cares if he can type or not? What about Angel Girl? What did you have to do with that?"

"I didn't do nothing, Bunk," he said, almost

pleading. "I was just a fuckin' bystander. That sicko Cheeves kills the girl. Everybody else has to live with it for the rest of their fuckin' lives. I'm a victim every which way you look at it. But sure, I understand you got a job to do. But I tell you this: I never hurt nobody. You're just going to take me and my family down. Emmie doesn't even know. She's been through so much with me already. God, this is just going to break her heart. Gonna do a lot of irreparable damage. Gonna ruin some fuckin' lives. I just want you to know that."

"Christ," Bunko said, shaking his head.

"Bunk," Eamon said quietly, "I don't see that we have a choice here."

"Kid, I need time to figure this," he said. "It's like what Cole here said. It's not so simple. You can understand that, can't you? The man's got a right to his feelings. If anyone has a right, he does. He didn't do nothing, really. Got drunk and typed some ill-advised letters. So should we fuck up his whole entire life because of that?"

"I think we need to get to the very bottom of it."

"Kid," Bunko said, authoritatively, "I'm going to take full responsibility on this matter. And I say we wait until morning before we do a damn thing. I need time to figure it. Besides, where's Cole going to go? He ain't going anywhere. Let's sleep on it."

Eamon knew it was a mistake, just knew it.

But what the hell was he supposed to do?

Cole was gone.

He wasn't surprised.

They were in the fancy gourmet kitchen, the one with the skylights and the stainless steel range out of some restaurant. They were drinking coffee at the faux marble counter, on the built-in stools. She was in her pink housecoat and slippers scrambling them up some eggs. She seemed nervous, and there were bags under her eyes.

"Well," Emmie said in her starchy way, "I'm sure he'll be back any moment."

She said she'd sent him out for bacon. That was her line of defense. She acted busy, but she didn't seem to be able to look at them. Eamon was guessing that he'd made a run for it. He was also guessing that she knew. Bunko was awfully quiet, probably just couldn't believe he'd been used.

"What's open this early?" Eamon asked. It was seven-thirty on his no-frills Timex.

"Oh, not much," she said. "That's why I'm sure it's taking so long. Probably went to the 7-Eleven. That's a bit out of the way."

Eamon had stayed awake as long as he could, listening for anything the least bit unusual. But he finally fell asleep around two. That gave Cole five

231

hours. He could have left any time in that period. They only had her word to go on. And he didn't like it.

But on the other hand, how far could he get? He was encumbered by a wheelchair, and they also had the plate number of his van.

So they waited.

By the fourth cup of coffee Eamon was ready to put out an all-points bulletin. It was eight-twenty. They were in that dramatic living room, pacing Norwegian wood. She was in her bedroom getting ready for work.

"Christ, I can't believe this," Bunko said for the umpteenth time. "It doesn't make sense. Why the hell would he try something so stupid? He didn't even know what I was going to do."

"Maybe he didn't need to know."

"What's that supposed to mean?"

"Maybe it was all catching up with him."

"What are you talking about, kid? He just wrote a few fucking letters. It's not like he killed anybody."

"How do you know that, Bunk? How do you know anything at this point?"

"Because the guy's in a fuckin' wheelchair, that's why. Give it fifteen minutes more. Trust me on this, kid. I've just got a feeling. I've always had good instincts about people."

"And I say we get on the horn with Montrez right away."

"Kid, don't be a prick. We do that, we might very well be out of a job. We already blew it with Cheeves. How's it going to look if we tell him about this? Just give it a little bit more time."

Eamon had never seen him this tense. He put the big TV on. It was one of those network morning shows. First they did one of those two-minute up-dates: The president was meeting with European

Community members in Brussels. He'd be flying back aboard Air Force One on Sunday. An Ohio drifter had confessed to killing and dismembering twenty-two young boys over a two-year period. The space shuttle liftoff was still being delayed because of tropical storm George. Boris Yeltsin was asking for an increase in western loans. Then the serious-toned newsman shuffled his papers, and they brought out the zany network weatherman. The weatherman appeared in a black witch's costume and used his broomstick to point at the satellite map. All in honor of the fact that tomorrow was Halloween. At least he had some kind of reason. Still, it wasn't easy to watch, a three-hundred-pound weatherman in a conical hat sticking pumpkin suns on the national map. Eamon turned away.

He went over to that wall of Briggs family photos. They were tacked to a huge slab of cork in a collagelike way, unintentionally spilling over and overlapping, no rhyme or reason. The healthy, glowing, all–American family. They played touch football together, they went snowmobiling and water-skiing. They camped at Yellowstone and did Disney World. The instant smiles and momentary displays of good fellowship. Only fleeting incandescence in the camera's eye. You never knew, really. All families looked the same in snapshots. Everybody smiled when you said cheese. It would have been interesting to see the Briggses after the click and the flash.

Eamon kept going back to the few pictures of Cole before the land mine, old yellowing black-and-whites of the strapping young hulk. They were standard fare, in front of the barbecue in an apron that said World's Greatest Dad, with his arm around Emmie in front of their old house, flexing his muscles at the beach à la Charles Atlas.

It took a moment, actually. He had known something wasn't quite right. But he had kept looking past it, as if his mind refused to believe it.

"Bunk," he said, in disbelief, "you better come over here and take a look."

"What now?" he said, getting up from the couch, totally disgruntled.

"Look at this picture of Cole at the beach. Do you notice anything weird about it?"

"What are ya talkin' about? A day at the beach. When he used to have legs. So what?"

"Look at the date. Just look at the fucking date."

"Jesus H. Christ."

It was stamped in the white border: Kodak. June 12, 1975.

They went right into her bedroom. Screw formality. She was in front of the full-length mirror. In a tartan skirt and blue jacket. She turned, eyes blazing.

"Don't you people knock?" she hissed.

"Usually we make a point of it," Bunko said. "But in your case we're making an exception."

"I demand you leave my bedroom at once," she ordered.

Eamon said, "So where's your husband? Where'd he *really* go?"

"I told you, he went out for some bacon. He must be having some kind of car trouble. Now just get out of here. Can't you see I'm busy?"

She stood there, rigid and impervious. Short iron-colored hair that looked like it had been cropped with garden shears. Tight, pursed face. Thinly colored, hard-bitten lips. No amount of makeup could hide that pent-up hatred. She didn't even bother. The hazel eyes burned red.

"Fuck you," Bunko said. "I want answers now. Otherwise I'm going to arrest you. I might do it anyway, but at least this way you got a fighting chance."

"I don't understand what this is—"

"Just save it, lady. Where'd he go? Let's start there."

"I don't know," she said, unyielding.

Eamon said, "So how did he wind up in the wheelchair anyway? It sure didn't happen in Vietnam. The war was over by the time he lost his legs. Isn't that right?"

She was the darkness, the utter, bitter, unforgiving darkness.

Eamon said, "So when did he leave? You helped him. That we know. Makes you an accessory right there. So maybe you should start talking."

"He ... left ... in the ... middle ... of the night," she said with profound distaste, like each word was an extraction.

"What time? Where was he going? C'mon. We've gotten this far."

"Oh, you'll find it out anyway. What's it matter now?" she said, sitting down on the edge of the bed. "He went to Washington. There, are you satisfied?"

"Not yet," Eamon said. "Why's he going there?"

"I don't know, he didn't tell me," she said, still surly. "I'm just tired of it. I don't want it on my hands. Said there was something he had to take care of. That's what he told me, at least."

"How did he lose his legs?"

"He had an accident, that's all," she said, sour as anything. "Leave it alone now."

"C'mon. We're going to find it all out anyway. What kind of fucking accident? Spit it out, for God's sake."

"In the basement. Building something. He's always been good with his hands. It was an accident."

"What would he be building that would ... "
Eamon didn't even have to finish his own question.

He knew, he just knew. "He was building a god-damn bomb, wasn't he?"

She was silent, the unapproachable darkness.

Eamon saw it then. Like he could look into her damned soul. He felt a chill go through him, the absolute evil of it all.

"You knew, didn't you? You knew what he did. He killed them, and you knew that. My God."

She didn't even bother to deny it.

"You even typed those fucking letters, didn't you? You're the goddamn typist in the family, aren't you?"

She didn't cry. She didn't fall apart. She didn't do anything. She just got off the bed and brushed the lint off her jacket. She said, "I'm late now. I have to go."

They let her walk away. They didn't know how to stop her. They didn't know how to do anything with a woman like that.

Bunko picked up the phone and called in. As he filled in one of Montrez's men Eamon remembered the nightstand drawer. He checked, and the Beretta was indeed gone. "Consider him armed and danger-ous," he called over. "Make sure to tell them that."

16

The idea came to him from the newspapers and TV shows. He'd never been there himself, but he knew the hold it had on people, especially the veterans.

It was just a guess, a crazy hunch.

But they didn't have anything left to lose at this point.

They asked Montrez what their orders were, and he told them that they should give serious consideration to a very long vacation. Maybe even a permanent one.

His men captured Cheeves Lundquist. It happened early in the morning, in Central Park. They didn't have the whole story yet, but Cheeves had told agents that Briggs had killed Lieutenant William Ford. Not Earl Shad. Not anything like it. Briggs killed Ford because he was going to testify about what had happened in Phuoc Linh. Briggs had been in love with Angel Girl. She was carrying *his* child. It wasn't hard seeing how the sergeant, a devout Catholic with a devoted wife and four children back home in Fort Dix, might have had a problem with this. It was just hard imagining anyone sticking a bayonet into a pregnant Vietnamese girl. Which is exactly what Briggs apparently did.

The rest of it was what you might expect. Bunce and Shad and Hurly and Robinson and Lundquist had at least one thing in common: They were unlucky enough to witness the rampage.

The Bureau was flying Cheeves to Washington, to continue questioning.

Bunko and Eamon, driving with a certain absence of caution, made it to the nation's capital by two in the afternoon.

Not that it really mattered.

They were just guessing, after all.

They could even have missed him by now.

But they were going to stake out the place anyway. They really didn't know what else to do.

They weren't talking about it, but they were both feeling the same anxiety: What if their bungling added up to an assassination attempt? They weren't so much worried about Briggs coming up to the president with a gun—after all, Secret Service and Bureau agents were on the lookout for him—as they were concerned about the unknown. This was one dangerous character. Someone with a knowledge of explosives. A guy who'd killed a bunch of people. And gotten away with it.

It was a brisk, cloudy afternoon, in-and-out sun and those big, fast-moving cumulus clouds. They watched the tourists pass through from their respective positions. They stood at the entrance to the memorial, opposite each other. The Vietnam Memorial couldn't be seen from the street. The walls came up over ground level just a tiny bit. Only from the other side could you see how it was dug into the earth. The black granite walls met in a V—and it was like walking into a shallow grave, which is just what Eamon figured the designer had intended.

He knew there'd been a lot of controversy surrounding the memorial. He remembered when they'd first put it up and the traditionalists were all up in arms. A lot of them had wanted a statue, something more like the Tomb of the Unknown Soldier. But Eamon liked the memorial; liked the fact that they'd bothered to list every single name of the missing and dead on those walls of polished granite. Everybody counted for something, everybody mattered. At least he wanted to believe that.

When they went in to check it out, the first thing that struck him was all those names, over fifty thousand of them, row after row after row after row. It wasn't just all those dead men. It was all those families. All those moms and dads and wives and sweethearts and children. Not to mention the friends and everybody else. It was kind of amazing when you thought about it, how many lives had been altered, changed forever.

At different points along the base of the wall there were little flags and bouquets and letter bundles tied in ribbons and all sorts of intimate memorabilia. He'd read about this, too—and if he remembered right, they had even built some museum to hold all of the stuff. At the end of the day some government man came around and collected everything. There was a lot to tag and inventory. People left the oddest things. Somebody had left a Corvette steering wheel. Another person had actually made an offering of a T-bone steak smothered in onions. More typical, though, were the photo albums and yearbooks, the comic book and record collections, the high school letter jackets and baseball gloves.

There was also plenty that was war-related. There were the medals, the canteens and helmets, the dog tags. Many of the veterans came to pay their respects in their old ill-fitting uniforms. Many saluted. Many welled up. Even Bunko. He'd just found the name of a fallen comrade. Which wasn't the easiest thing. Names weren't listed alphabetically. It was all done in the order in which they had fallen. Of course, there was a directory you could consult.

"Jesus, I've never seen you cry before," Eamon said. "I didn't even know you were capable of feelings."

"I'm not crying," the big guy replied, tears streaming down his cheeks.

Eamon walked away, regretting he'd said anything in the first place. He felt outside of things. What did he really know about Vietnam? It was just some place on the other side of the world. He hadn't been drafted, didn't have to run to Canada. He'd missed everything by a couple of years. And he certainly hadn't lost anybody to it. No father or older brother. It wasn't his war. He'd missed it completely.

But why did he feel such a knot in his stomach? Why did his own eyes well up so?

He felt it passing the names. Passing all those solemn men in their badly faded fatigues. Passing all those other people, too, every kind of family and individual, these people he didn't even know.

Eamon looked up Lieutenant William Ford. He really wasn't sure why. It was just a name etched in stone. It wasn't like he was buried there or anything. It was just a name in the dark gloss, among so many others. Eamon hadn't intended to, but he made a promise to the name, to Justine's dad. Then he said a quick prayer for his immortal soul, something he remembered from Catholic school, from long ago.

The rest of it was pretty much hopeless.

For the most part they stood sentry, waiting and watching. Every time they saw a wheelchair approach—and there were a lot of them—they'd get ready. But it was one false alarm after another. Bunko didn't even bother to complain. He was past

240

that, past even grumbling. The whole situation had humbled him. Briggs. The wall. Everything. Eamon wished for his old blustery self.

They waited until darkness.

Until closing time.

Nothing.

They called it a day.

They came back Saturday, the very next morning.

They didn't know what else to do. In some ways, they were just doing penance, doing time.

At least now they knew Briggs had definitely come to D.C. Agents had found the Voyager in a downtown parking lot late yesterday afternoon. Bunko and Eamon had spent a good part of the evening with Montrez's team, checking motel and hotel registries in the area.

It was the same weather as yesterday, the same thing.

Hour after hour.

The tourists arrived with their Instamatics and Polaroids and videocams. They went in talking easily and confidently among themselves, in great anticipation. They'd read about it, too. They'd seen it on "20/20." Hugh Downs and Barbara Walters had given it their televised stamp of approval. It was an *experience*. Everyone had to experience the experience.

And then the tourists came out. They departed in silence, not a heavy silence exactly, but a kind of beatific quiet, a quiet that came with experiencing something. It was what they'd wanted in the first place. People wanted to feel it, to feel something.

You could hardly blame them.

The tourists. The veterans. The families. They came and they went. Hundreds. Thousands. Every hour. Every day. It made you wonder how big this was, how far it stretched.

Sometime in the afternoon they gave into their
hunger and walked across the street to an umbrella
cart. The chef-proprietor slathered onions and
greasy sausage on an Italian hero. They shoved it
down with a couple of Dr. Peppers.

"Jesus," Bunko said with a mouthful of sandwich,
pointing across the way. "It looks like your hunch
paid off."

Eamon saw him, too. Somehow he was not
surprised.

They checked their guns; they got ready.

"We'll try to approach him from behind," Bunko
said. "Get him completely by surprise."

"Bunk, don't forget, the guy's a fuck. Don't give
him a chance. Or else he might use it."

They moved quickly. Redemption seemed close
at hand.

It happened in the space of a minute.

Coleman Briggs had not wheeled himself far. The
problem was that he saw them coming. He was near
the first great panels of wall, reflecting back in the
dark gloss.

He had his nickel-plated Beretta out, momen-
tarily glinting in the sun.

People scattered, not needing instructions. A man
in a wheelchair with a silver gun. Other men con-
verging with their own dark hardware.

"Drop it, Cole!" Bunko yelled, his thirty-eight
drawn and raised.

Eamon was right behind him with his own Smith
and Wesson.

They were fifteen feet away.

Cole didn't say a word. He smiled. He actually
smiled. He put the silver-glinting gun to his temple.

Bunko yelled, *"No!"* He let his own gun drop to
his side without thinking.

It was all Briggs needed.

Without hesitating he turned the glinting weapon on Bunko. He fired away.

The big man was falling.

Eamon didn't need another reason. Holding his gun with two hands, he emptied the chamber, not even aware he was doing it. He kept squeezing until there was nothing left.

Every shot hit its mark. Six bullets right into Briggs's chest.

The reverberation. The sick smell, like sulfur.

The gun suddenly felt heavy again, felt real.

It took a moment in the absolute stillness to remember Bunko.

Then he was ripping off his shirt and trying to stop the bleeding.

17

Eamon was anxious to get there. It was a long drive, and the fidgety, odd-looking fellow beside him wasn't making it any easier. He hadn't said a word for at least an hour. You could tell he was nervous, riding out his own deep and quirky train of thought. Eamon wasn't at all sure he wanted to hop aboard that crazy locomotive. He slid in a CD to drown out the uneasy quiet.

It wasn't good to let it fester; that's what he knew.

You had to resolve the things in your life. Otherwise they stayed with you. They sneaked up on you at the oddest moments, took you down.

It might not have been the wisdom of the ages, but at least it was a small, clear truth. It was something to hold onto.

Eamon was going to resolve the things in his life. He'd made up his mind.

The first thing he'd resolved, with some help from Bunko, was how he felt about killing a man.

The truth was he did not feel all that terrible.

Bunko had said, "Kid, you done him a favor. You put him out of his misery."

Who knew if that was really true? But it was the truth Eamon was buying into. It made it easier to let go. Life was all about going on and leaving the past behind. It was all about living.

Who knew how he would have felt if Bunko hadn't made it? Who knew how that might have shaped his thinking? But the big guy was going to be okay. Briggs had shot him twice in the left side; one just missed the heart. The other went into the lung, filling it with blood; it was close enough. He was going to be in the hospital for at least another week. But that was not his problem. That was the problem of the doctors and nurses. Bunko was not what you would call a happy camper. He did not like wearing a puke-green gown with his tush hanging out; he wasn't particularly fond of consommé and Jell-O for dinner; he had a slight problem with large, bossy attendants taking his cigarettes and Jameson away. God help the poor, unwitting staff of Washington General.

It was great to be alive, though.

It was great to be in his Pontiac, whooshing down the highway on a beautiful sunny day.

It was great to have a sense of purpose again, a destination in mind. It wouldn't be long now. He remembered the first time he'd come this way. That day with Justine would probably stay with him always.

He didn't know. Maybe it wouldn't work out. Maybe the damage was irreparable. But he wasn't going to worry about it. It would happen, or it wouldn't happen. He just didn't want to think about it for the rest of his life, wondering about the what-might-have-beens, kicking himself all the while. After all, how many times did you fall in love in your life?

He was going to hope for the best. At least he wouldn't have any regrets. At least he would go the distance.

He wasn't sure about his surprise. It might be a

mistake, but he didn't really think so. Besides, Cheeves had been so insistent. It was something he needed to resolve in his own life. He needed to talk to Justine, needed to tell her some stuff about her dad. It was such a small little thing he wanted, just a beginning.

They were almost there, just outside of Crisfield. Cheeves still hadn't said a word. At least he was trying. He hadn't had a drink all day. He'd gotten a haircut and a shave, and he'd borrowed a tie and some clothes from Eamon. He stank of some cheap cologne, and his hands shook when he lighted his cigarettes.

"Pretty day, isn't it?" he finally said. "It's a good traveling day."

Eamon turned the volume down on Sade.

Cheeves said, "I think we are driving in a dream. You know, a time ago, in one of my other lives, I came this way. It was a day very much like this one, a November gift. And we were on this very road, I kid you not. We'd run off in the MG for the weekend. And we stopped at one of the roadside picnic tables. We had cold shrimp and goose liver pâté. Louise was fond of such things. She poured Chablis. We clinked glasses. She had one of those expensive picnic basket ensembles one buys at, say, Bergdorf Goodman. It was all perfect. She gazed lovingly at me. And I tried to return the favor.

"But it was not something I could do so easily. Because I knew. I saw it coming. I really did. It was there all along. She was thinking of charming bed-and-breakfasts while every particle of me was self-destructing. I was just trying to hold it together, to keep from cracking and breaking.

"It's hard to understand, I suppose. I had everything—and yet I knew in the most inarticulate and perverse way that I would lose it all. I would fall into ruin and disgrace, go to the utter depths. I knew that sooner or later my outer world would begin to mirror my inner world."

"You're talking about Ford and Angel Girl, right?"

Eamon felt dumb asking the question. But he wanted to be sure he understood Cheeves. Sometimes he was so oblique.

"Yes. I carried that with me. I watched a girl die in the most savage way imaginable. I saw a brave young lieutenant get murdered. And I did nothing. I was just plain scared. Unless you've been through something like that, I don't know if you can understand. It is the rawest, most cowardly humiliation. I didn't want to get hurt. I didn't want to be next. So I sacrificed everything. If only I knew then what I know now."

"Okay, I'll bite. What do you know now?"

"Oh, just the obvious. That physical pain, even death, is preferable to a lifetime of spiritual agony. If somebody put a bullet into you, at least it's over in a flash. One way or the other."

"Cheeves, I've got to ask you something. It's been bothering me more than a little bit."

"Shoot."

"That metal box they found on your boat. The one with the money. There was also a piece of paper in there. It had Briggs's address and phone number on it. What was that all about?"

"Oh, that. Well, it ties into the books, too. The ones you so astutely noticed before I made a mad dash for it. Those incendiary cookbooks. Well, I probably shouldn't tell you, but I don't see how it matters now. I was going to kill him. I was going to figure some way to put explosives on that stinking wheelchair of his, and I was going to blow him to Kingdom Come. I really was. I was building toward it. I was full of resolve."

About the Author

SEAN MCGRADY lives with his wife, Inge-bjorg, on the North Shore of Long Island. He is currently at work on the next two Eamon Wearie novels, *Sealed with a Kiss,* and *Town Without a ZIP.*